David Raymond

Time Noir

To my ageless, wise, and beautiful Aunt Lynn,
who always told me I would be tall, dark, and handsome—
two out of three ain't bad!

Love Always, David

1

Sea-crets

In an oceanfront penthouse on Miami Beach.

I've always had dual settings: breathlessly fast or Buddha slow. I can't remain in between. Oh, I've experienced that state. I light on middle-ground for a nanosecond, a fleeting tourist. I know, I know, that's the existence most others live. For me, going the speed limit is not an option. I blow through life, a tormented shooting star. I can't be contained by any space. I don't fit. Never did. I'm not even sure I belong here. I think I come from another time, another place, another dimension. Hell, maybe another planet? The Planet of Obsessive Thoughts and Perpetual Motion, ruled by a mad, dragon-riding barista, brandishing a never empty blender of expresso, hot sauce, and marbles. *Drink this. Don't mind the glass shards. Free refills! And, no, we don't have any damned whipped cream. Fire-breathing dragon—Duh!* Another planet would explain a lot. Still, I long for middle-ground; if only for a moment's respite.

Water. Water slows me down, so I stand in the shower, long, long after I am clean, gazing out the window into *now*. It's a Miami

Beach day. The kind of day the sun levitates over the ocean like a giant orange, waves break like foam on a café con leche, and it's hot enough to fry plantains on the sand. Lucky for me, I like it hot. I delight in the steamy water washing over my body as I regard the waves. Water quietens me. As long as I am wet, energy envelops me, a misty blanket of comforting skin, my own membrane too slow for the job. Water. My personal force field. Protecting me. Imprisoning me. Allowing me to remain in the moment. In the *now*. Water stops my cells' constant, frantic vibrations I can't contain on dry land.

My relationship with water has been this way as long as I can remember. The wetness of the shower reminds me of my childhood. When I was 4, I worshipped my time in the bathtub. Playing with my toys—small boats with orange and blue snap on tops, plastic fish, and of course rubber duckie. If I held my yellow duck underwater and squeezed out the air, it filled with water I used to rinse the shampoo from my hair. It took forever, but I enjoyed the experience of the erratic streams hitting my head, gently pushing the hairs around my scalp. Even at 4, I felt it. The sensation of water molecules washing over my skin, harnessing the excess energy escaping my cells. I stayed in that tub until the water turned ice cold, Mother whispering through the door, "Freddy Fluid, get out of there, my exquisite little fishy, before you grow gills." Mother said it 3 times. Always 3 times, softly, consecutively, each repeated sentence the same cadence. I think that's what started my obsessive-compulsive disorder. (*Some days, I do more counting than a stripper sorting out singles at the end of her shift.*) After the third "little fishy," I forced myself to open the drain, shivering in the coldness of the empty tub until the last drops of water glugged down.

I loved my bathtub, but in life, most good things have a shelf life. Some good things leave with such force you are vacuumed headlong into a dark, slimy well. Sometimes the force of a good thing leaving is so intense, it creates a vortex the size of Sedona, attracting more good things to you. Other times, if you're lucky as a rabbit's foot like me, a good thing leaves and transports you along on its wondrous journey, only at the time you feel like the rest of the rabbit—limping along with a missing foot. When I was 5 years old, Mother took me on a journey. A road trip to Naples Beach. Unlike Miami, the sand was white and silky soft, the water shallow, warm, and calm. Bliss! We stayed in a hotel. There was no bathtub. To say I freaked out would be an understatement. Mother slept through all of it. Or so I thought.

I bounced around the hotel room like an ice cube on a hot skillet until 3 a.m., springing from bed to bed, imagining myself a beached baby dolphin, frantically flapping my tail; flippers futilely digging into the sand until I surrendered. Surrendered to the fact there would be no long soak in my tub to slow me. Water. I had to get to water. Even at 5, I knew it was imperative to get wet. I was drying out, dehydrating! Into the shower I hopped. Like most first childhood experiences, it was simultaneously exhilarating and terrifying. While I missed being submerged in my tub, I relished the sensation of water droplets striking my body. It was like playing outside shirtless on a rainy day. With no rubber duck, I held my head back to wash the shampoo from my hair. As my cells screamed out in pain, I gasped. I was drowning! It wasn't from water rushing onto my face. No. The water nursed me like mother's milk. I was drowning in air! This is when I first glimpsed my secret.

If I speak these words aloud, I know what will happen. I always know what happens *next*. I know what people are going to say; what people are going to do. I know what happens *next*. That's part of my secret too, but I'm getting ahead of myself. As usual, I'm getting ahead of *everything*.

2

The pool boy

In a modest, waterfront home on Biscayne Point, a gated island on Miami Beach, an old couple sits on the couch.

"June. I told you, I've been cleaning this pool for 43 years. What makes you think we need a pool service?"

"Please go look at it, Jerry."

"I can see it fine from here, June. Look at that color!"

"I am looking at the color, Jerry. It's green."

"Ah! You're crazy. It's as blue as the color of your lovely eyes, June."

"My eyes are green, Jerry."

"Green! What are you talking about? Just loo… I could have sworn you had blue eyes."

"No, dear. That was Wendell, the Australian Shepherd."

"Oh, right. Wendell loved to swim in the pool. What were we talking about?"

"The pool, Jerry. I called a service. They're sending someone out this morning."

"This morning! We didn't even discuss this. Once they see we live on Biscayne Bay, they'll charge double. I built that pool, and I'm not—"

"Sorry to interrupt, dear, but we talked about this yesterday, and the day before."

"What! Whadayamean, we talked about this before? You're making that up," Jerry says, leaping off the couch with more vigor than he had shown in years.

"Come here and sit down, Jerry."

"Why should I sit down? You're trying to gaslight me. After all these years, you treat me like a little kid. You do this every damn time, June, and I'm not—"

"Jerry, my love, come, sit by me," June calls out slowly, and loudly, patting the cushion next to her like she is training an ancient hearing-impaired dog.

"All right. But no funny business."

"Jerry, dear, watch this with me."

June hits the play button on her iPad video app. Jerry sits down when he sees himself on the screen.

The recording plays, "Why do we need a pool cleaner, June? I'm perfectly capable—"

"Do you need to see more, Jerry?"

"What's the big deal? So, you know how to make a video on your iPad. Whadayawant, a medal?" Jerry yells, as he bounds from the couch, then promptly trips, righting himself.

"Jerry, dear. You know I love you. Please, dear, look closely at the video, and stop jumping around. You're going to hurt yourself."

"What's the big deal? You know how to record a video, and if you ask me, I look pretty good for 95, right, huh? And I jumped off the couch like an Olympic gymnast. Not bad for an old man. Right?"

"You still look like the handsome devil I married 70 years ago, Jerry. Now, take a look at the clothes you are wearing today."

"Whatsamatter, I got stains on my pants or something? You know, my damn prostate, no matter how many times I shake, the damn thing still drips."

"No, dear. No stains. What color is the shirt you are wearing today?"

"It's yellow. So what? You always told me you liked me in yellow."

"You look dashing in yellow, Jerry."

"Thank you, June. So, what am I looking at?"

"What color is your shirt in the video?"

"What? What are you talking about, June? You just filmed me. It's yell..." Jerry stops talking, holds his head in his hands and sits down. "I wore my red shirt yesterday. The one the kids got me, because I thought they were coming for dinner."

"Yes, dear, you did."

"And they didn't come. God, all day yesterday I thought it was Thanksgiving. I thought fighting in WW2 was bad. This getting old crap ain't for sissies. Last week I bought LED lightbulbs that last 22 years. Whoop-de-doo for the light bulb. I'll burn out long before those damn bulbs. Maybe I already did? When did I get to be such a fricking mess, June?"

"Years ago, Jerry, but you're my fricking mess."

"I'm lucky to have you, June, but I think you did this so you could have a hot, young, pool boy over every week. I've seen those movies. The pool wasn't the only thing they stuck their nets in."

"Why, Jerry, after 70 years, you're still jealous. I like it! Now be nice. The pool boy is pulling up, and I need to show him the equipment."

"You never mind his equipment. If anyone is showing this kid the pool equipment, it's me. You stay here."

"But, Jerry, you don't remember where everything is."

"I may not remember where everything is, but this is still my house, and my pool, and MY WIFE! You stay away from him."

"Oh, Jerry, I can't remember the last time you were so passionate about anything. Maybe after you show the pool boy around, you come back to me for a big kiss."

"Fine! But stay inside, and no bikinis when he's around!"

"Oh, Jerry. You sound like your old self. Come back soon," June says, secretly hoping the pool boy would be hot—he is. June watches the man as he follows Jerry around. He isn't exactly young; maybe 40. More of a pool man, but he is handsome. He has long brown hair, amber eyes, wears board shorts, and a white tank top which displays his tanned muscular arms and chest.

Even at 90, June likes having a young buck around. *A girl can fantasize, right?* June sees flashing lights on a fitness watch. "Oh God, forgive my thoughts. Please don't take him. He's old and losing it, but I love him." The amber lights flash faster as June runs out the door, screaming. "Oh, Jerry, Jerry! Please don't take him. I love you, Jerry. Don't go!!"

"Go? Go where? I was just showing this young fellow around. Hey, I told you to stay in the house, June."

The pool boy winks at June as the lights on his watch flash faster and faster, until he, and his net, vanish.

"Fucking aliens! Oh, thank God. It was the pool boy's watch flashing. He was just here, Jerry?"

"Who? Who was just here, June?"

"Why, the pool boy."

"Pool boy? What pool boy? You better come inside and sit next to me on the couch, June."

"The couch? Why yes, Jerry. I think maybe I'll sit on the couch."

"You go right ahead, dear. I'll be right in. I just need to add a little chlorine to the pool. It's looking perfect. Same color as your eyes, June."

"Yes, Jerry. Same color as my eyes."

3

The disappearing act

Back in Freddy Fluid's condo.

It's not like I'm clairvoyant. No! That would be a crazy claim. The thing is, I'm always a moment ahead. I'm ahead of almost everyone, and everything. I realize it's unbelievable. I've only told one person about this, Grace. She didn't believe me at first either. Who would? Shit! Time for work.

I force myself to shut off the shower. Even now, at almost 30, I hate leaving the shower. If I'm not covered in water for at least 25 minutes, I spend the rest of the day wheezing like a 4-pack-a -day smoker. Our Ocean Drive penthouse has 4 bedrooms and 3.5 bathrooms. I don't have a bathtub. If I did, I would never leave. I would sit there all day with the drain slightly open, hot water trickling over my toes, just enough to maintain the perfect tub temperature; 94 degrees. Did I mention I have obsessive-compulsive disorder? No bathtub for me. Mother was the only one who could whisper me out of the tub. God, how I miss her.

When I want to be immersed, I sprint a few blocks to the Miami Beach Marina, jump in my boat, and go diving. There are so many reefs just offshore, especially in Biscayne National Park. The first thing they teach you in scuba school is to never dive alone. The problem is, nobody can keep up with me underwater. When I say keep up, what I really mean is slow down.

Did I mention I can breathe underwater? So why bother with scuba school? Well, I'd look pretty damn suspicious diving with no tank and staying underwater like Aquaman for 10 hours, right? When I'm in the ocean, I move effortlessly, floating from coral head to sea fan, watching the colorful tropical fish with nothing else on my mind. I picture myself a stoned otter, blissfully bobbing from place to place, making metaphorical love to the seafloor. Every breath is slow, deliberate, intoxicating. Every so often, tiny bubbles escape my scuba regulator. Each movement like an underwater ballet. Nothing like the frenzied, sometimes spastic movements of my body on dry land. I long for an underwater companion to share this with, but my tank of compressed air is just for show. It lasts me, well, forever, whereas my failed diving buddies run through their air supply in 90 minutes at best. I once dove with a girl who stayed down for 4 hours. I thought I finally found her—my perfect diving buddy. After she almost drowned, I found out she was on Molly and cocaine that she got in a club on Ocean Drive the night before. *Miami Beach—a planet all its own.*

Reluctantly, I dry myself, run deodorant under my arms, throw on my scrubs and fitness watch, and sprint to the kitchen of my empty penthouse. Grace is already at work for early rounds. I miss her morning face. I grab a protein bar, pour juice into a tumbler, scoop up my keys, dash out the door, bolt down 9 flights of stairs, and jump into the Maserati. God, how I love this car. *Sure, there's more performance cars on the streets of Miami than Cuban coffee shops, but how many have Neptune's trident for their grill ornament?* I feel at home when the engine is revving, even if I'm going nowhere. It's incredible pushing this pedal. The engine revs, providing ultimate relief; *like a long pee first thing in the morning.*

Oh, God! My cells are humming, ever so slowly. This car speaks to me on a cellular level. My entire body is chanting *Ohmmmm!* I know, I know, this isn't how it should work. My muscular body should be pumping adrenaline, fueled by the excitement of listening to this beast of an engine. No! Not me. I rev the engine again and my mind comes to a happy halt, like that little doze after sex—while driving a Maserati! What the fuck is wrong with me? I mean, besides the OCD and living in my own time zone? Floor the pedal, Freddy! Who needs adrenaline? I'm calm, peaceful, on the verge of ultimate delight.

What the hell is this? Flashing amber light consumes me. It's the color I see when I close my eyes on the beach. Vision escapes me. *As an eye surgeon, I astutely recognize this is not a good thing.* Lifting my fingers to my eyelids, I find my eyes fully open. I'm in my office parking lot on Alton Road in my spot next to Grace's car. It's the oddest thing. I have no recollection of how I got here.

No time to ponder. Time is precious. I turn off the Maserati. The engine pings to a stop, sucking my ecstasy away like the end of a roller coaster ride. I pat her firm red leather seat. *See you later, my love.* Walking through the back door, Liz, my favorite assistant, greets me.

"Good morning, Dr. Fluid," Liz says, handing me a cup of coffee.

"Thank you, Liz," I return without looking up, or stopping. A bit of coffee spills on the floor as the cup transfers hands, and our pinkies touch. "Get that, will you please, Liz?" I ask as I leap over the spill.

"Yes, Doctor," Liz says as she watches me.

The staff are always watching me. Timing me. When will he get to the next patient? They have to work hard to keep up. It takes 11 of them, and often I find myself looking at my watch; the seconds slip away, no next patient lined up. Everyone else moves so damned slowly. Mine is a life of constant inconveniences.

Liz is still watching me. She smiles, thinking of saying how handsome and charming I am. She wants to ask me for a drink. She longs to tell me she dreams of holding hands across a candlelit table, lost in my penetrating amber eyes. Now she's daydreaming about another kind of penetration. I do not smile back. That would be trouble. Plus, I'm hoping to convey I am taken, but she knows. Everyone does.

Did I mention I'm always thinking about what everyone else is going to say? It's the OCD. It's also part of being ahead of everyone. Not that I'm clairvoyant. No. We've established that. I simply see and hear *next*, tuned to an always on-demand channel of other people's visions which transport me to their future, 1 minute ahead of the moment everyone else exists in. Yes, I can see 1 minute in the future. Trust me, I've timed it. Still, 1 minute from now is the future, the *next*, and that's the space I live in. A moment ahead of everyone; except Grace.

I hear people's words before they speak them, see their visions before they occur. Sometimes, people like Liz cast their words into an unspoken future only I see, rattling in my mind with the rest. Futures real and imagined. My future, my *next* is, well, it's complicated. You see, OCD has plans of its own, directing my mind to create my fictional future to keep up with everyone else, making me as anxious as a virgin in a room full of good-time girls. *OCD, you little slut you!*

Time to wash my hands—again. Scrubbing each finger down and up, then up and down precisely 11 times. I think one of the reasons I went into medicine is so many OCD rituals are seen as professional. I know because I hear my patients' *next* thoughts whenever I walk in the exam room. *'I can't wait to see Dr. Fluid wash his hands this time. He's the cleanest doctor I've ever seen.'*

Sure, I'm clean, pushing soap and water onto my hands as if Brillo-ing a pot bottom caked with burnt soup, but at the end of a day's work, my hands look like a jellyfish had its way with them. Nevertheless, the water snaps me back to my happy place, where I can focus on the *now*.

I stop at the nearest patient room and pick up the chart hanging on the door. Scanning it, I walk inside, and without looking up, wave hello to the patient. Mrs. Nelson. She's a feisty one. Macular degeneration. Awful eye disease. I'm working on a cure, you know. I'm so close, but until then, there's the barbaric practice of monthly eye injections to seal the leaky blood vessels. There's the tray containing a syringe with a 30-gauge needle. *What, you may ask, is a 30-gauge needle? It's sharp and pointy, okay?*

"Numbing drops, Liz?"

"Yes, Dr. Fluid. I administered 12 drops. Right eye, 10 minutes ago," Liz replies with an embarrassed smile, as though she knows I heard her naughty thoughts, or wishes I could.

Liz watches as I whiz past her so quickly, she feels a draft, shivering in my peripheral. I plop on my stool, spin around, look at Mrs. Nelson's eyes through the slit lamp, push back so fast the stool spins when I stand, and put on my gloves.

"You're doing fine, Mrs. Nelson." Here comes her *next*. She's going to pick on me about how young I am. She's going to tell me about her arthritis and diabetes, and something about not paying for her visit. *Odd? The last part is fuzzy, like I'm out of the room when she says it.*

"Fine? How can you say I'm fine, Dr. Fluid? What do you know anyway? What are you, 12? My underwear is older than you. Fine! Ha! Between my arthritis and diabetes, I'm barely able to leave the house."

"I meant your macular degeneration is holding steady. Ready, Mrs. Nelson?"

Before Mrs. Nelson responds, I pick up the syringe. I'm about to plunge the sharp pointy needle into her eye and Mrs. Nelson exhales screaming, "Oh, shit!" as my fitness watch glows bright amber.

Abruptly, time ceases. It's as if I'm in water, but am I going fast, slow, or not moving at all? What the fuck? The syringe floats in the air, then shatters on the floor. I'm light—weightless. Looking down, only my sneakers remain; already pointing toward the next exam room. My last molecule evaporates. I silently laugh as the 95-year-old Mrs. Nelson jumps from her chair and shouts, "I'm not paying for this visit! Fucking aliens!"

4

Meet the aliens

The spherical spacecraft sits stationary. Two creatures aboard anxiously await the coming. Miniscule specks of amber lights skip in all directions—amorphous.

"Did it work, #2?"

"His molecules departed his earthly form. All we have to do is retrieve them. Easy peasy, as the Earthlings say."

"That's what you said last time, #2."

"Don't worry, #3. I got this. I've adjusted the photonic reflectors."

"Wonderful! #1 will be pleased. Not like last time. I'm surprised he didn't banish you."

"Shhhh, #3! You're distracting me."

"Oh, sorry. It's just the last ti—"

"Shut your yap, #3! I need to concentrate."

"Yes in-deedy. You go ahead and concentrate. I'll let #1 know."

"Just hold your flippers, #3, and shut the zalk up."

"Hey! Don't get testy with me. If it weren't for me, #1 would have sent you back to Rolexa centuries ago, or flippers forbid, Timexa."

"Timexa! He wouldn't. Would he? Shhhh, now! I'm trying to concentrate. Here he comes! Here he is. Hah! GOT HIM! Yes! I'm the greatest! Go zalk yourself, #3."

"I don't think you are concentrating, #2. It's written right on it—not from concentrate," #3 says, watching a half-gallon container of orange juice floating in the spacecraft chamber.

"Honest mistake. They're both kind of orange."

"Honest mistake? How can you say that, #2?"

"There's a lot of orange stuff floating around. It's Florida."

"Thirsty, #2? This stuff is delicious," #3 says, sipping juice from the jug.

"#2. # 3. Report?" Comes a British voice enveloping—everything.

"Hello, #1. Lovely day, isn't it?" #2 asks nervously.

"#2. Don't be a twit. Time is precious. Don't waste it. Progress?" #1 demands.

"Yes, #1. Time is precious. Apologies. We're so close, you can practically taste light specks everywhere," #2 responds.

"Right-o. Let me know as soon as #009 arrives," #1 says.

"Yes, #1!" #2 and #3 answer in unison.

"And, #2, you do remember what happened last time?" #1 asks.

"Don't worry, #1. Won't happen again. We won't let you down."

"Cheerio. Contact me when he's here," #1 says as he flashes away.

"Yes, #1."

"Hey! What's this *we* stuff? Holy zalk! I'm just an observer," #3 says.

"Thanks for having my back, #3. Don't forget, if something happens to me, you are next in line to take over this job."

"Holy zalk, #2! I never thought of that. Don't worry, I'm sure you will get it right next time."

"That's the spirit, #3."

#3 swims off, drinking orange juice, muttering, "He is so zalked."

5

That sinking feeling

In the middle of the spacecraft, Dr. Freddy Fluid floats.

Where am I? Why am I moving so slowly? I'm floating. What are all those little specks of light? Oh, shit, it's me. What the hell? How did I not see this coming?

"Ahhhhhhh. Very good. #009. I've been waiting for you," booms a voice from nowhere and everywhere.

"Hey! Who are you? Who the fuck is #009? My name is Freddy. Freddy Fluid. Dr. Freddy Fluid!!! There must be some kind of mistake. Who are you!!??? What the fuck is going on?" *I can't see what happens next. I'm rudderless without next; like searching for a lighthouse through a cataract, on a foggy night.*

"I'm #1, and you are #009."

"#009? What the hell are you talking about? Who are you? Where am I?"

What the fuck?! I'm floating. My molecules are all made of light, bouncing around empty space, as if each of my cells has a destination in mind, leaving me to explore, then returning to form the outline of my body. It's a dance of sorts, like fragments of kelp, slowly breaking off in pulsing underwater waves, then returning to their underwater stalks. Holy shit! I'm not floating in air. I am moving slowly, very slowly, as if I'm underwater.

"Hey! Hey you! #1! Is this water? Am I in water?"

No response. This is nuts. I don't have eyes, but I can still see all around me. What is above me? Small waves. Those little amber specks. They comprise my form, dancing toward the surface. They are almost up to those waves above me. Go! Get the fuck out of here! Wait! They're heading back before they make it to the waves. What the!?

"Hey, #1! This is water. I'm in water! Right?"

"Water indeed. Welcome home, #009. Welcome home."

Home? Fuck! I think Miami Beach finally sank!

6

A fallen Leif

The larger of the two creatures swims to a chamber in the bottom of the spacecraft. Amber specks swirl and dance inside. One creature waves his large, broad tail, and another creature approaches.

"Are you sure you got him this time, #2?"

"Yes, #3. I've adjusted the chromatic filters. I've isolated the pattern. All I have to do is extract his beams from the others using the Rolexa Algorithm, and VOILA!"

"But how can you be certain? You remember what happened last time, #2?"

"How could I forget?"

"#1 was furious."

"I know, #3."

"Ever since then, your name has been associated with, let's just say, #2," #3 chortles.

"Yes, yes. How could I forget? Every time I visit this planet, you yell, '*watch where you're going, you don't want to step in any #2.*'"

"That's timeless, right, #2? Over 2,000 zircs ago, and it still gets me right here," #3 chuckles, pointing her front flipper at her rear end.

"You're a regular comedian, #3. Too bad you're not funnier, though. We could use a comedian around here. Oh, wait, a life form is coagulating. I can see the form taking shape. Definitely humanoid. It's him. Definitely him. Got him!"

"Uh, #2, I don't think this is #009."

"Well, these humans all look the same to me. Look! He has amber eyes. It has to be him. Go ahead, you ask him, #3. I'm too nervous."

#3 swims to the side of the chamber and sends a telepathic message to the humanoid.

"Are you #009?"

"Get away from me. I know karate," the pool boy shouts, while thrusting his pool net all about.

"Hey, #2, I don't think this is him," #3 says with a furrowed brow.

"Maybe he doesn't remember his birth name? Ask him again. Ask him!"

"Okie-dokie! Ohhhhh, mister, are you Freddy, Freddy Fluid?"

"Freddy, who the hell is Freddy? I'm Leif Netter," the pool boy responds, panicked.

#3 laughs hysterically. "Leif Netter! You're killing me."

"I work at my dad's swimming pool business. Our last name is Netter. See the Netter logo on my shirt? Anyway, the moron thought it would be funny to name me Leif…and why am I explaining this to you? What the hell are you anyway, a talking fish? I knew I shouldn't have done those shrooms before work. Dad is going to fire my ass for sure this time."

"Fish!" #2 says, descending on the chamber like nightfall.

"Hey! Who turned off the flashing lights? Where did the fish go? Can I at least have my vape pen?"

"Nope, I don't think this is Freddy, #2. Nope! Oh, this is bad, #2. When #1 finds out, he's going to be so pissed, and remember what happened last time."

"Shut up, #3."

"Don't you worry, #2. You'll get him next time," #3 says.

"That's more like it, #3."

"Sure, #2. You'll get him all right," #3 says, muttering under her breath, *"He is zalked. So, so zalked!"*

7

Yo-Yo Hah!

In the middle of the spaceship.

I'm pulling apart and coming together, as if my molecules were a school of baitfish fleeing a marlin. I enjoy this sensation of my atoms releasing and returning. It's the feeling I used to get whilst playing with my yo-yo. (Yes, I say whilst—deal with it.) I loved making my yo-yo spin in place, flicking my wrist and watching it return to my outstretched hand. Sometimes it would spin so long, I felt like I froze time in an ice cave. My mind was cool and clear of thought. Any thought. I was alone in my head, and no one was speaking; not even me. It was wondrous, as if I discovered some secret yo-yo method of manipulating time and space; even energy itself.

"#009. It is time."

"Time. Time for what? And I keep telling you, I'm Freddy. Dr. Freddy Fluid."

"It's time."

"You're not making any sense. I'm being held against my will. Don't I get a phone call?"

"You are free to come and go, #009. You always have been."

"Great. Let me go home."

"You are home, #009."

"What the fuck are you talking about!!? This isn't Miami Beach. Where am I?"

"Home."

What the fuck is this? A giant cloud of light specks is enveloping me. I'm moving *slower than a sloth in a school zone.* The specks beyond me seem to be dancing with my light specks. They are flowing in and out of my space. Wait! This is not my space at all. These molecules make up more than my form, more than the space around me. They make up—*everything.*

"Who are you?"

"I am #1, dear boy."

"#1! #009! Knock this crap off. Tell me who you are, and where I am."

"You are still thinking, #009. It is time for you to be."

"Be what?"

"Everything."

My throat is closing. I can't breathe! Anger and frustration always do this to me. Deep breath in, deep breath out. Stay calm, Freddy, you're an eye surgeon, for God's sake. Keep your cool. *I'm shaking like Ricky Ricardo's maracas.* Stop shaking, Freddy! Breathe. *Breathe.* In and out. In and out! Good, Freddy.

"Good, #009. Breathe. Your molecules are returning to your being, to all of us, like long-lost companions. Like your yo-yo. Yes, very good, #009. Breathe. In and out, slowly. You can do it. You can move slowly here, lad. Breathe."

Floating. Damn it! That's why this feels familiar. They must have me suspended in some type of liquid infused with oxygen. People think there is no oxygen in water; that fish breathe water. *They don't.* Fish gills extract oxygen from the water, but water contains only 1% dissolved oxygen, whereas the oxygen-nitrogen air we breathe on Earth contains 20 times that. If there were enough oxygen in water, humans could breathe in it. Really!

In medical school, we super-infused a tank of water with oxygen, then placed a mouse in a cage in the tank. The mouse was able to breathe water for an hour before we removed it from the tank and gave it a good shake to get the water out of its lungs. The little fellow lasted a week, and then died of pneumonia. I guess we didn't shake *all* of the water out.

Oh shit! I'm going to die like the lab mouse. Another breath, Freddy, then get the hell out of here. He said I could leave. Wait! There's something about this place, this state of being. I felt it before. "How did you know about the yo-yo?"

"I've always been here, #009?"

"Been where?"

"With you. Always."

"Fuck! I knew it."

"Ah, you sensed me. Very good indeed, #009. We're making progress."

"Sensed you? Hah! You're crazier than me."

"Then what is it you knew, #009?"

"I knew I should have taken those psych meds Grace prescribed."

8

The comedian

In a small, mission style home in El Portal, a quaint, peacock-filled village in Miami, a lonely lady longs.

I hope I see him today. God, he's so sexy, and that dog of his; what a couple of cuties. "Time for a walk, Millie. You'll like it here in El Portal. And wait until you see all of the peacocks. Come here, girl, so I can put your leash on." I only adopted this stupid dog so I could have an excuse to talk to him. This better work. 7:15 p.m. He's usually in Sherwood Forest Park by now. I hope his adorable dog likes Millie, and if that doesn't work, this ought to do it. My tightest shirt—no bra. This has to get his attention. I don't even know if he's married, or straight.

"I know, Millie, I'm 52. What am I thinking?" Crap, now I've become one of those people who roam the streets talking to their dogs. "Come on, Millie, enough sniffing already."

"Cute dog. What's its name?"

Holy crap. It's him. Oh, he's even cuter up close, and so is his dog. Look at those eyes. They're amber. That's so hot. I can't believe he's talking to me. Holy crap!

"Um, Miss. Are you okay?"

"Sorry. It's Patricia."

"Patricia. Come here, girl. Come, Patricia," he says, getting down on his knees and thrusting his hands out.

Did he say, 'Come, Patricia?' If only. Shit! I told him my name. He's going to think I'm an airhead. Pull yourself together, girl. "Sorry, I'm Patricia. I just got the dog today. Her name is Millie."

"I'm Burt, and this is, wait, promise you won't laugh?"

Holy crap! Even his voice is gorgeous. What did he just ask me?

"Patricia?"

"Sorry. Yes?"

"Do you promise?"

"Yes. I promise not to laugh."

"This is Ernie."

"Burt and Ernie. Hilarious!"

"Go ahead, you can laugh now," Burt says.

"No, I promised."

"I never saw you with a dog before. Is Millie yours, or are you pet sitting?"

"You've noticed me before?" Shit! I can't believe I said that out loud. I'm such a ditz.

"Yes, I see you walking every evening. This is my favorite part of our little Village, and Ernie's favorite sniffing spot. Welcome to El Portal, Millie. Can Ernie say hello?"

"Sure."

Ernie's such a cutie. I love dachshunds. "No, Millie! Don't growl at him." Holy shit on a shingle. Go figure I would adopt the most anti-social dog ever. Maybe I can return her? Lots of people want dogs these days. Sure. I can bring her back. She seemed so sweet and friendly at the shelter. What's he doing now?

"Mind if I try something, Patricia?"

"You can try anything you like." Oh crap! Shit! Crap! Shit! Did I just say that? I sound like a soft porn actress. He's going to think I'm a slut. Maybe that's a good thing? Shut the hell up, Patricia, and talk about the dog. Well, at least he's laughing. And look at those amber eyes. I can't stand it.

"Here you go, Millie. Try this."

He's giving her a treat. Millie likes him. She's licking his hand, and his face. Lucky little shit. "Wow! You certainly have a way with dogs, Burt."

"Thanks. It's mainly the treats. I have more dog friends than people friends. Dogs are direct and honest. You can tell right away what's on a dog's mind just by watching their body language, how they carry their head, or wag their tail. Little Millie here, she's a good one. In a week or so, she'll come out of her shell. Look, she's already sniffing Ernie's nether regions."

I'd like to sniff Burt's nether regions. It's been so long since I've seen a naked man. "Lucky girl. I'm so proud."

"Good one! I thought you might be funny."

"Oh, what made you think I was funny?"

"Just from watching you walking around the neighborhood. You usually have a mysterious smile on your lips."

Holy shit. He noticed my lips. I'm going to lose it, either that or walk over there and kiss him with these noticeable lips. Control yourself, Patricia, and for God's sake, say something, anything.

"Yep, that's me. The mysterious smiler."

"It was a pleasure meeting you, Patricia, and welcome to the neighborhood, Millie. I've got to run. Work."

He's leaving. Say something, you idiot. "Um, yes, it was nice meeting you too, Burt and Ernie." Don't laugh, don't you dare fucking laugh, Patricia, oh no. "Hahahahaha!"

"It's okay, Patricia. Nobody ever keeps that promise, but that's what I was going for with the name Ernie. Can I tell you a secret?"

"Sure, anything." I'm such a moron! Shut the hell up, Patricia. He's coming closer. Oh God, he's going to whisper in my ear. I can't stand it. He's brushing against me. My nipples are tingling.

"Ernie is a girl. I only named her that for the laughs."

"Hahahahahaha." Compose yourself, idiot. Say something intelligent. "Heading to work so late? What do you do, Burt?"

"I'm a comedian. Stand up."

"NO WAY!" I shout, pushing his arm so hard he stumbles.

"Way! And, boy, you pack a wallop like a wallaby."

"It's my special training routine—Pilates, followed by two hot fudge sundaes," I say, making a muscle and kissing my bicep.

"Funny. Are you a comedian too?"

"I wish. I love stand up." Oh, God! Comedians are so cool. I can't believe he's a comedian.

"Stop by my house. It's the blue one, right over there. I'll leave you tickets in my mailbox for tonight's show."

"Holy shit. I mean, thanks, Ernie. Sorry. I mean, Burt." What an idiot, Patricia. Stop talking. God, he likes me. Stand up straight, Patricia. Boobs out. Tickets! I can't believe he's giving me tickets!

"I knew you were funny. See you tonight. Maybe we can catch a drink after my set?"

"Awesome!" Oh, God, you sound like a teenager. Just shut your mouth, Patricia, and hit him with your mysterious smile. He's waving. Wave back. Oh, crap! His watch. It's blinking effing amber.

"Noooooo! You can't take him now. Not now! Come on, he's a hot comedian. Burt, come back!!!"

Crap! Shit! Crap! He's gone. Look at Ernie. She looks so helpless with half of her severed leash hanging from her collar. Oh, God, now she's whining. "Don't cry, boy. I mean, girl. You can come home with us."

Great. Just my luck. Instead of having a cool comedian boyfriend, I'm running an effing kennel. Oh well, at least I'm not going home alone.

"Come on, Ernie, Millie. This place is going to the dogs. EFFING ALIENS!!!"

9

Finding Grace

In the middle of the spacecraft, Freddy Fluid contemplates his circumstances.

This is amazing. I have no idea how I'm surviving in this liquid. Maybe I finally grew those gills Mother warned me about. I appear to be an assembly of frolicking light beams. I wonder what I look like to this #1 character. I'm not vain, well, maybe a little. When you grow up hearing how good looking you are, it's hard not to think about your looks.

Since I was very young, all of my relatives remarked about how gorgeous I was. In fact, one of my earliest memories was Grandmother talking to Mother about me. The flickering lights! My memories are coming to life in light, like a holographic projector scattering 3D images all around me. There's Mother, and Grandmother. I can hear them speaking like it's taking place here and now. I know it's a light show, but it's so real, I can even smell Grandmother. *Her ever present, and overwhelming scent of perfume and cigarettes permeating the air, like dead flowers in a wet ashtray.* I can hear them talking as if they were right here.

"That Freddy, he's a looker. That kid is going to get laid all over town."

"Mother! You're terrible."

"I call 'em like I see 'em. Do you think his deadbeat father will ever show up, or at least save up?"

"Save up? For what, Mother?"

"Condoms."

"Mother! You're terrible."

"I never saw Freddy's father, but he must have been a gorgeous lay. Where did you say he was from again? And why hasn't he shown up? He must have been one hell of a beautiful man. Just look at the kid. You know I love my grandson more than life itself, Fiona, but he's such an odd duck. If I didn't see you give birth, I would swear Freddy was the secret love child of Sheldon Cooper and Guy Noir."

Despite her noxious scent, Grandmother was such a righteous bitch. *Grandmother hugged everyone like she was measuring them for a coffin.* She went out of her way to be critical, about everyone and everything. Conversely, when Grandmother thought something was great, she touted it like a carnival barker at a peep show. I knew if Grandmother said I was gorgeous, and a tad peculiar, it was true.

When Mother took me outside, people would go out of their way to stop her to say what an attractive kid I was. Really! I was smart enough to realize the gift of beauty I was granted, and learned to use it to my advantage. It was then, at age 6, I learned the power of my smile.

All I have to do is smile, and people are charmed. It's because I flicker. When I smile, my eyes, they flicker. Gazing into my eyes is extraordinary, like watching millions of minuscule goldfish scales glistening through a sunlit bowl, *or so I am told.* I didn't know about the flickering until I found her.

Most people never find grace until they become grandparents, find themselves, or religion. I found grace on the corner when I was 6. I was riding my bike around the block like Lance Armstrong, and Grace stopped me in my tracks. She looked like a little elven princess, sans the pointy ears. *I have a thing for pointy ears, okay?*

Wait! This is crazy. Grace is taking form here, in these lights. She looks just like the day we met. So do I. There she is on the sidewalk, the next block over. I'm right here too, only I'm 6 years old. This is insane. Breathe, Freddy. Breathe!

"Hey, #1! What the hell is happening to me? Hey!!!! Talk to me!" Silence fills the air, and the light show continues.

This is nuts. I'm right here, staring across the street like when I was 6. I'm not allowed to cross the street. Neither is Grace. We stand like bookends waving to one another. Unlike my light brown skin, hers is alabaster white. Grace's hair is glistening gold in the sunlight. When she smiles, I smile. She looks angelic.

The thing I want most in life, right now, is the same exact thing I wanted then, to cross the street and hold her hand, like we're the only people on the planet.

"Hi!"

"Hi!"

"I'm Freddy."

"I'm Grace."

"I not allowed to cross the street, Grace."

"Me neither, Freddy. My father won't let me. I'm only allowed to go around the block."

"What could it hurt if I walked over there right now?" I ask.

"Oh, I don't know, Freddy. You might get in trouble. Is your father mean? Mine is."

"I don't know."

"Huh?"

"I never met my father."

"What? You never met your father?"

"No."

"That's sad."

"Nah. I have my mother, and she's never mean, but she gets disappointed in me when I don't listen."

"I guess you better not cross the street, then."

"I guess not. See you tomorrow after school," I say, smiling.

"I'll bring a ball. We can play catch."

"Good idea, Grace. Nobody told us not to throw anything across the street."

"Hey, Freddy! Did anyone ever tell you your eyes flicker when you smile? I can see them all the way across the street."

"They do?"

"Yes. They're absolutely magical. Well, bye, Freddy."

"Magical, huh? Bye, Grace."

Yep, that's the first time I knew about the power of my smile. I'm not sure if Grace drew the flicker out of me, if she was the first person to notice, or maybe it was just their time to shine? In any event, my friend flicker was here to stay.

Grace and I were such goodie two shoes. I didn't cross the street until I was 7 years old when Mother gave me permission, but it didn't stop Grace and me from talking every day. She went to Holy Cross, and I went to Biscayne Elementary, so we only saw each other on the street corner. Back then, it took what seemed to be forever before we stood face to face.

Wait! Not again. The lights are fast forwarding a year ahead to when we're 7 years old, or is it 22 plus years behind the present? What's happening to me? This is crazy. I could never go back in time before. Always ahead. A minute, but I always go forward.

"Hey, #1! What the hell are you doing to me?" Silence fills my being.

10

This ain't Sesame Street

In the bottom of the spaceship, lights emerge.

"Are you #009?"

"#009? Huh?"

"Sorry. I should have realized; you probably go by your humanoid name."

"Humanoid name? Where am I? Why can't I see anything but light?"

"I'll explain in a sec. Do you know why you are here?"

"I'm not sure where here is, but I think so?"

"Good, good," #3 communicates, as #2 floats up to the chamber.

"Please tell us why you are here," #2 nervously messages telepathically.

"Well, I'm not 100% sure, but I think I just heard someone say they needed a comedian?" Burt answers.

"Comedian? So, you're not Freddy? Dr. Freddy Fluid?" #2 asks.

"Who the hell is Freddy?! I'm Burt. And where's Ernie? What did you do with my dog?!"

"You're Burt and your dog is named Ernie?" #3 roars hysterically.

"Yes. I'm a comedian, and—"

#3 cuts Burt off, "A comedian. Burt and Ernie!!!" #3 guffaws while holding her belly. "You are so zalked, #2. You made a real #2 of this! Why, that's not Freddy. Nope, not Freddy at all. He does have amber eyes, though. You are so zalked!"

"Hey. At least that guy's dressed for the occasion," Burt remarks, pointing to Leif Netter. "You should have told me the dress code. I would have worn my swimsuit too."

"We really did need a comedian around here, #2," #3 adds as she watches the pool boy flopping around the ship's chamber, swiping his pool net at the moving lights.

"Sorry, dude. You're not Freddy either, right?" Burt asks.

"Freddy? Who the fuck is Freddy? I'm Leif. Where am I? What did that old dude do to me?"

"Who are you calling old? I'm not a day over 40,000,000 zircs!" #2 replies.

"40,000,000. Why, you don't look a day over 39,000,000. Oh, and you—Leif. Really, Leif?"

"Even better. His name is Leif Netter, and he's a pool boy," #3 says through a fit of laughter. "Oh, and, Leif, where are my manners? This is Burt, as in Burt and Ernie, only Ernie is his dog, and #3 probably scattered its furry atoms to Alpha Centauri."

"Leif Netter. Did you guys set me up? Is this one of those kidnap the standup comic reality shows? What did you do to Ernie? I'll kick your fish asses if you hurt my dog!"

"This guy cracks me up, #2. You were right. We needed a comedian around here," #3 chuckles.

"I wasn't calling you old, Flounder. How the hell would I know what an old fish looks like anyway? I meant the old guy who was showing me his pool pump. I was right there in his yard, and then, poof. Did the old dude slip me some Molly?" Leif implores.

"Apologies, Leif. There is no Molly here, just Burt and you, but you see, we are trying to find Freddy. I don't suppose you know him? Dr. Freddy Fluid? Of course, you wouldn't. Anyways, we will have this sorted out in a jiff," #3 states.

"Jiff? You guys say jiff too? What exactly is a jiff? It always makes me think of peanut butter, and that stuff never moves quickly, especially when I give some to Ernie. She just sits there and licks her mouth for hours," Burt adds.

"Enough out of you, human," #2 says, as he kicks his tail, sending a wave of light specks hurtling toward Burt's mouth.

"Humph." Burt struggles to reply as his mouth fills with tiny lights.

"Ohhhh, #2, what are you going to do with this one? Can we keep him? He looks like a strong one. I bet he could hold his breath for—"

"Hey, #3!" #2 interrupts.

"Yes, #2?"

"Go zalk yourself!"

11

Wynwood balls

In the artsy area of Wynwood, Miami.

Karla Katz sits in her windowless, not so artsy office thinking about the people who worked in this building in years past. In the 1940s, the building was filled with immigrant women glued to their sewing machines for 12-hour days. In the '80s, through the turn of the 21st century, the building served as a social service agency. The huge warehouse was still a sweatshop of sorts, filled with people with developmental disabilities, packaging ceiling fan bolts and nuts into little plastic bags at a rate of 2 pennies per bag. Wynwood was a pit back then. In present day, the Wynwood district bustles with art dealers, tony restaurants, bars, and shops; their multi-million-dollar buildings adorned with commissioned graffiti art. Karla ponders all of this, and just how lucky she is.

Karla graduated from FIU and landed an entry-level job at Designs R Us, a one-stop marketing firm for authors, and other creative types, hoping to turn a profit off their labors of love; or at the very least, not wind up homeless. Karla loved the vibe of

Wynwood. It's a place where hipsters and old hippies mingle, enjoy a cocktail, and immerse themselves in cool art. Even in the muggy Miami heat that hangs on you like a wet rug, there is a dynamic energy in the air. People come alive at the ever-present graffiti covered Wynwood Walls, as if they discovered ancient cave drawings. Lately, the walls bear the images of goofy aliens.

Today, Karla can't stop thinking about how lucky she is; especially to have found Bob. Karla is 23, has ordinary brown eyes, fair skin, freckles, and stands at 5'3" tall. She is self-conscious to a point of distraction. No matter how she dresses, or what the scale tells her when she steps on it each and every morning, she always hopes to lose another 15 pounds. She never imagined a man like Bob would give her a first, let alone a second, look, but he was meeting her after work for their third date. It was now 5:40 and 6 p.m. couldn't get there soon enough. Tonight, she is planning on going all the way. It isn't like Karla never had sex before, but never with anyone she loved, nor with anyone she thought cared even a tiny bit about her.

Karla's cell phone dings with a text.

Oh, God. It's him. My heart is racing as I read his text. *"Running about 10 minutes late. Sorry. I'll meet you at your office. Wink emoji-Bob."*

I'm so nervous. I better make sure nobody else is here, for the fourth time. Hallways-clear. Offices-empty. As usual, I'm the last one. That's why the boss gave me the keys to lock up every night. The rest of the staff have lives, but tonight, it's all going to change. I'm wearing my sexiest outfit. A lacey, low-cut teal top, with my shortest tan skirt, and silver high heels, which I squeezed into when Bob texted. I hate walking in heels, but I can carry it off for a few blocks. Besides, these are my lucky heels, the ones I wore the night I met him.

Bob is going to fall in love with me tonight. I know it. I've got it all planned out. He's such a great guy. Who would ever think anyone would fall in love with me? I guess it really took someone like Bob, who spends his day working in the food stamp office. I hope I'm not just another charity case to him? No, no. NO! Shake it off, girl. He's really into you. He likes chianti. I'll open this bottle and put it on my desk with two wine glasses. There! It looks perfect. Bob is texting again. *"I'm here. Come out to play?"*

My heart can barely contain itself. Come on, feet, all we need to do is make it to the front door. Thank God the printing bay is still empty. It'll just be the two of us. Oh geez, the veins in my forehead are tingling. Just turn the doorknob, Karla. Hold it together. Now, open the door. Just look at him.

"You are so handsome," absent-mindlessly slips from my mouth.

To the average onlooker, Bob is not your traditional beauty. Bob has pasty skin, slight shoulders, a small mouth with permanently pursed lips, and he's so tall he walks like he's constantly ducking under a doorway. *In fact, Bob is the kind of guy who looks so nerdy he makes the guy wearing socks and sandals look cool.* Through Karla's love-struck eyes, though, Bob looks like Justin Timberlake.

"You look pretty damn cute yourself," Bob says, as he kisses me on the mouth.

I wink, take Bob by the hand, and lead him to my office.

"Just what are you up to?" Bob asks.

"You'll see!" I say playfully, and wink again.

Bob sees the open wine bottle and glasses on my desk. He pours two full glasses, hands one to me and downs the other. I take an extra hard gulp of wine, put the glass down, and shut my office door. While Bob might appear dimwitted to others, he is actually quite intelligent. Bob jumps on the opportunity, and me. What is that warmth on my back? It's him. He's kissing the back of my neck. He's so tall. Geez. What is he, 7 feet tall? Even with my heels on, he towers over me. What's he doing now? He's turning me around. Oh, he's kissing me. This is such bliss. I feel like we're floating away. I'm in love. I'm in love! Don't spoil the moment, Karla. Shut your damn mouth, Karla, don't say it. Don't say it, Karla, you moron!

"I love you, Bob."

"I know," Bob replies, and laughs.

Good grief! I really screwed the pooch. Gee whiz! What is this feeling? It's my heart crumbling. I can't look at him. Turn away, Karla. Oh no! Don't cry, you little wuss. Don't do it! Great. Here come the tears. What's that? Bob's touching me. My face. He's holding my face so delicately in his hands. I'm looking at him again.

"Hey, look at me, please. You said it in such a cute way, it made me laugh. I love you, too. I love everything about you, Karla."

Blinking, I look deep into Bob's amber eyes, which are glistening in the LED ceiling lights. My stars! He said it back. Am I dreaming? My mind is racing faster than my pulse. This is the greatest moment of my life. He loves me. Finally, a man who loves me. Just look at those eyes, those beautiful amber eyes. They're so sexy. They almost twinkle.

What's that beeping sound? Why is Bob's fitness watch flashing a bright amber light? Just look at him. His face looks blissful. The lights. The flashing lights. What the heck???!!!

"BOB! Come back. No!!!! Not him!! Please don't take him. Please. Not now!!!!!" As Bob vanishes, Karla yells at the sky, her outstretched arms grasping at air, tears racing down her face.

Karla screams, "WICKED, WICKED ALIENS!" louder than any sound she thinks could ever come out of her, and it scares her. He's gone. He's really gone. It's not just a rumor.

She throws her heels against the wall, picks up the wine bottle, takes a giant slug, then walks outside, chianti in tow, leaving the door to her building wide open. Making her way to the Wynwood Walls, she sits down in front of one of the many wall paintings of aliens, and yells, "BALLS!" Karla feels like a bag of wet onions on a hot sidewalk, and before she knows it, she's crying again. Though an accomplished crier, this time, she can't for the life of her remember what she's crying about.

12

Her father, the racist

In the middle of the spacecraft, amber lights are still putting on a show.

Here I am, still in the past, age 7. It's my first time crossing the street myself. I'm in such a hurry, I trip over my own feet, and face dive onto Grace's concrete sidewalk *like the roadrunner just dropped an anvil on my neck*. The feelings from long ago are all too familiar—pain, exhilaration, shame, but they all vanish when Grace touches my back.

"Are you okay, Freddy? You poor thing."

"I'm fine," I reply, hiding my shame, with as much indignation as my injured 7-year-old self can muster.

"You really are fine," Grace says with a tone of admiration. "Why, Freddy Fluid, I couldn't see you as well from across the street. You're downright pretty."

That should have told me there and then about Grace, but there was something so innocent in how she said it. And when I stood up and finally got to look at Grace up close, the words spilled out of me.

"You're pretty, too."

I'm right here, reliving decades past. I must be losing my mind. I'm here. I mean, there. It's happening all over again. Grace takes my hand. We walk around her block. She introduces me to her father, Jim Whisperer. He's as tall as an oak, and just as strong, wearing a policeman's uniform. He has a big gun, a nightstick, and handcuffs hanging off his belt. Jim reminds me of Batman, only meaner. Because when he looks at his daughter holding my little brown hand, there it is. That look. That racist look. It's the first time I saw it, but certainly wouldn't be the last.

"Young man! Why are you holding my daughter's hand?"

"Oh, Daddy, I took Freddy's hand. We've been talking across the street for a year. We're good friends."

"Friends or no friends, it's inappropriate, young lady."

"Oh, Daddy."

"Young man. Didn't your father teach you about holding hands with young ladies!!?"

There it is again, but this time there is a fury behind it. I see Jim's plump face turn pink, and his eyes are drawn tight with sparks of hate glistening in the Miami sunlight. This is the first time I became interested in eyes, and what they could reveal about a person. *I would later learn Shakespeare said eyes are windows to the soul, or some shit like that.*

"No, Sir," I say. *All I want to do is run home, as fast as I can, but something is holding me here. It's Grace. Despite her father's tone, her hand sticks to mine like superglue.*

"Now, Daddy, Freddy doesn't have a father, so we should be extra nice to him."

"That explains a good deal, young man."

This comment triggered something deep inside me. The feeling came from a place within me I didn't recognize at 7 but would become all too familiar to me later in life, triggered by bigotry, ignorance, and plain meanness. *I call it my asshole meter— what can I say, it's a gift.*

"My father was a great man, Sir. He was royalty in his land."

To this day, I don't know why I made that up, but it felt good to push back against this angry man—still the myth about my father was planted in my brain and even I believed it. I never met my father. Mother was white—very, very, very white, with red hair, and green eyes. When Mother wore a sundress, and the wind was blowing just right, she looked like she was plucked from a bleach commercial in the Irish countryside. All she would say of my father, was he was a great, and noble man. A veritable king from another land. When she told me, I always added—he was like Aladdin, with skin like mine.

Fathers are mythological creatures to most young boys. They get the beautiful maiden, slay dragons, conquer empires, or at the very least, teach you to shave. When you don't have a father, well, it sucks; *and you cut yourself shaving—a lot.*

As I got older, I figured my father was some Middle Eastern dude who got deported. I guess he didn't give a shit about me, or about her. But, deep, deep down, I had a strange feeling, and even at 7, I knew one thing for certain; my father, wherever he was, whoever he was, wasn't as big an asshole as Jim Whisperer. *Yep, my asshole meter never fails me.*

"I think it's time for you to go back to your side of the street, young man."

Before I can stop my tongue, it spills out. "Yes, Sir. And I think Grace is very fortunate, Sir."

"Why?"

"Because clearly she takes after her mother," as I say these words, I see Jim's face turn from light flamingo pink to cardinal red, and then the birdbrained bigot screams, "GRACE! INSIDE! Right this minute," and he grabs Grace by her free arm.

"Bye, Freddy. See you tomorrow."

"OH, NO YOU WON'T, YOUNG LADY!!!" Jim shouts at the top of his lungs.

This was my first big lesson about the color of my skin. After that, Grace wasn't allowed to talk to me on the corner, and I knew better than to go to her house. The bright red color on Jim's face, and the hate in his eyes, forever emblazoned on my retinas. In retrospect, his eyes became a warning beacon to me for future asshole racists. I learned to guard my tongue, and my time.

Approximately 3 years later, Jim had a stroke. He couldn't move or talk. Surprisingly, I had no feelings about the matter. They put Jim in a nursing home. Thankfully, Grace's mother was much more open-minded about race. She didn't mind me hanging around at all. She even took up with the mailman, who happened to be Haitian. That would set Jim's eyes ablaze. Grace, being a dutiful daughter, went to visit her father every Sunday. When we were 10, she took me with her, and here we are, together again.

"I don't think this is a good idea, Grace."

"Oh, come on, Freddy, he doesn't even know I'm there when I visit."

"Okay, but only to keep you company."

"Thank you for keeping me company, Freddy," Grace says, patting my shoulder, *like I'm a hungry service dog walking into a bakery.* We enter the drab hospital looking room, and there he is— Jim Whisperer. He doesn't move a muscle, and compared to the last time I saw his face, it is now a drab gray. I decide to chance it.

"Hello, Mr. Whisperer. I'm sorry you are unwell."

"Oh, Daddy. It's my friend, Freddy. Freddy Fluid, remember?" Jim doesn't budge.

"You see, Freddy. I told you. He doesn't even know we're here."

"Well, then I guess we can do this again," I say as I take Grace's hand. It's a fricking miracle! Jim opens his eyes, looks at Grace, then me, then at us holding hands. His face regains a little color— a *ghoulish gray with a hint of candy striper pink.*

In retrospect, it's the first time I saw the future, but it wasn't because of my powers. I knew exactly what was going to happen a moment from then because Jim's face turned as red as a vampire's tongue in a room full of hemophiliacs. The same thing happened to my great Uncle Larry right before he died. It was going to be awful, but I stayed, for Grace.

"Oh, Daddy, Daddy, you're awake."

With this, Jim reaches out his hand, points at me, and tries to speak. No words come out, but I hear the death rattle.

If you've never heard the death rattle, it's sort of a slurping sound you make when your soda glass is empty, but you keep sucking the straw. Only with the death rattle, it's your last soda. I imagine it's poetic justice. You come into this world, and they give you a rattle, then when you leave you, well—more rattling.

Jim takes a shallow breath and dies. I'm not shocked or scared. I know it's coming. Grace does not. She collapses against me, and we slide down to the floor together. I hold her as she softly weeps. Not knowing what to say to console her, I look at her and smile. I always smile when I see Grace, and I see my flickers reflect in her eyes. She brightens up and smiles back at me, because how can you not smile back when I flicker? *Just saying.*

Grace composes herself and addresses me like an old English noblewoman whose cherished Cavalier King Charles Spaniel just died. "I know he wasn't perfect, but I know he loves, I mean, loved me. Daddy's in a better place, Freddy." *I'm thinking, that's good, because this place smells like piss.* I keep smiling because she's so full of grace.

I see them reflecting in her eyes. My flickering lights. They're moving very fast, and the room fills with what looks like stardust.

This happened 20 years ago. And now, looming all around me in this liquid prison, there they are. Flickering stardust lights.

"#009. Are you finding your way?" #1 asks.

"My way? Where am I going?"

"Everywhere," #1 responds.

"Stop talking in riddles. Where am I? Tell me right now?"

"Nowhere."

"Everywhere, nowhere? Knock it off. What are you, some kind of Zen Warden? What a bunch of crap. Can't you give me a straight answer? You kidnapped me, have me floating in some kind of underwater prison, have me reliving my life, and you won't even answer my simple question. WHERE AM I??!!"

"Maybe you are asking the wrong question, #009," #1 responds.

"Wrong question? What the fuck? Do you think you're Buddha or something?"

"Ahhhhhhh, Buddha. Nice, chap. For such a quiet bloke, he had some wild parties. Why, one time, there was a set of Siamese twins who could… Sorry, I digress. Apologies, #009. Why don't you try asking *when* you are?"

"When? When?! What difference does the time make?"

"Time makes all the difference, in everything, #009. It's very disappointing you don't know this. I knew I waited too bloody long to retrieve you."

"Retrieve me? Time?! Enough already!!! WHERE THE FUCK AM I?" I roar. I hear a loud clattering sound, like someone dropping an aluminum bat on a porcelain floor. "What's with all the racket?"

"Bollocks! Excuse me, #009. It's #2 and #3. I thought I could keep those ninnies otherwise occupied looking for you."

"Looking for me? I'm right here."

"Yes, but they don't know that. I gave them the wrong coordinates. #2 and #3 mean well, but they're a couple of real wankers. I shall return shortly."

"Wait! Don't leave me here. You didn't even tell me where we were?"

"Ah, Freddy! You're not hearing me, old chap. It's not so much about where, as when."

13

Don't just Bob there

Back in the bottom of the spacecraft, millions of tiny amber lights abruptly appear.

"Ohhhhh, #2uuuu?"

"What is it now, #3? Jeebacrom! Can't you see he's coming through now?"

"Oh, he's through all right."

"He is? Why didn't you tell me, #3?"

"Uhhh, because I don't think Freddy is this tall. #1 told us specifically, he's 177 centimeters. This one is well over 2 meters. Yep, well over."

"Hey, you? Mister???" #3 asks.

"Me?" a startled Bob asks.

"Yes, Sir-eee Bob," #3 replies.

"You know my name?" Bob pleads.

"We do if it's Freddy," #2 quickly probes.

"No. My name is Bob. The other fish over there just said it."

"I am not a fish," #2 curtly responds.

"Well, you could have fooled me. What's your tail for, then? And how about those fins?" Burt teases.

"They're flippers! Enough out of you, human!" #2 shouts.

"Not much of a joke if you ask me, Burt," #3 remarks in a disheartened tone.

"How's this? Hey, new guy?" Burt shouts.

"Me?" Bob asks.

"What do you call a guy floating effortlessly up and down in the water?"

"Seriously? Is this really a time for stupid jokes?" Bob asks.

"Bob. His name is Bob, get it? Because he's floating in the water," Burt replies.

"Why is that funny?" Bob asks.

"Look up, look down, look all around," Burt responds.

"Holy crap!" Bob says as he discovers he is immersed in liquid.

"Now that's funny. Isn't that funny, #2?" #3 snorts.

#2 looks at Burt, Leif, and Bob in the chamber and silently sighs to himself. I am so zalked!

14

The day of the lips

A confused, but determined, Freddy remains in the middle of the spacecraft. To an outside observer, absent an assembly of amber lights, the chamber appears empty.

The flickering lights are devouring and feeding me simultaneously. Some of them are taking shape. I'm back in the past, again, on a very special day. *The kind of day that makes you glad you were born with lips.*

7th grade. The first year we attended the same school. The same class—science—and we get to be here for 2 hours, including lunch! I'm sitting on a tall stool, at a real lab table with gas burners, sinks with tall faucets, beakers everywhere, and they assigned us goggles. Oh, and Grace is next to me, plus goggles! Grace is a vision, with her long golden hair, twinkly violet eyes, and the first girl in middle school to get them—boobs. Grace is also the first girl my age to tell me I'm good looking. *She told me when I was 7, but at 13, it makes me smile inside.* My inner geek is alive. I feel myself smiling, and my eyes twinkle faster than usual. Grace smiles at me in a brand-new way.

"Hey, good looking. Why don't you move your stool over here and have lunch with me?" Grace says as she winks.

She's never winked at me before. No girl has. My heart beats fast, my hands sweat, and the rest of my body is awash in a flood of unprecedented bliss, mixed with a healthy smidgeon of fear.

"Hi, Grace. What's up?" I ask, *trying to be as cool as one can be while unwrapping a hummus sandwich.*

"Are you going to the school dance on Saturday?"

"I'm not a good dancer, Grace."

"I'll bet you are, Freddy. Any boy who looks like you just has to know how to dance. Or you could just stand next to me looking pretty."

"Cut it out, Grace," I say without blushing.

"Come on, just look at you, Freddy!"

"What?" I say, putting goggles on my forehead.

"Oh, Freddy, Freddy, Freddy. Your skin shines like caramel. Your thick black hair is always perfect. I don't think one lock would move out of place in a hurricane. And your features. Oh, Freddy, *Freddy,* you look like you were fashioned by Michelangelo himself. Come to think of it, Freddy, you look like the picture of Jesus in my old school—without the beard, of course. Yes, that's it, you look like Jesus. I think more than anything, it's your eyes. They're the color of stars. They flicker when you smile, as if they're made of starlight. Oh, forgive me, Freddy, I can't bear it any longer! If I don't do this right now, I'm going to burst."

And with that, on a stool in a science lab, wearing goggles on my forehead, Grace's lips burst all over me. *I never thought I could love anything more than science, until this moment.* When I was 6, I couldn't even cross the street to see her. At 13, I'm crossing into a river through her lips. The kiss slows me down—Buddha slow, and I'm not in the water! It must be Grace. She takes my breath away. Literally. She is sucking my face hard, and it feels like she's vacuuming my lungs. Thankfully, Grace is a quick study and perfects our first kiss before our lips part.

In retrospect, I thought the feeling was true love, but it could have just as easily been a combination of the lack of oxygen and addition of moisture. The innocent moistness of our teenage mouths. Water in the form of saliva is still water, and water always slows me down. Something else happened that day and as naïve as I was at the time, I knew it wasn't from the moisture. I was bewitched.

What's this strange feeling in my loins? Tingling, desire, trepidation. Puberty hits so fast I feel my armpit hairs growing, and in a flash, I get my third superpower. Well, fourth if you count my asshole meter. I swear it's as if everyone in the class is speaking directly into both of my ears through the world's tiniest EarPods, and I hear everyone's *now* and *next*. Everyone but Grace.

Joe says out loud, "The Dolphins were robbed last night. They should have won!" Immediately, Joe's *next* thought pops into my mind like a sprung mousetrap, '*No sand monkey. I can't believe Grace kissed you. And what's with your eyes?*' Joe's mouth isn't moving, but I hear it just the same. I'm terrified; not of his racist words— I've heard them too many times before. I'm freaking out because I'm hearing what he's going to say *next*. Should I ask him what he's thinking about? Maybe he's practicing ventriloquism? I saw a guy on TV do that with a dog puppet. That must be it. Will he tell me? He only got a B in science last year, and sand monkey! *Why would I care what this moron is thinking?*

"Hey, Joe, are you practicing to be a ventriloquist?"

"No, sand monkey. I can't believe Grace kissed you. And what's with your eyes?" Joe says, punching me in the arm. Sand monkey. Joe definitely gets a ping on my asshole meter. Just because I look different, this a-hole has to insult my heritage, and I don't even know where half my family is from. *And FUCK! I did hear his next thought!* I'm about to punch Joe back and smirk, like *screw you, racist*, I kissed the most beautiful, amazing person in the Universe, when said amazing person dons her goggles and adjusts them *(safety first!)* and grabs the lighter for the gas burners on our lab table. Grace brings the lighter toward Joe's crotch, and says, like a graceful princess about to pull the guillotine, "These lighters are highly sensitive, Joe, and with you being at our lab table all year, we want to be very careful nothing *important* catches fire, burns off, and falls to the ground in a heap of ashes. Right?"

Joe nods in terror, *like someone is holding a lighter next to his junk, because, like I told you, Grace is amazing, and really rocks those goggles.*

"Joe," Grace says *very, very slowly, like she's talking to an idiot, because, she is,* "Don't you have something you want to say to Freddy?"

"I'm sorry, Freddy," Joe says immediately, *like his junk depends on it.*

Brenda says out loud, "I hope someone asks me to the dance."

Doesn't this tramp have any self-respect? By the time she's in college, she'll be dancing with the entire football team, if you know what I mean by "dancing." Then, Brenda's *next* shoves its way into my consciousness, like a fat guy cutting in line at a deli. *'Freddy is gorgeous. I should have kissed him in third grade. I should kiss Bill before some slut does. I hope they don't give us more stupid chemistry homework. I have to get home and feed my kitty.'*

Personally, I love chemistry homework. I can't believe Brenda wanted to kiss me—Ewwww. *Not with that filthy mouth of yours, young lady!*

"Hey, Brenda, if I asked you what you were thinking about a minute ago, would you tell me?"

Brenda blushes. "Oh no, Freddy. A girl has to have her secrets."

"Tell me, please. Was it about chemistry homework and your cat?"

"Freddy Fluid! Who told you I got a cat last night? I didn't have a chance to tell anyone yet! And I hate stupid chemistry homework." *Brenda adds the last part as if I should know this.*

"There's cat fur on your sleeve. Little white hairs. And who likes chemistry homework?" *There wasn't any fur. What a dunce. Brenda is only in this class because her father's the assistant principal. And, as I said, I love chemistry homework. LOVE IT!*

"Freddy Fluid. The dance? Saturday night?" Grace whispers in my ear, momentarily silencing the havoc invading my thoughts. I realize I only hear Grace's *now*. I carefully try to tune into her brain, her *next*, like searching for a radio station on a desert highway. No *next* reception.

She speaks, and I hear it, Grace's *now*, "Say yes, Freddy. Please! It will be fun."

"Huh?"

"The dance, Freddy," Grace says.

I hear Grace speak, no *next*, and I'm relieved. Maybe I'm imagining everyone's *next*. Great! Something else to obsess on. *Sure, Freddy, now you can see the fricking future. What are you thinking? FREAK!*

Grace is silent, waiting for me to respond. That's the thing about grace, sometimes it comes in true silence. Mine doesn't last. *I hate dancing, but Grace made the next go away, and the tension falls from me like a silk nightie off a newlywed's shoulders. I want to tell her she is rescuing me from my insanity, that I can't imagine my life without her. That our kiss was the greatest moment of my entire life. That I love her. That I always will.*

My own words shatter the silence. "Dance? Oh, sure." Not my finest moment, nonetheless, a more than adequate response, prompting Grace to put her hands in the air and shake her hips.

"We're going to the danc-ance! We're going to the danc-ance," Grace says just loud enough for the class to hear. For Grace, this is shouting. Grace never shouts. It throws me and invites the outside clatter. All of the other *now* conversations and *next* thoughts rush me like a sacked quarterback, and flickering is everywhere, in every beaker, flask, desk surface, window and wall. The flickering, the voices, the *now* and *next*. I squeeze my eyes tight as I remember the unyielding flickering is shooting from my own peepers, and the whir envelops me. *My brain vibrates like a paint can in a broken mixer, on a cracked concrete floor.*

Opening my eyes in time, I see flickering reflecting in Grace's goggles and *next* disappears. I smile as her open mouth once again floats toward mine. My eyes flicker faster and brighter than ever. *Maybe it's all the glass in here?*

"Oh, Freddy, your eyes are sparkling so much, it looks like a fairy disco in here. I love you," Grace says, then our mouths touch, and I know in every geeky, goggle wearing, stardust shining quark in my being, I love her. I am enraptured until she pulls away when the teacher enters the room.

I'm scared, but not of Grace. I'm never scared of Grace. It's the voices. I hear all of them at once. *Everyone in class, their nows and nexts flooding my brain, and anxiety grips me like a fish in the talons of a flying eagle. Make that a handsome, starry-eyed fish plucked from a calm lake into the extremely sharp talons of a ginormous soaring eagle, with balls—big ones—and I don't understand what is happening to me, and even though I'm frozen in place, my body pulses faster than anyone, or anything around me, and my lungs can't keep up, and I can't fucking breathe!*

"Breathe, Freddy," #1 says as the lights flicker and I'm back in the spaceship. "Just breathe, lad."

And I do. Look like Jesus, that is. As I got older, I let my hair grow out and sprouted a beard. I look like Jesus's handsome younger brother— the one who went into modeling.

15

Cruising for a bruising

At the bustling Port of Miami, on an exceptionally sunshine-filled morning, a couple embarks a cruise ship.

"Geez, Al, look at this. Champagne when you walk on the boat. So fancy!"

"It ought to be for the money I paid for this cruise, Candy. And they call it embarkation."

"Embarkation? Is that a special French champagne? Geez, you're so sophisticated, Al."

"Not the champagne, moron! Embarkation is what they call it when you board a ship."

"Ohhhhh! Can I still have a glass?"

Geez. What a ditz! I can't believe I'm going to be stuck on this ship with her for 14 days—8 at sea. Sure, she's great in the sack. But what the hell do we do for the other 23 hours, 58 minutes of the day? Well, if I sleep 9 hours a day, and spend the rest in the casino and buffet line…

"Sir. Excuse me, Sir?" the ship's officer asks.

"Oh, sorry for holding up the line," Candy says.

"Quite all right. Welcome to your vacation. Champagne?"

"Yeah. Champagne would be good. And one for my charming companion here," Al says.

"Oh, Al. You're making me blush. Do I shake his hand?" Candy whispers into Al's ear.

"Sorry. She doesn't get out much. Go ahead, doll. Be yourself."

"Oh, hello there, your Honor. I mean, Captain. Sorry, this is my first time on a big boat like this. I'm a little nervous," Candy says.

"It's called a ship, doll. Geez. Like I said, she doesn't get out much. But she has other good qualities, if you know what I mean?" Al says, making an hourglass figure in the air with his hands.

"Quite all right, Miss. It's a common mistake. Generally, ships are larger, and meant for ocean-going journeys. One easy way to tell the difference is from an old saying, *'a ship can carry a boat, but a boat can't carry a ship.'* Notice the lifeboats hanging from the railings."

"Oh, you are so smart, Captain. No wonder they let you drive this big boat. I mean, ship."

"He's not the captain, doll. Do you think the captain would be handing out drinks to passengers on the gangway?"

"Oh, God. I'm such an idiot. Sorry," Candy says, slapping her forehead.

"Oh no, Ma'am. It's quite the compliment. My name is Riptide. Ensign Rodney Riptide. I am the assistant purser. My card. Anything I can do to make your stay better, please do not hesitate to call me, Missus…?"

"It's Miss. Miss Cotton, but my friends call me Candy—like Cotton Candy, only backwards, it's Candy Cotton. Funny, right?" Candy says, abruptly sticking out her hand.

"It's quite humorous, Miss Cotton. It will be a great pleasure cruising with you both," Riptide replies as he kisses Candy's extended hand, and shakes Al's.

"Oh, how sophisticated. And I love his English accent, Al. Isn't it swanky? It's so swanky, right? I can't believe you took me on this boa—I mean, ship," Candy says as she kisses Al on the mouth.

"Hey, Riptide. Are the room's ready, because it looks like this one is! Know what I mean?" Al says, winking at Riptide.

"Al. Stop. You're embarrassing me," Candy says.

"Don't worry, doll. This ain't Riptide's first cruise. He knows what a girl like you is doing here."

"Al, please stop!" Candy admonishes, turning red, tears streaming from her eyes.

Ensign Riptide leans close to Al and whispers in his ear. "I certainly don't, Sir. Miss Cotton appears to be a delightful young lady. If you don't mind my saying, respectfully, Sir, I think you are taking this a bit too far."

"HEY! Who the fuck do you think you are? Just 'cause you're on a big fancy ship at the Port of Miami doesn't give you the right to talk to a paying customer like this. I paid good money for this cruise and bought this bimbo a whole new wardrobe. So how about you just serve the drinks and shut your fricking limey mouth before I shut it for you."

"Apologies, Sir."

"Now that's more like it, Ensign."

"Apologies for this, Ma'am," Riptide says as he cocks back his arm and strikes Al full force in his right eye.

"You son of a bitch. I'm going to kick your stuck-up British ass, then get you fired, then sue this cruise line. You fancy prick!" Al yells, taking a swing at Riptide. As Al's arm travels forward, he sees it. His wristwatch flashing amber. "Fucking aliens!" Al screams as he vanishes.

"Oh, my God! I never thought I would see it happen, and right before my eyes. He's gone. He's just gone. I heard they could disappear us, but if I hadn't seen it with my own eyes."

"So sorry, Miss Cotton. And I must apologize for my behavior. I shall immediately submit myself for discipline to the captain."

"Oh no, Ensign Riptide. You're the first guy who's stuck up for me since I was a kid. This can be our little secret."

"How kind of you, Miss Cotton, but certainly the captain will want to discipline me for my transgression."

"Well, I don't know about the captain, but seeing as I'm all alone now, why don't you come back to my room when you get off work, and I can discipline you myself."

"That certainly is a titillating offer, Miss Cotton."

"Don't you worry, doll, there will be plenty of titillating," Candy flirts, adjusting her bosom. "And, doll. I mean, Ensign Riptide?"

"Yes, Miss Cotton?"

"You can call me Candy. You'll find out another reason my friends call me Candy later."

"I look forward to that with great anticipation."

"And one more thing, doll."

"Yes, Candy?"

"Wear that little hat of yours. It's so YMCA."

16

The day of the lips, revisited

Back in the middle of the spaceship, I take a deep breath into my belly.

"Good, Freddy, breathe," #1 says with encouragement. "It's all part of your journey."

"Hey! What journey? What are you doing to me?"

"Me? You are the one with the controls at hand, lad." #1 chuckles, and shoots me a look, like I'm a stoned teenager with a learner's permit and his dad's car keys.

"I'm 13 again? We were just here! Give it a break, #1. #1?"

How do I describe what was going on in my brain in science class, the day of the lips? Actually, it started the night before when Grandmother took me to a sports bar. The one with cute girls in tight white t-shirts, greasy chicken wings, big screen TVs plastering the walls. *You know the place.* I ordered beer—well, root beer. Grandmother ordered 2 plates of wings, 1 for each of us, and a gin martini, followed by 3 more martinis with olives. *I hate olives.* Grandmother drank, ate olives, and picked at a wing. I demolished both plates of wings and 3 root beers. Everyone in the bar was talking, glasses clattering, knives thrusting against plates, pitchers of beer flowing, big screen TVs erupting football, baseball, fishing, soccer, and slow-motion replays from all directions, and I didn't like it! I frantically stabbed my straw in and out of my root beer while counting to myself. 29, the number of TVs in the bar. If I got to 29, everything would be okay, *but I did, and it wasn't.* I was overwhelmed by all of it, the talking, the restaurant noise, the TVs, the replays. I was moving breathlessly fast, and not only on the inside. My hand was shaking. So was my right leg. My nose and mouth couldn't keep up with my own demand for oxygen. *I desperately bobbed for air, like a 2-headed puppy trying to dislodge a bone from my throat, and, and, and I couldn't fucking breathe, until a whiff of something medicinally strong under my nose shocked my airway open. And, I'm back in the bar, with Grandmother.*

"Here, kid. You look like you need this more than me," Grandmother says, and touches her martini glass to my nostrils. I gulp it, olives and all. I want to scream, but my breath is absent, and I want to pass out. The room is spinning too fast for me to find a landing spot, and Grandmother says, "Breathe, Freddy. Breathe! You don't want them to think you can't hold your liquor, kid." I smile at her and puke across the table, my magical flickers washing away in a flood of undigested gin, root beer, wings, and olives. Yuck!

Yep, science class, the day of the lips, is like being in the sports bar. It's as if I can see every play occurring, but instead of watching instant replays on the big screen TVs, I see the plays that will occur a moment from *now*—who will catch the ball, who will drop it, what giant fish will be caught, and which will escape. Our first day of science class is just like the sports bar, without Grandmother, sports, the TVs, booze, olives, or cute waitresses.

I'm here again with Grace, hearing the classroom conversations and my classmate's *next* thoughts all at once. *Now* and *next* invade my mind like a colony of ants attacking a melty ice cream cone on a hot day. I'm dizzy. I hope I won't puke in class. *Yuck!*

"Way to go, man. You kissed Grace. This is a good ham and cheese sandwich, Freddy. I'll trade you half for half your hummus. It appears you have sub-atomic meteor remnants traversing your eyes," says George Smelt, who perpetually smells of ham and cheese. I also hear his *next* thought, although an entire half of a well-stacked ham and cheese sandwich fills his giant maw, and he's not speaking, *'I'm asking Mom to make me ham, cheese, and hummus tomorrow.'*

Disgusting! Sorry, I have little patience for George, although for a 13-year-old, he has an extraordinary understanding of physics, organic chemistry, and animal husbandry. It's a shame rather than using his advanced brain to end world hunger, George Smelt's greatest accomplishment will likely be crossing a pig with a hunk of sharp cheddar.

"Did you see Grace and Freddy kiss? Why are Freddy's eyes full of fireworks?" Flora asks out loud, as her *next* thought pops into her and my head. *'I wonder if George will taste like ham and cheese when he kisses me.'*

Yuck, and yes, just look at him. Every pore in his body oozes ham and cheese.

My struggle for air quickens. *Now* fades, replaced by 1 minute from *now*—*next*. George wants to go home and feed his ferret. *I didn't know ferrets liked ham and cheese?* John wants chocolate ice cream after his salami and pickle sandwich *(again, yuck!)*. Mary is thinking about Grace's boobs. *Hey! Cut that out! Oh, fine, she's wondering when hers will come in, and they're all thinking about the stardust in my extraordinary eyes.*

All the *nexts* in the classroom attack. Only *next* exists, and I'm frantically stuck 1 minute in the future drowning in all of my classmates' *next* thoughts. *Stop! Please, please make it stop!* My brain churns *next, next, next.* All of their *nexts* commingle sickeningly in my skull, *like when you put big scoops of everything from the buffet table on your tiny dessert plate and eat every bit. Not a good idea, by the way.*

My brain can't stop, *next* is feeding it like a coal stoker on a runaway steam ship, and only *next* exists. My throat tightens, my mind so stuck in *next* it forgets to tell my lungs a simple *now* message—breathe! I'm light-headed and sick, *like after a bad carnival ride. Make that a bad carnival ride after 2 orders of greasy wings and a gulp of Grandmother's martini, with olives.*

Next takes over, and the next thing I experience in 7th grade, after collapsing to the science laboratory floor of Nautilus Middle School, is Grace Whisperer. She sits next to me, cradling my head in her lap, wearing a white shirt, and looking infinitely prettier than any of the sports bar servers. Grace strokes my hair, mellifluously tells me I'll be okay, and *next* retreats, washed away by her whispers. We smile at each other. I feel like an unadoptable puppy finally being lifted out of a bin by a happy child, and it's all I can do to keep my tongue in my mouth and not lick her all over her face. Grace finds me, and I know I will never be graceless again. She is mine, and I am hers, forever. Yeah, this is what's going on in my 13-year-old brain, as I try not to puke all over Grace's perfect lap.

I blame my physical state on yesterday's wings and martinis. Grace showers me with a concerned look, and I wish above all things *next* would appear, but only Grace's. What is she thinking? But it doesn't matter, because there, in front of the entire classroom, Grace kisses me again and she's still wearing goggles. *Goggles! I love this girl!* My eyes flicker, as does everything in the classroom, and in the quiet, I see it. Hovering outside our classroom window—a translucent twirling orb the size of a bumblebee, surrounded by millions of teensy-weensy stars. Must be a tiny drone. As it gets closer, it looks like a glistening soap bubble, and I feel dizzy again, but in a good way.

That was one helluva kiss, all right! Despite her worried look, I didn't say anything to Grace about *next*, until after med school. I wanted to tell her everything. I didn't think even Grace could handle hearing about *next*, and I was scared she would think I was losing my shit. Maybe I was? *Impressive reasoning for a 13-year-old, right?* I can't believe I just relived 7th grade. Shit! I'm back in the flickering amber lights of the round chamber, realizing there is something very familiar about that bubble orb.

17

Al aboard!

"Did you get him this time, #2? I see something else materializing in the chamber. It's flashing. Wait for it. Wait for it. There!"

"I got him for sure this time, #3!"

"Who the fuck are you two? Where am I?" a very pissed Al asks.

"Uh, #2uuu, I don't think this is Freddy."

"Freddy? Who the fuck is Freddy? Where's that limey Love Boat dropout? I'll kick his ass so far across the Atlantic, he won't need a cruise ship to get home," Al shouts.

"Definitely not Freddy, #2. Nope. Not him at all."

"Let me out of here! Who the fuck are you?" Al questions, pointing to Burt, who is sitting on a stool with a microphone in his hand.

"Don't mind me. I'm just the comedian."

"Comedian? I didn't sign up for no entertainment. What is this, a shore excursion? Did the ship sink? Am I dead? What the hell kind of cruise is this!!???"

Burt swims over to the chamber Al occupies and speaks. "So, two aliens walk into a bar…"

"Fucking comedian. This must be Hell. I knew I shouldn't have offed that choir boy. My sister told me I would go to Hell for that. Let me outta here. See if you're cracking jokes with my foot up your funny ass," Al blurts.

"Don't mind him, Burt. Good one. Don't you think he's funny, #2?" #3 asks.

"Hysterical," #2 replies.

"Whew! Tough crowd. At least you're not throwing tomatoes. After my last show, I could have made a salad," Burt responds.

"Is that the best you got? Poor excuse for a comedian," #2 says.

Before Burt can respond, a voice pierces the air. "Status report, #2?"

"Any minute now, #1. Any minute."

"Keep me advised, #2," #1 says in a tone #3 doesn't like at all.

"Let me the fuck out of here and I'll kick your alien asses," Al yells, throwing himself against the side of the chamber, to no avail.

"Hey, #2! #3! You want to know what I think?" Burt asks.

"Not really," #2 quips.

"Yes, Burt? I want to know what you think," #3 queries.

"You are so zalked!"

18

Myiasis

Back in the middle of the spaceship, Freddy is beamed to a place no man has boldly gone before.

"Oh no, not this. Please, #1, not this. No one should have to see this! Can't we fast forward to the good parts? There are good parts, right?" I plead.

"I keep telling you, old boy, you're the one driving this bloody bus," #1 says.

"More of an out-of-control train with no brakes, if you ask me, but who's asking? Can't I skip this part? #1? #1!!!" Fuck! Guess not.

When I was a teenager, when I wasn't in school, studying, or making out with Grace, I was in my happy place—the shower. *And no, not because it's all soapy in there.* The great thing about growing up in South Florida is even if you have OCD, you're living in the fricking sub-tropics. Beaches, coconut trees, lush greenery, scantily dressed people, sleek boats, fast cars, and flip-flops. Lots of hot, sweaty outdoor activities; so many excuses for a shower or swim. Yeah, it's hot, but it's Miami, and people love it. What's not to love? *I'll tell you—bugs! Well, bugs and traffic.*

There're too many insect species to name, but there's one in particular I despise. You see, when I was in school, learning, homework, and my classmates' *next* thoughts occupied my gray matter. In the summer, weekends, pretty much any time I wasn't busy, I created my own frequently miserable steaming pile of *next;* and I became *OCD's little bitch.*

Here's the thing, if a person with OCD gets ill, they are typically good at getting well. They take their meds on time, obsessively check their temperature, remember to drink plenty of fluids, get lots of rest. But if an OCD person only thinks they are ill, their own body terrifies them. They google every disorder known to man and are convinced they have the rarest of the lot. Even now, as a skilled physician with medical knowledge that my stomach cramps are probably gas, a time bomb *tick, tick, ticks* in my head. Cancer! I must schedule a colonoscopy. No, a colonoscopy and an endoscopy. Might as well check my upper GI tract while they're up there. *I really hope they clean off the endoscope between procedures. Who in their right mind wants a colonoscopy?*

Shit, here I am again, back in my past, age 14! At least it's a beautiful day outside, not that I noticed at the time.

The shower's magic slows me down after a hectic summer day of watching Star Trek, eating everything in sight, and making out with Grace. I'm blissfully Buddha slow until they show up. Three tiny black worms fall to the aqua and beige tiles beneath my wet feet. As I wash my nether regions with the shower wand, it occurs to the science nerd in me, these worms are infinitesimally small life forms, corporeal pieces of sewing thread. Despite their stature, they are mightily swimming against the swift current heading to the drain. Momentarily fascinating, until these 3 minuscule worms send me on my first of many OCD journeys to Hell.

My stomach throbs, my breath deserts me, my panicked thoughts rattle off each other. *OCD is at the wheel, and it didn't bother to take driving lessons.*

What are these worms? Are they venomous? Where did they come from? Wait, what was I just washing? Did the worms come out of me? *Ewwww!* I urgently rinse off the rest of the soap, leap from the shower, and slip across the bathroom floor into my towel. My brain is in full gear worry mode. I can't focus on anything but worms, worms, worms. Well, worms and butts, and also genitals. *Again, yuck!* It's all so gross, but where else could those worms have come from?

I race to my bedroom, google parasitic worms on my laptop, and fight off images of the creature in the movie *Alien* ripping through my stomach. Paranoia takes over. My breathing is labored. My gut aches. My body releases a layer of cold, sticky sweat. Worms! I'm going to fucking die! Paranoia takes over. Nobody else is in the room, unless you count the fucking worms, yet someone is coming for me—*and it's me!* Anyone who ever walked down a dark street alone on a moonless night, sure someone is following you, knows the feeling. You tell yourself it's all in your head. You're being paranoid, Freddy. Yeah, sure, paranoid, but they're worms! *My fingers frantically click the mousepad, like a horny teenager waiting for a porn site to download on a slow computer.* Come on already! *Tick, tick, tick.* The time bomb is set.

In my frenzy, I knock my printer to the floor. I don't know who's steering my brain, but it's certainly not me. Something takes over. I feel like a crazed character come to life in a video game; a character someone else controls. I laugh maniacally to see if it will clear the command. *It doesn't.*

"Are you okay in there, Freddy? Sorry, dear, I heard a noise? I know how teenage boys like long showers and privacy, but what's with all the noise?" Mother asks through the door, in a voice that could calm a cyclone. My brain comes to focus, like a clear, cool morning. *Get it together, Freddy, you freak!*

"Fine! I'm fine, Mother."

"Okay, Freddy, my love. Dinner in 10 minutes."

My brain bounces around the Google search results at warp speed. So far, I found hundreds of parasitic worms and the term myiasis. *I freeze like an asthmatic squirrel.* I fight myself for the limited air coming in rapid, shallow breaths. I can't read the computer screen. I need to answer Mother. I hear her *next* thought. *'Cheeseburgers.'*

"Freddy? Did you hear me?"

My circuits are fried. Myiasis? I may have worms in my ass. Shit, I better read this.

"Freddy?"

Answer her. "I hear you, Mother. Cheeseburgers, 10 minutes."

"Okay, Freddy. Hey, how did you know I was making cheeseburgers?"

I want to say, "I smell them." *I don't.* I want to say, "You told me before, Mother." *She didn't.* My first big act of omission to Mother is, "Lucky guess," and it's followed by no response for a full minute. I don't hear her *next* thoughts either. Just an image—an orca in a tiny orb bubble? Then my brain goes back to smashing itself against my skull over, and over, and over again. Shit! I have myiasis!

Mother's *next* dares to interrupt my OCD, and I know she will say *'Love you,'* and I blurt, "Love you too, Mother." Another moment's hesitation from Mother. This one lasts longer, and her silence mercifully holds OCD at bay.

"You sure everything is all right, Freddy, my love?" Mother asks.

"Fine, Mom." *I never call her Mom, and she knows everything is far from fine, because, well, mothers know these things.*

"Okay, baby," Mother says. *Yeah, more like Rosemary's baby!*

Precisely 6 hours, 14 minutes, 16 showers, and 268 Google searches later, I fall asleep at my laptop, until terror jolts me from a dead sleep at 2:01 a.m. My eyes pop open. My insides feel like they touched a hot book of matches, immediately followed by an ice water plunge into fear. Chill, Freddy. Chill! They're just worms, and even if you have them, you'll probably just take some pills and be fine. Don't worry about the worms. *My brain screams STOP, but OCD screams louder—I'll see your logic, Good Sir, and raise you 10,000 worries!*

My *next* fills with the worst possible outcomes; and, and I'm going to die of worms! *Next, next, next pounds away at me like a chisel to my spinal cord. Nobody talks about how painful OCD is—let me tell you, it fucking aches like the flu.* I somehow fall asleep and wake up a few hours later to a starring role in my own Hitchcock flick; The Worms! Exactly 5 hours, 6 minutes, 48 seconds, 349 more Google searches, 6 more showers, and 3 rolls of scotch tape stuck in my butt last night as worm traps *(don't ask)*, and I'm as spent as a gravedigger after a massacre. I walk into the bathroom for shower number 23. Mother comes in carrying a teapot full of boiling water.

"Sorry, Freddy dear. I'll just be a minute."

"Weird place for teatime, don't you think, Mother?"

"Oh, Freddy, you're a trip. We have sewer moths. I saw their larval worms in the shower. Hot water down the drain kills them. That, and putting tape on the drain at night. The moths stick to the tape when they hatch in the drain and try to fly away." I stand dumbfounded, wanting to tell Mother everything, to expose my

OCD for the wretched villain it is, but instead I am humbled by her superior Google skills and appropriate use of tape.

"Sewer moths?"

Mother pours boiling water around and down the shower drain. I watch 2 tiny worms shrivel as OCD is vanquished. *Mostly.*

"You missed 1," I say casually, as I notice another worm clawing its way to the corner of the shower. (*Worms have claws, right?*)

"Oh, you saw the worms, Freddy?"

"Yeah," I say, feeling like I've just survived an exorcism.

"A couple of nights of this should do it," Mother says, tickled, hoisting the tape and teapot into the air as if she were taming a lion.

The rest of my teenage years were a blur; fast and furious. Just my pace! Until I turned 18.

19

Now! Wow!

The lights are back.

"Hey, #1! Are you coming back?" Fricking guy just leaves me here. "Hey, #1! If you want me to see my life story like *A Christmas Carol*, can't you at least run the commercial free version with a narrator, or better yet, pop in every once in a while, and tell me WHAT THE HELL IS GOING ON!!??? #1?? You still here?"

Fucking guy. Wait! The lights are flashing. It's my 18th birthday, senior year of high school, and this memory is worth the commercial announcements, *speaking of which*. Every person should have a great love affair once in their lives. Sometimes it lasts a minute, sometimes years, a few last a lifetime. Our love affair is infinite, *like lint on a lollipop in the bottom of an old purse.*

Did I mention Grace looks like an elven princess, sans the pointy ears? Like I said, I have a thing for pointy ears. I joked about it while nibbling her ear when we first made out. Memory like an elephant, that Grace; she never forgets a thing, is extremely thoughtful by nature, and turns out she knows her way around a

3D printer—like I said, infinite, if not geeky, love. She fashioned a set of elf ears as a birthday surprise. Clever girl, that Grace. She still has the ears. She wears them for my birthday, Halloween, or when she's feeling a little naughty. They're extremely realistic. She can even wiggle them. When Grace wiggles her elf ears and winks, I shake like Jell-O. If we were stranded on a desert island and I could only pick one thing for Grace to bring for the rest of our days—elf ears, hands down.

Our love formed the first time Grace took my hand, then it cemented with our first kiss, and the first time we made love, it turned diamond hard. *So did I. Well, I did!* Here we are, walking, not sneaking into the science lab in our senior year in high school. I had keys, a benefit of assisting our physics teacher, Mr. Sanderson, with his unsanctioned after-school experiments creating a new distillate. For something Sanderson claimed would cure the world's ills, it smelled a lot like Grandmother's Irish whiskey—not the cheap stuff either.

"God, you're beautiful," I say, sitting next to Grace on my lab stool.

"You're not so bad yourself," Grace says and kisses me.

It is a deep, long, wet, but not sloppy kiss. *I hate sloppy kisses.* Grace's mouth tastes of chocolate and sunshine and seawater, and it calms and excites me all at once.

"I have a surprise for you, Freddy Fluid," Grace says coyly. *Grace is never coy.*

"Surprise? You already told me we were having sex today, Grace. I'd have to say, intercourse is a pretty damn good present, but it's not a surprise, not that I don't appreciate it. I think it's the best present anyone has ever gotten me; maybe even better than my truck."

"Open it, Freddy," Grace says, taking out a small box wrapped in silver, with gold ribbon.

"Perfect job on the wrapping, Grace. Just look at how you tied this cute little ribbon."

"Thank you, Freddy, my love. I used a little surgical knot, and—Hey, wait! Now you have me doing it. I know you're nervous, so am I, but open it, please. I think it will help."

"Nervous, me?" I say, untying the ribbon, my hands moving over the box as awkwardly as butterfly wings on a windy day. "They're beautiful, Grace. Absolutely anatomically correct. Wow! They feel real. Maybe a little cold, though. You know, Grace, I bet if we put these in a warming dish in the autoclave for just a second," I suggest, holding the ears to my head.

"Freddy," Grace hums, turning her perfect alabaster white skin a shade of pink. "They're not for you."

"Not for me? I would hardly call that a birthday surprise! Ohhhhh," I say, smiling apprehensively as Grace slowly puts the ears on, coquettishly smiling at me, having the appearance of an elf bound for a mischievous journey. She kisses me again, and we slide to the floor under the tall black lab table. *Grace removes her sundress. It's so yellow against the black floor, it looks like butter melting on the center of a sunflower, and I wish I were a tub of popcorn.* I remove my clothes, and as I kiss Grace, I transition into a delightful Buddha pace.

"Put it in, Freddy," Grace says, and she winks, making my body quiver. "And remember it's delicate, Freddy."

I put it in, and the quiver turns to a shiver which surprisingly extends beyond my loins to my entire being. "Delicate! Why, that's an understatement. Do you know how many nerve endings there are in entrance to the female reproductive system alone? Why there's—"

"Freddy," Grace interrupts, "just because we're in the science lab doesn't mean I want a lesson. At least not the book kind. Now, where were we?" Grace hushes me as she playfully, and forcefully, kisses me.

And *now* is exactly where we are. It's the most wonderful *now* I've ever felt, until my *next* starts, even though it's a good *next*. I want to feel like this for-fucking-ever. Stop it! Get out of your head, Freddy, the big one. Be *now* Freddy!

"You okay, babe? Your face is scrunched up. It's not like you're fighting a tiger, Freddy. Relax. Enjoy yourself. I am," Grace says as she grinds slowly against me and smiles.

"Oh, Grace," I breathe out, holding her stunning face in my hands. "How could you be even more beautiful and perfect than you are? I don't know, but you are right now, and those ears, why they are even better than my truck, and I always want to feel this way, like we are lying in the middle of a hot fudge sundae in enormous spoons, and it's cold, and hot, and melty, and delicious, and tastes like the best thing ever created, and infinite—like our love," I say as I pull out of my geek nosedive, into the most epic kiss ever delivered to a girl—*or so I've been told*. I lose all sense of *next* and am bathing in *now*, and it's the most *now* I've ever felt. Our breaths, heartbeats, pulses, delightful movements, touches, kisses, all unite in *now*.

"Now, Freddy. Now," Grace whispers as she nibbles my ear.

I almost stop to ask, now? Now what? Because I'm already in *now*, and I never want to leave the *now* that is Grace; that is us. There's flickering, with increasing frequency and intensity reflecting in Grace's eyes. I smile at her, because, well, she is Grace and smile-worthy from everyone on the planet, let alone the person she is gifting with her *now*.

My brain moves Buddha slow, but my body moves faster and faster in rhythm with my flickers and Grace's body, as we meld together like writhing sea snakes in the current, and flickering bliss is shooting out my eyeballs, making all the glass in the science lab glow amber. I move fast, and I'm not breathless, and I move slow, and know this has to be what Buddha felt when he attained enlightenment, and it's, it's, it's—fricking heavenly.

Grace winks, and I know exactly what *now* is as she melodiously moans, like a tiger cub discovering a piece of catnip encrusted meat, dipped in chocolate and fried, and her elven ears wriggle like she's a happy bunny in a field of fucking clover and sunshine on a spring day, and *now* explodes between us like a quiet storm, and for the first time in my disorienting, *now* and *next*, flickering, OCD mess of a life, I am at peace, *like a tiger cub in a field of clover and sunshine, digesting a fucking chocolate bunny—dipped in catnip, and fried.*

20

The adulterer

In the 1960s and 70s, Greynolds Park was the hippy capital of Miami-Dade County. Weekends found the park's tall grassy hill full of barely, if not colorfully dressed young people, who were smoking a different kind of grass. In present day, the park's patrons are mostly young families, and residents, looking for a walk through nature. The wood and stone boathouse and castle topped hill stand sentinel from the center of the urban forest as an older woman takes a trip down memory lane.

46 years ago today. It's hard to believe it was that long ago, and I really can't believe I lost enough weight to rock my wedding dress. Our wedding in Greynolds Park, on this grass, next to the boathouse. The row boats and paddleboats are gone now, but the boathouse looks the same as it did in 60s. Why are there no more boats? They made this place even more magical. Back then, this little lake was filled with rowers and paddlers, small children hanging their feet in the light brown water, Muscovy ducks loudly

flapping their wings, squawking at the shoreline, the large males running off their competition, trying to impress the females.

He's holding my hand. All this time, and I still feel the same way every time he holds my hand. My heart thumps a bit harder than usual at the touch of his fingertips grasping the back of my hand. I love the feeling, except in the summer, when his skin is hot and sticky, and before I can control myself, I say, *"Ewwww. Too hot."* He always laughs and touches his butt, with the same reply, *"Why, yes. Yes, I am hot. How can you possibly keep your hands off of me?"*

We must have had this exchange a thousand times over the years, and I still smile, and smack his butt every time. For a while there, I thought he might like getting spanked. I tried it once in bed, and he pulled away as if he were a toddler being admonished for running into the street. I'll never forget the pained look in his eyes. I asked him if he had ever been abused. *"Who hasn't?"* he replied with a damaged smile, as he turned me around and did me from behind. That was hot too, but I could feel his detachment and pain coming through his very being—poor thing. We've been through so much. It hasn't been easy; especially on the kids.

I remember the Miami Dolphin Game in 1972 when we met. Dolphins versus the Patriots. His eyes sparkled like they were right out of a Carpenters' love song. I love Karen Carpenter. She was quite the song stylist. The Dolphins were on their way to an undefeated season and the energy in the stadium was palpable. Every Sunday, Will, me, and the kids would arrive 3 hours early, bringing sandwiches, a football, blankets, and we'd party on the west lawn of the Orange Bowl.

Will was a good guy, a bit shorter than men I dated in my youth, but he was a decent guy, with southern family roots like mine. We dated in high school. Then we went our own ways, hooked up one night at a bar a few years later, and decided to move from our hometown of Rome, Georgia, to North Miami Beach. That was right after our shotgun wedding. The sex was good, at least what I thought was good at the time, and before I knew it, we were having another kid. Will had a good-paying job at Florida Power & Light, working on the overhead power lines. It could be very dangerous, but he was small and wiry, and fit well in a bucket truck. Our house was nice enough, although too small, with two bedrooms and one bath. So, there we were, the perfect little family. House-check. Children: boy-check, girl-check. The children really did need their own rooms, though.

Everything was fine, until I met Harvey. It was those sparkling amber eyes. And he was so tall and broad. Like the boys I used to date before Will. At first, it seemed the only thing we had in common was the tailgating spot we shared at the Orange Bowl. As the season went on and the Dolphins dominated the NFL, there was an incredible excitement in the air outside and inside the Orange Bowl; an excitement that spilled into our encounters. While Will and Harvey's wife, Lois, joined the kids in their tag football games, Harvey and I sat on our blankets, drinking wine, eating sandwiches, talking about music, food, and books. I couldn't believe it when he told me he loved Hemingway, Willy Nelson, and Orange Nehi. A few weeks later, we were parked in his van at Greynolds Park, drinking wine, and having the most amazing sex of my life. I sat in my kitchen every day for a week after, drinking myself into bottomless anguish. I must have screwed Will a dozen times that week, hoping to feel a drop of the passion I'd felt with Harvey, but it never came. Neither did I.

I told Will it was over. To say he took it hard would be an understatement. The kids wanted to stay with me. Who could blame them? I was the fun one. Will bought a motorcycle, had his van painted with giant cobras, got a tattoo, and became a pothead.

Harvey left Lois and filed for divorce. We bought a house a few blocks from Greynolds Park and went "parking" there every week. Back then, Greynolds was so happening. These days, with the exception of a few music festivals, the once bustling hippiedom is just a park, but a lovely one at that.

Here we are. Harvey and me. At the boathouse again. He looks at me with those sparkling amber eyes, and as has been the case for 4 decades, I turn to mush. My mother told me, when you're young, sex is like a sport. When you get old, it's like a cozy conversation on a warm couch between two people who love the shit out of each other. Yet another thing Mom lied about. I still liquify the second Harvey kisses my neck. Our lips touch and I feel a power I never felt before. It's electric.

What's flashing? Oh shit! His watch is flashing amber. He's disappearing. "HARVEY!!!!! He's mine, you hear! Find someone else! Not now! Please! For God's sake, it's our anniversary," Helen yelled at no one in particular. As she walked toward the boathouse, she muttered, "Fucking aliens! Just when I finally fit into my old wedding dress!"

21

Loop Road

In the middle of the spaceship, the flickering lights transport Freddy Fluid to his college days.

Grace and I lived together through college and med school. We took all the same classes. I'm fricking brilliant. Did I mention, I'm brilliant? *If I haven't, don't worry, I will.* I always find a way to bring it up.

When I was in middle school, I couldn't balance the future thoughts I was hearing from my teachers and classmates, and the present moment. Overload! To put it mildly, I struggled emotionally—*Okay, okay, I was a fucking mess of a kid.* Thankfully, Mr. Garlitz, my favorite teacher, recognized something special in me. That's what the mean kids called me, "Special." Some children can be real assholes. Garlitz had me tested. My IQ is off the charts. So is my OCD. *What can I say? I'm an overachiever.* I'm a doctor. I don't need to tell anyone I'm smart, but I do. A shrink will tell you I am overcompensating for feeling dumb as a kid. Bullshit! I felt misunderstood, lonely, and anxious as a kitten in a kennel full of

Dobermans. I didn't fit in with the other kids, but I always knew I was brilliant.

In college and med school, I knew the answers to all of the tests, but just to verify, I probed the instructor's *next* for test clues whenever possible. Never can be too careful, or too OCD. *I own the shit out of my OCD when it serves me.*

Grace and I were inseparable. Everyone was charmed by her. The jocks, the nerds, the smooth talkers. But as us eye surgeons say, *"She only has eyes for me."* Every single day we came home together, and then we came together, *if you know what I mean.* Afterward, we collapsed into each other, spent and blissful, waking up at 4:30 a.m., off to class. Lather, rinse, repeat.

Just because the sex was fucking amazing doesn't mean I was easy to live with. Grace tolerated my OCD, even calling it a positive quality. She joked to her friends that our home was always remarkably organized. A place for everything and everything in its place on steroids. I was lots of fun at art fairs—NOT!

"Babe, don't you love this painting."

"Sure, Grace. It's a lovely portrayal of a baby frog in a flower. Where are we going to hang it?"

Of course, I was right; there wasn't wall space, but I could have found a spot, moved something to another wall, made an effort. No, instead my tight-ass OCD wall went up. A place for everything. Everything in its—Wait! There goes my asshole meter—and it's pointing to me. Still, I can be fun—*really, I can!*

On rare days off, we snuck away to Loop Road in the Everglades. In the early 20th century, Loop Road connected Miami to Naples on Florida's west coast. A lazy crawl through a trail of unparalleled, soggy wonder—if you know where to look. Since the state built Alligator Alley to the north, and the southern Route 41, Loop Road is a remnant of times past. A largely unknown, hard-packed rock, bumpy side road, winding through native trees and along creeks, flowing from the ever-present River of Grass.

Thousands of people whiz past the entrance at Monroe Station doing 80 miles per hour, not realizing one of the most beautiful, accessible parts of the Everglades lies within. Once you visit, Loop Road beckons you back to its magical mystery tour. Don't go in the summer, though. The biting insects are fierce; there's so many no-see-ums, you can see-um.

Revered by nature lovers, locals, fishermen, and good ole boys and girls with 4WD trucks and Jeeps, the Loop was our special place. It's one of the only places on land I can go slow. I attribute it to the ever-present sawgrass. Water, water everywhere. That and the rumble of my classic 1999 4WD Tacoma truck—a present from Mother. My truck is solid. I still have it. Mint condition, of course. This is how I maintain all of my possessions. If not, I fix or discard them. Imperfection is not an option when you're OCD. The Tacoma emits a lovely *vroooom* sound, which vibrates at my frequency, allowing me to be still. *Did Mother know about the vibrations calming me when she bought me the truck?* You can drive through the Loop in an hour or so to get to the other side, but you would miss the good stuff.

In the Everglades, you have to stop and smell the mucky sawgrass. Wear your waterproof boots. Get out of your vehicle, walk over to a creek, look for fish, alligators, turtles. Walk into the woods, turn over a rock, find a snake. The trees hold their own wonders, like native orchids. Those folks in Colorado with their Aspen trees think they're all that. Come to the 'Glades and watch the Florida Red Maples glistening in the 50-degree winter sunlight. Beats 22 below in Colorado! Roseate spoonbills, red-shouldered hawks, kingfishers, lining the cypress trees. Blue herons fishing the shallows. Alligators sunning on the muddy banks, one eye open, hoping for a bird's misstep, or a farsighted turtle. *Hey, animals have eye conditions too!*

I keep a waterproof mattress in the truck bed, and blankets and pillows in the back of the cab. After a day of exploring, Grace and I pull off the main drag, find a cozy spot, and spend the night.

The flashing lights are bright now, transporting me to one particularly cold winter night. I'm looking at the moon through my binoculars. Moon over Miami, sure it's beautiful, but when you view the moon on a clear winter night in the Everglades, far from the lights of Miami, it's mystical. Tonight, the moon is a glorious mass of gray splotches, with contours and odd shapes of gray and silver. Contrasted against the harsh whiteness of the light of the moon, the gray craters first appear as they usually do. Then the craziest thing happens—*well, the craziest thing tonight.* The longer I look, the more the craters move about. I'm tired. That's it. I put down the binoculars and rub my eyes. When I look again, the craters form the shape of a huge, smile-less dolphin. No more Adderall for me, no matter how many hours I need to stay awake and study. What the fuck is that? A perfectly spherical silver ball the size of the moon starts orbiting it. Slow at first, then quicker.

"Hey, Grace. Are you seeing this?" I call to Grace, who is already under the covers.

"I see your cute little ass-crack sticking out from your jeans, Freddy Fluid. Come to bed. I'm freezing and all alone under here. Come warm me up," Grace says in her *come get me* tone I never can resist. *I resist.*

"Look at the moon, Grace. Don't you see it?"

"I see it. Another beautiful moonlit night in the 'Glades. So romantic. Now get under here and service me already."

"Don't you see it, Grace?" I ask, still watching the giant sphere circle the moon.

"See what, Freddy?"

"A giant sphere orbiting the moon? It looks like a giant soap bubble. It's shimmering purple and gold."

"Freddy, did you take Adderall again? You know it makes you loopy."

"I took one 2 nights ago. It's worn off by now. Never again, I promise. Come see this, Grace." Grace finally sits up, pulls the blanket snug over her nakedness, and crawls over.

"This better be good, Freddy. I think my nipples are frozen. Look!"

I look, and they are magnificent, but there's a giant bubble circling the moon that's unfortunately more distracting.

"Look, right there, Grace. It's huge."

"It certainly is," Grace says, playfully grabbing my crotch.

"Thank you, Grace. Please, look at the moon."

"I don't see anything but the moon, Freddy."

I can't believe she doesn't see it. Maybe she's fucking with me. Grace has a habit of making light of my occasional, well, not so occasional craziness. *Let's face it. I'm a nutcase.* As an example, I see a fricking sad dolphin on the moon's surface and a round spaceship? Maybe a satellite? Sure, that's it.

"Here, look through the binoculars, Grace. Tell me what you see. Please, Grace," I beg. *Grace hates when I beg.*

"Give 'em here, Freddy," Grace says, grabbing the binoculars and pulling them to her eyes.

"Ouch!" I scream, *because the binocular strap is still around my neck.*

"Sorry, babe. Okay, I give. What am I looking at, Freddy? It's a beautiful, romantic full moon."

"Don't you see anything else? On the moon's surface, or around the moon?"

"Oh wait, I think I see something. Look, Freddy, the moon is so close you can touch it," Grace says as she turns and drops the blanket. "Here's a full moon for you." She laughs, turning to reveal her glorious backside. Grace's butt is spectacular, and under normal circumstances, I would pull her to me, kiss her, and jump her beautiful bones. *Not today, butt. Not today!*

"Seriously, Grace. You don't see anything weird about the craters, or anything else?"

"Sorry, babe, no. Now come warm me up."

"Okay, it's just—" I can't finish my sentence. The sphere comes closer and closer, whizzing to within a few feet of my truck, and I yell, "LOOK OUT, GRACE!"

"Come on, Freddy, enough already. There's nothing here. But your eyes are flickering at warp speed."

I can't speak. The bubble is enormous. How can Grace not see it? *Oh, God, I need help. I'm going to the psych clinic tomorrow.* Wait! What the hell? It's leaving, spinning off a trail of specks of amber lights. It looks like they are forming shapes. Huh? They're letters, words. What are they spelling?

"You okay, Freddy? Your eyes are flickering awfully fast."

Grace interrupts my concentration, springing me from what I imagine is my impending madness. I am speechless. I focus on Grace, then at the ginormous bubble in front of us, then the words being spelled in front of me. "You sure you don't see this, Grace? You're not just screwing with me?"

"I don't see anything, babe, but I'll be screwing you if you ever get your cute little ass under these covers. You sure you're okay, Freddy? Your eyes look like one of Carl Sagan's wet dreams."

I look at Grace, her stunning, loving face, staring at me like I'm perfect, like she always does. Only she and Mother ever look at me like this. *Like I said, I'm misunderstood.* I forget about the moon, the sphere, and all I can think of is Grace. *She will make the bad man go away.* I pull back the covers and climb in next to her. She puts her head on my chest, and I hold her tight.

"Sorry. I'm so lucky to have you, Grace." I know this, and don't acknowledge it as often as warranted, because I don't want to give her a big head. *Besides, mine is big enough for the both of us.* Grace sighs and nuzzles my chest like a warm puppy. I look at the sky, and there's nothing odd now. I must have been imagining the whole thing. Probably the Adderall leaving my system. It's gotta be a satellite. Whew! No looney bin for me.

Blinking, I look at the moon. Perfectly normal. Nothing to see here. As I turn to kiss Grace, I see them, out of the corner of my eye. Flashing words in the sky! Like a blimp. Sure, maybe it's a blimp. *Double whew!*

I convince myself it is, in fact, a blimp. Amber lights, big shiny thing in the sky, but my eyes are drawn in. It's like staring into fireworks. Not the big ones in the sky. The little ones you light in the street as children. Flashing little flickers everywhere. No smoke. I read the flickering letters, the words they form—SLOW DOWN, FREDDY!

22

Tough crowd

"Er, #2, I think you did it again!"

"Shut the hell up, #3. You're making me nervous."

"This one is too old, #2."

"Argggghhhh! Not again," #2 shouts, looking at the older man with dashing amber eyes.

"Hey, old-timer, welcome to the party. Want to hear a joke?" Burt asks.

"Young man, I'm in no mood for jokes. I was just walking with Helen. Hey! Where's Helen? What is this place?"

"So, a couple of aliens, a pool boy, a gangster, a geek, an old man, and a comedian, walk into a spaceship. Stop me if you've heard this one?" Burt kids.

"Young man, you don't want to see me get angry," Harvey growls.

"Tough crowd!" Burt says.

"Where's Helen!?!" Harvey shouts.

#3 swims to the chamber. "So sorry, Sir. We're having a few technical difficulties. Well, more than a few, if you ask me. You see #2 over there. Oh, sorry, we haven't been properly introduced. I'm #3. Hey, #2, wave hello to our new friend here."

#2 does not look up from his instrument panel and does not respond.

"Well, you see, that's #2 over there worrying." #3 swims close to Harvey and whispers, "Anyways, #2 made quite a mess of things around here. It's a real #2, all right."

Burt laughs. "Yep, it's a real shit show, all right. Don't you think so, #—" Burt's mouth fills with light, and he finds himself paralyzed.

"I've had enough out of both of you!" #2 shouts, and with a flick of his tail, he circles the chamber at light speed. "One more word out of either of you, and I'll beam you to the Bachezoid colony."

"Oh, you don't want to go there, Burt. The temperature is 100 degrees Celsius in the shade. Talk about hot and dry. Worse than Vegas in the summer. No, you don't want to go there at all," #3 whispers to a silent Burt.

"ENOUGH!" #2 shouts as light floods the room, filling the space completely.

23

A musical interlude

Back in the middle of the spacecraft.

"That was you, right, #1? Slow down Freddy over Loop Road, that was you? Hey, #1, where'd you go? #1?"

"Sorry, lad. I had to pop off. Business in another galaxy. When are you off to now, #009?"

"You tell me? Wait, you were in another galaxy?"

"No time to chat, Freddy, looks like you're off again," #1 says, and I'm flashing back to after medical school and residency. It was a time when my life wasn't absorbed with study, thus opening up plenty of free time for my own *next*, which could be my best friend or worst enemy, and had to be fought off with *now*.

Listening to the right kind of music keeps me on the edge of *now*. Stringed instruments, violin, viola, cello, bass, mandolin, banjo, and especially guitar, all speak to me, as if they are hardwired into my being. When I bike, jog, do research, or clean the house (yes, I clean my own house, and it's cleaner than a surgical ward—OCD, remember?), I pop in my EarPods, crank the volume to blaring, and *next* can't get a foothold. Oh, *next* still pops in for a quick stopover, but it's more like teatime than *next's* usual 9 course feast of Freddy. Hearing music is great, but what temporarily binds me to *now* is playing music.

How do I know this? Grace bought me a guitar. She thought it might help channel my OCD. As usual, Grace was correct. I taught myself to play. Locked myself in our bedroom for a month until I could play one particular song, plucking the steel strings until my fingers bled, until I perfected each chord, each note, every strum. A month later, I called Grace in to hear my rendition of 'Hotel California'. And…I rocked it. I spent a year practicing 4 or 5 hours every night until Grace decided it was time to ramp my volume up.

"Freddy, come to bed. Look at your fingers. They're all blistered."

"They're calloused, Grace. I don't feel a thing."

"I know how much you enjoy playing, Freddy, and you're getting pretty good."

"Pretty good?!! I'm awesome," I say, *because I am—sort of.*

"I think you should join a band," Grace suggests.

"A band? Not this idea again, Grace? You know I don't do well in groups. This is a very bad idea," I say, *because this is a very bad idea.* Grace doesn't know all of the band member's *nexts* would fill my head like cold lumpy oatmeal.

"I disagree, my love. It would be a good way for you to connect with other humans, Freddy. You can't just hang out with me all the time. Besides, it would be good for your OCD. Get out of your head and tune in to other people's vibes," Grace says.

Oh, the irony of her statement. Besides, I play music for myself. The frequency of my guitar music informs my moods. It calms me, excites me, and makes me happy—*Okay?* Still, I must force myself to do something social. Something inside me is telling me to get out of my own head. Be with a group. When there's more than one person in a room with me, I don't lock in on anyone in particular's *next* thought, instead they all sort of get spread out. Maybe this could work. *Join a band, she says. It'll be fun, she says.*

By day, Dr. Constantina Contraction, is a fine obstetrician who guides babies into this world in a most respectful and caring manner. By night (*weekends and holidays, schedule permitting*), Dr. Contraction plays lead guitar for the band, Billie and the Baby Catchers, and they happen to have an opening on rhythm guitar. I show up 15 minutes early. Nobody is in the garage. *I'm not happy.* Finally, 16 minutes later, she shows up.

"You're 1 minute late," I say, *because she is.*

"Sorry, C-section ran late. I'm Constantina. My friends call me Billie. Grace is great, by the way. She's helped one of my bi-polar patients with their anxiety. Coached them through the entire delivery. It was like watching a birthing film."

"Yes. Grace is wonderful. I wouldn't be with anyone who wasn't," I say, and Billie looks at me like I'm a cocky dick, *although I think the term might be redundant,* and I hear her *next* thought. *'He's a looker. I wonder if Grace would share, or maybe even a thre—'* I'll have to stop this *next* right here. *Nobody is talking about my Grace that way, nobody.*

"Let's see what you got!" Billie says, which puts me on edge as I hear her *next* thought, something about a strap-on. I am relieved as she straps on her guitar, and 2 others join us in her garage, which smells of fertilizer, gas, and cypress mulch. "Hey John, Paul. This is Freddy."

"Freddy. Too bad, I thought maybe we'd finally get lucky and land a Ringo or a George," John teases, then sticks out his huge meaty hand which feels like a thawing pork chop.

"You must be the drummer," I say, *and I get no next from this guy. Interesting?*

"How'd you know?" *John asks, laughing and shaking his pork chop mitts in the air.*

"Hey, Freddy. I'm Paul on bass," Paul says, and I hear his *next* thought. *'He's a looker.'*

Great! Now there's two of them fantasizing about me. I need to start playing—soon.

"Hi, Paul. Are we ready to start, Billie?" I ask.

"You want a beer or something stronger, Freddy?" John asks, holding out a joint.

"I've never tried it," I say, *but what I really mean is, give me a hit of that joint.*

"Hey, you're all right even if you ain't named Ringo," John says, and hands me the pot, which looks tiny and harmless in his pork chop hand, so I take a big hit, cough deeply, and I am fuuuu-ccccc-kkkk-ed uppppp.

"Let's jam," Billie says, and they start playing an Eagle's song.

I jump right in. Sounds pretty good. We seem to be on the same wavelength, and there're no *nexts*; not from a single one of them. Hey, maybe Grace was right. Being in a band is fun, and it is, *for exactly 3 minutes and 20 seconds*, until Billie jumps into a snappy Django Reinhardt number and it all goes to shit. They don't have any sheet music, so I listen for the chord changes and try to discern the upcoming chords from their *nexts*, but *next* must have floated off on a musical interlude, so no dice.

These guys are good. Really, really good, and this gypsy jazz shit is hard. *Really, really, really hard.* I don't know these chords progressions. *Did I tell you I'm stoned?* I am soooooo stoned. I have no guiding light to follow—fucking *next*, you picked a great time to go AWOL. I play an A minor, because I think that's what Billie is jamming on lead, but too late, her fingers are flying off to some unknown destination, and so am I. This pot is really strong. *Did I tell you I'm stoned?* Well, I am. I try to follow along, but this gypsy jazz stuff is crazy hard. *Did I tell you it's hard?* I'm lost—lost and *horrible*, to be precise, and the sound I hear is a putrid cacophony, and it's coming from me.

I've never been horrible at anything except sports. I don't like sports. I don't do sports, unless you count swimming, in which case I'm an Olympian. I do like music, but what I am playing is far from music, and Billie, John, and Paul stopped playing a while back, and are watching me, but I am too stoned to notice. *Did I tell you I'm really high?* I shouldn't smoke. *Pull it together, Freddy!* I come out of my fog, and their flood of *nexts* hit me in the head like a giant tuning fork. *'What's up with this guy's crazy flickering eyes? This guy sucks!'* John thinks. Billie's and Paul's *next* thoughts also contain the word suck, but I shan't repeat them. I have a girlfriend! Shame on both of them! Speaking of shame, I never felt so humiliated.

"I can't play in a BAND!!!" I shout as I find myself back on the spaceship, with a flashing bundle of lights, wishing I still had that joint.

24

The environmentalist

A couple of miles off the coast of Miami Beach, a laboratory technician lowers a silver cylinder 100 feet into the smooth patch in the waves, known as the boil. The boil being the outfall of a sewer line dumping 90 million gallons of treated sewage into the glistening, tourist filled waters of the Atlantic each and every day. Even a frozen drink with a little umbrella won't numb the smell when the wind is blowing right.

"Did you see that?" Sam asks, as the rope he was holding a moment ago zips through his hands, like a snake escaping a weasel.

"Bull shark!" Tim yells.

"Shit. That's the second test cylinder I lost this month. Those sharks are getting nastier by the minute. Luckily, I brought a spare," Sam says, loading a collection bottle into another cylinder, and tying on a rope.

"Keep your hands away from the gunnels, man. You might get a repeat performance. I'll bet you gave that bull shark a stomachache. He might want revenge," Tim jokes.

"Good point. I'll lower this slowly. Now, I just pull the rope like so, the cylinder flips, filling the collection bottle with nice fresh sewage effluent from 100 feet deep. Care for a swig?" Sam asks.

"As good as you make it sound, Sam, I'll stick with Corona."

"Can't blame you at all. It's either too much chloramine, or too many bacteria. Choose your poison. Will these idiots ever figure out they are destroying our planet? Every time my tests show coliform bacteria, you know the ones living in human digestive systems, my boss makes me rerun the test, but the test takes 72 hours, and by the time I retest the water sitting in my collection fridge, the bacteria are dead. It's so damn frustrating, Tim."

"What the hell are you going to do about it, Sam. You're just a little science geek cog in a big governmental wheel."

"I wrote a letter."

"You doing the whole pen is mightier bit. Very noble, dude."

"Here. Wanna read it?" Sam asks, grabbing the letter out of the back pocket of his uniform pants, handing it to Tim.

"Damn! You came loaded for bear! Did you send this to the newspaper yet?" Tim asks after reading the letter to the editor of the Miami Sun.

"Emailed it this morning, right before work," Sam replies.

"You're brave, and a little crazy, man. You know they're going to fire your ass. You sure you don't want a beer? This might be our last ride out, Sammy boy."

"Nah, I'm in the union. And there's a whistleblower law. I'll be fine. I can't stand these fuckers acting like they care, and improperly dumping shit—literal shit—into our ocean."

"In the old days, the only kind of shit we'd find floating out here was a few bales of weed. Those were the days, Sammy boy. Did I tell you about the time I found three bales? Hey, Sam! Are those fuckers watching you or something?"

"Why?"

"Your watch is flashing, Sam."

"I've heard about this. I'll bet they don't pollute their planets with chemicals and waste."

"Heard about what?" Tim asks.

"Aliens!"

"Aliens! Do all you science dudes have X-Files fantasies, or what?" Tim says, turning around to grab another beer from the icy cooler as Sam vanishes in a barrage of amber lights. Tim turns back around. "Hey, Sam? Sam? Where'd you go, buddy? Sam, this isn't funny. SAM!!!! Damn!"

Tim sighs, holding his ball cap over his heart in respect, eyes cast into the choppy water, "FUCKING BULL SHARKS!"

25

The jig is up

Back on the spaceship, Freddy's journey into his past continues.

After residency, Grace and I were still inseparable. We established medical practices in the same building on South Beach. Our home was a stunning oceanfront apartment on Ocean Drive, and we met for lunch most days. It was a challenge to keep my secrets from Grace, but I thought it was better this way, until *last month.*

We were waiting at the Alton Road crosswalk. *Did I mention I hate waiting? Waiting is horrible, like driving uphill, in a slow car with four flat tires.* So, we're waiting. Arghhhhh! My brain is tuning in on the people at the crosswalk *nexts* words. Instead, dreadful images flood my senses. A terrified mother screaming. Maybe someone nearby is having a daymare. I look all around. I don't see the mother's face I saw in my vision. When will this damn light change? If only I could hear what technology will do *next.* Then *next* takes control of my body like I'm the star of a crazed puppet show. I fly into the middle of Alton Road. *My feet are moving like*

Fred Flintstone's starting the Flintmobile. I don't know where they are leading me, yet I follow.

Before I can think again, there's a toddler in my left arm, my right arm in front of me, in a near Nazi salute. I yell, "STOP!" A Dodge Charger's brakes screech. *I hate Chargers!* A mother screams. It's the lady in my vision. My body once again yields to my brain's commands. I calmly walk to the crosswalk and hand the mother her sobbing child. Perfectly good waste of tears.

"Don't cry, kid. You're fine," I say. The mother throws her arms around the child. She's crying, rocking her kid, and shouting, "Thank you, thank you!" I don't take it in, I'm too busy worrying. Oh, God! I hope nobody videoed me doing a Nazi salute! A post like that on social media could kill my practice. The light changes. I take Grace's hand and force a smile, which barely flickers my eyes. *Come on, eyes, turn on your stardust charm, I beg myself, but nada.* "Come on, Grace. I'm starving." Grace doesn't budge.

"You just saved a child's life. And you moved like The Flash. Freddy Fluid, you got some 'splaining to do," Grace says in her best Ricky Ricardo accent. *Grace is the funniest person I know. Perfect timing. Everything about Grace is perfect.*

"Saw the car out of the corner of my eye. You know me and my perfect vision. I'm famished, Grace," I say abruptly, again pulling Grace's hand to cross the street. Grace holds her ground.

"Freddy! You never lie to me. You moved as if you were that child's guardian angel. Tell me what's going on, please," Grace pleads with a heartbroken look on her face.

I can't resist Grace. I'd like to think everyone has a guardian angel, but logic tells me it's rubbish. My heart, on the other hand, tells me Grace is mine. She loves me unconditionally, which ain't easy. It's time. I almost told her in middle school, high school, then a million times since, but now I have no choice. With my gifts, omission is second nature, but I can't really lie. Lies clog up too many neural pathways and mine are already overworked.

"Fine, but let's eat, please. I'm starving."

"You should be. You just burned about 5,000 calories a second."

We walk in silence to Café Havana and get an outside table. Grace is never silent, and she's quiet as a snake. *Not a good sign.*

"That's long enough, Freddy. Spill it," *Grace says like a sexy CSI detective, and it erupts out of me, like popping the cork off a hot bottle of champagne—shaken, not stirred.*

"Remember the first time you kissed me?"

"How could I forget? What a great first kiss."

"Yes, it was. That's not the point, Grace. Remember after the kiss, when I passed out?"

"Sorry. I think I sucked too hard. It took me a second to perfect my technique, but you didn't seem to mind, Freddy. I practiced all week on a plum."

"A plum?"

"It's a very popular technique. Really."

"I didn't pass out from your kiss, Grace. It was the voices, all of them coming at me at once."

"Oh, Freddy, you're hearing voices and you never told me? Me?" Grace grabs her name tag off her white coat and tosses it across the table. "Grace Whisperer, psychiatrist, nice to meet you. Come on, Freddy, give."

"They're not those kind of voices, Grace. These are real."

"Go on," Grace says in her soothing psychiatrist pitch. *I never can resist her voice.*

"I have… let's call it a gift," I say, holding my breath for a second.

No matter how well I see the future, without actually hearing or seeing what people's *nexts* are, I am terrible at guessing what anybody might do next. Face it, without my predictive powers, I'm an emotional klutz.

Grace gives me her *you can tell me anything, I love you* look and says, "You can tell me anything, my love." *What can I say, sometimes I get one next right.* Now she's winking. Shit! The wink. Grace's superpower. Over me, at least. I exhale slowly, pull the Band-Aid off my tongue, and my secret floods out—part of it anyway.

26

The politician

In the beatific, tree filled, funky, Village of Biscayne Park, a community comprised of 3,000 plus highly creative, intelligent, slightly eccentric residents, along with a myriad of animals ranging from the ubiquitous squirrels to coyotes, iguanas, manatees, bats, birds, and butterflies, the Village Commission meeting may just end early tonight, at 11:55 p.m.

Another evening of riveting local government for the six people in the audience, and three people on Zoom, who stayed until the bitter end. Like most local government meetings, there was a great deal of talk, with little to no action. Who in their right mind would want to be involved in local politics? At least the setting was nice.

The Log Cabin, which serves as Town Hall, was built in 1935 via the Works Progress Administration under President Franklin D. Roosevelt. It seems fitting one of his namesakes was elected to the Biscayne Park Commission. Max Roosevelt, no relation to FDR, was first elected to office in a landslide. He ran his campaign on the principal of improved communication, a trait Max excelled in. Prior to running for office, Max spent an inordinate amount of time communicating at commission meetings, on social media, and talking to neighbors about how to make Biscayne Park the best little village in America.

In other words, Max had a big mouth. Thankfully, the size of Max's mouth matched his large brain, heart, and allegedly another large body part which shall go unnamed. This made Max a local folk-hero to many Village residents. Many of Max's ideas were commonsensical, and gained support from residents, so of course, at first, most were rejected by the commission. Not because they didn't make sense, but because they were attached to Max. Over the years, the other Commissioners put their personal feelings aside, were replaced by other, more logical humans, or were just plain worn down. Max was elected mayor.

Unbeknownst to anyone, including Max's husband, Max was in the Witness Protection Program. Over the objections of the U.S. Marshals Service, Max thought the best place to hide was in public—very public. So, he moved to Miami, changed his name, dyed his hair, married a dude, and became a politician. The other thing nobody knew was that Max snuck off to Chicago to see his ex-wife Sheila every month.

Despite this, Max wasn't really a bad boy at heart. He started out on the straight and narrow. Fresh out of college with a communications degree, Max was hired by Carlo and Carmela Cacciatore to help them establish a brand presence for their line of frozen meals. Their food was delicious and tasted like their motto, 'Just like Mama makes.' Max, being a creative, and energetic young man, learned how to use targeted search engine optimization and other marketing strategies in and around the Chicago area to promote the hell out of their food. Sales increased 10,000-fold, and the family expanded to a giant warehouse/kitchen/distribution center, with a chain of restaurants bearing the Cacciatore name. Carlo and Carmela's success made their great Uncle Cesar Cacciatore very happy, and very, very rich.

Besides bankrolling their food business, Cesar headed the second largest crime syndicate in the Windy City. There was nothing Cesar loved more than making money; except maybe a good calzone. One day, while Cesar was touring the new warehouse, he saw the bar-coded scanners on the shipping boxes, the bank of computers, and the fleet of delivery trucks, and an idea sprouted. What an operation to launder drugs and money. Cesar called for a family meeting, which included Max, who, due to his ingenuity, became a 5% not-so-silent partner and director of operations. While hesitant at first to dirty the waters of an, up to now, completely legitimate operation, Max was won over by the offer of a cut of the profits, and the opportunity to avoid another kind of cut; to retain his scrotum—an option Uncle Cesar casually proposed if Max opposed him.

A few years later, Alzheimer's got the better of Uncle Cesar, and he sometimes forgot where he was, or who he was talking to. One day, while at the urinal in one of the family restaurants, Uncle Cesar let it leak. That is, he dangerously leaked information about the Cacciatore's operation while peeing next to a DEA agent. Uncle Cesar's brain was so shot, he mistook the agent for their long dead cousin Alfredo. Unfortunately for Max, he happened to enter the restroom at the exact moment Uncle Cesar was finishing his leakage.

"And here he is now, Alfredo, the man who made it all possible. Get over here, Max. Did I ever introduce you to Cousin Alfredo?"

Max's eyes drifted down to the man's dangling equipment—as well as his gun and Drug Enforcement Agency badge, and he had two immediate thoughts. One—this isn't Cousin Alfredo, and two—I might be bisexual.

Max and Dick Narc, the DEA agent, struck up a mutually beneficial relationship, whereby Max fed Dick key information about the Cacciatore's business, and Dick fed Max grapes off his hard abdomen. Dick also placed Max into the Federal Witness Protection Program. After the trial, Dick was promoted and moved to DC. He never saw Max again. Max left the Windy City and moved to The Magic City—Miami.

"We're on Item 12e solar panels," Max announces to the Commission.

"Oh no, Max, not this again. It's late. I'm tired," Commissioner Glum says.

"Commissioners, this village is going to be the greatest little community in South Florida when I'm through with it. We are going to maintain our historic charm and character and propel us into the forefront of technology and self-sufficiency. Every house will have solar panels if it's the last thing I do. We'll place the panels on biodomes covering the medians, and sell all the excess electricity back to Florida Power & Light. We can make enough money to hook up the entire village to sewers. No more septic tanks. And due to the triangular shape of our village, when the solar panels are connected and viewed from above, by a plane, or let's say aliens from a spaceship—"

"Please don't get started on this alien crap, Max. I'm tired," Commissioner Blank interrupts.

"As I was saying, the panels will camouflage us from the aliens," Max says.

"Max!!!!" Commissioner What yells.

"I know how it sounds, but I get these visions. You've all heard the rumors," Max says.

"Max look!" Commissioner How says.

"Look at what?" Max asks.

"You're glowing," Commissioner Blank remarks.

"Thank you. I've been using this new tinted sunblock and—"

"No! Your watch, Max. It's flashing," Commissioner Glum says.

"I told you there were aliens!!" Max shouts as he vanishes into thin air.

"I'll be damned. He was right," Commissioner Blank says.

"He usually is, you know!" Commissioner How says.

"FUCKING ALIENS!" the Commission shouts in unison, which is the first time they ever agreed on anything.

27

The truth, the whole truth, and well, you get the point

Back on Lincoln Road.

"Oh, Grace, what a relief. I've been meaning to tell you since middle school. You see, the way I rescued the child. I call it my gift. I can see, well, it's more like hear and visualize the future, but only 1 minute ahead of time. I know, I know, it sounds nuts. But I do know what people are going to say *next*. It's not like I'm clairvoyant. I was just made this way, I guess. That's what happened before, with the toddler. It all unfolded in my mind before it occurred. I heard it, saw it, the child in the street, the screeching brakes, the woman screaming. Before I knew it, my body exploded into action. Sort of on its own."

Grace looks at me blankly. Fuck! I shouldn't have told her. Shit! What should I do? Tell her I'm trying to be funny, like her. Yeah, that's it. You idiot, just keep talking. You can't keep this to yourself forever.

"Is this making sense, or are you ready to commit me, Grace?"

"Freddy dear. You just experienced a trauma. It's your brain's way of processing it. That child nearly died. You're a hero. It's just too much for you," Grace says sheepishly, grasping for answers.

Grace never struggles–with anyone or anything. Fuck it. No more secrets—about this anyway. I blather like a teenager caught sneaking in their bedroom window at 3:00 a.m.

"Oh, God, it feels so good to finally let this out. It's odd, though, because this time my body took control. I didn't know my feet could move so fast, Grace. It never happened before, in the outside world, at least. It happens when I operate, but obviously not with my feet. When I'm operating, at times, my body takes over, guides the scalpel, the laser, my fingers, my own eyes, I fix whatever problem was about to occur because I see it coming, 1 minute ahead." The look on Grace's face isn't hard to read; amusement combined with pity.

"Hey, I'm the funny one around here. We're always honest with each other, Freddy. Now tell me the truth."

"Truth," I say with my hand in the Vulcan salute. *Grace knows I would never disrespect the live long and prosper salute.*

"Okay, Freddy, I'll play along. Tell me what I'm going to say next," Grace says in a serious tone.

"I can't, Grace."

"Oh, good. You had me scared for a second."

"I can't because it doesn't work on you."

"Please, Freddy."

"I know you think I'm nuts. You want to test me?" I ask, realizing she'll never look at me the same way. "Pick anyone in the restaurant, Grace. I'll demonstrate."

"Really, Freddy? Let's go back to my office. You need rest."

"Please, Grace, pick anyone."

Grace looks at me, narrowing her eyes as she agrees. "Okay, Freddy." She scopes out the room like a kid who lost their balloon at the carnival, and smiles when she finds it. Grace comes back with a man who could be Santa's grandfather.

"Dr. Shotzky, meet Freddy."

"Hello, Freddy," Grandpa Santa says. "Grace was in my abnormal psychology class. She tells me this is your first date, and you're a magician trying to show her your latest mind reading trick." Grace winks again, and I am a bit shaky. *Well, I am.*

I hear Grandpa Santa's next thought—*'what a fruitcake.'* Disappointing. Fruitcake isn't what I expected from a psychiatrist. Something a bit more clinical, but I provided just cause. Still, my heart sinks.

Expectations are what really fuck us up. Even people who can't see the future expect the next thing to unfold in a certain way, and when they don't, well, this is why relationships are so difficult. No matter how perfect a human is, we all have the potential to disappoint. Don't expect too much; you won't be disappointed.

"Freddy, just text me what you think Dr. Shotzky's next thought is," Grace says, tossing me my cell phone. I text Grace, "What a fruitcake."

Grace looks at her phone, laughs, and shows it to Grandpa Santa, who smirks.

"Not exactly a stretch, young man."

"That's okay, Dr. Shotzky. Just a parlor trick. It's not like I want to convince some girl on our first date I can jump ahead in time." *Okay, yes, I want to convince her.* I hear Grandpa Santa's *next* thought and blurt, "Alice in Wonderland," having no idea of the relevance, other than Grandpa Santa imagining I went through the looking glass and wasn't coming back. Grandpa Santa lets out a laugh that would sleigh Rudolph— (get it, sleigh Rudolph? Never mind.)

"Why, that's quite the trick, young man. Alice in Wonderland is exactly what I was thinking. Forget magic, you should take this guy to the racetrack to pick some horses, Grace. He's good. Real good. I have to run. I have an appointment at Macy's. Can you believe it? They want me to play Santa, again." *I believe it.*

I delve back into his parting *next* thoughts, and blurt them out loud, "Alice in Wonderland Syndrome. A rare psychiatric disorder, which includes time distortion."

"Extraordinary! I think this one is worth a second date, Grace," Dr. Shotzky says.

"Thank you, Dr. Shotzky. So nice to see you. Yes, the racetrack might be fun. Be well," Grace says, squeezing Grandpa Santa's arm, and winking at him—*lucky guy.* Grace plays with her spoon and doesn't look at me. She sits in silence for several moments. I hear laughter. It's coming from me. What a relief to finally tell her. I don't say a word. I'm laughing, deep, honest, real laughter. Then I hear it again, but it's not coming from me. It's Grace laughing. I don't know if this is a good sign, or bad. She keeps laughing.

"I swear, I know it sounds crazy. That I sound crazy, but it's true. I wish it weren't, but it is. Please, Grace, please, you must believe me," I plead. You don't have to be a mind reader to know she doesn't. I finally tell someone, and this is the reaction. Laughter. Like I said, people disappoint you. But then Grace gets up, walks to my chair, and plops on my lap. *I love it when Grace sits on my lap. I feel desired, loved, virile—unless she squishes my nutsack. Well, it's happened before.*

Despite people disappointing you, they often surprise you. Mother led by example. She didn't give much advice; when she did, I soaked it in. Mother told me to never underestimate people.

I'm still a work in progress on this one. I'm so busy thinking about a minute ahead, oftentimes I miss the big picture. Thankfully, this was the only occasion I underestimated Grace. She kisses me hard.

"This is going to be a hoot, Freddy Fluid." Grace winks. I smile and feel the blood returning to my head. Then we laugh until we cry. *I never cry. Perfectly good waste of aqueous solution.*

"Yes, a real hoot!" I nervously say—*like an elephant in a room full of squeaky mice.*

The flashing lights return. I'm not alone.

28

The lover

In the waters off Key Biscayne, an island paradise, a short causeway or boat ride away from Miami. The water temperature in the ocean off Key Biscayne is a delightful 77 degrees. *Nothing like winter in Miami.* Tourists and locals sun topless on the white beach, drink $20 foul-tasting pina coladas from the concession stand, and swim in the ocean. The water is shallow. Just offshore, lurks a variety of sea creatures ranging from benign to benevolent. The rare few are treacherous. A handful are just plain horny.

The mullet are schooling off the sandbar, not far from the water treatment plant. A deadly tiger shark swims within a few feet of the shoreline, its lifeless eyes locking on a teenage boy snorkeling in the murky water. The shark swims by once, close enough to bite, but decides instead to circle its prey like a cat toying with a baby bird fallen from its nest. The monstrous beast turns rapidly and opens its toothy jaws for breakfast. The boy doesn't see it coming—neither does the shark. A bottlenose dolphin, half the shark's size, rams it like a Mack Truck that lost its brakes on a downhill curve. Blood pours from the shark's gills as it sinks dead to the ocean floor.

Beachgoers are shouting and yelling, "Look! Dolphins!" There is only one dolphin and one shark at the time, but tourists aren't very good at distinguishing the dolphin's friendly rounded dorsal fin from the terrifying triangular fin of a shark. The clueless teenager hears the commotion and turns in time to see a dolphin fin and a tiny waterspout and goes back to looking for shells on the seafloor.

A pod of four dolphins swim to the victor. Nuzzling it, rubbing fins, bumping tails, and playfully leaping about. One dolphin swims to the victor's face and gives it a toothy kiss.

"Yo, Dicksee! You da bomb, biiiitcchh! Screw that Flipper dude. You da real deal, girl," a larger dolphin says in a series of clicks and whistles. Ironically, across the road, the iconic TV Flipper, or at least one of its many namesakes, swims in endless circles around a cement tank in an outdated tourist attraction.

"Thanks, Special, keep spinning those whistles. This morning's playlist was dope," the victor replies, along with a tail slap.

"Yo, Dicks! Why'd you wait so long? I thought the kid was toast," Special says.

"More like Fishburger Helper, bro," Trixie clicks. Trixie is aptly named, because she loves to do tricks: backflips, summersaults, tail-walks, and the crowd favorite, suck the puffer. "You wasted his ass, Dicks! You da bomb! Here, girl, you deserve this," Trixie whistles, passing a puffer fish to Dicksee's snout. Pufferfish, otherwise known as puffers, blowfish, or blowies, puff up and release a defensive toxin when threatened. Their meat is considered an Asian delicacy, if one knows how to prepare their flesh and avoid the toxin. The toxin is lethal to many life forms. Dolphins, on the other hand, can't get enough of the stuff.

"Damn! You got the good stuff, Trix," Dicksee excitedly clicks.

"Word! How 'bout you share the love, Dicks, and pass the fish around. You know, there's nothing I like better than a blowie," chirps Lil Big Fin.

"You and the rest of my boyz. Catch you in a beat, Lil Big," Dicksee clicks.

As Special approaches, Dicksee sucks down the last hit of blowie. Dicksee whistles in a series of happy high pitches, and within seconds, she is indeed high and happy. Very high and very happy.

"Don't you ever want to sneak off, just you and me?" Special clicks.

"You know I love you, Special, and nobody do me like you, but you know Mama only named me Dicksee 'cause I want every dick I see."

"Don't do me like that, Dicks." While Special loved everyone in his pod, really, really loved them, he dreamt of a life alone with Dicksee.

Like most cetaceans, dolphins are social mammals, working together for a common good. Dolphins combine forces to drive fish into circles for the pod to eat, they protect each other, and beyond all other pod instincts, they display an overwhelming urge to make baby dolphins. To put it mildly, dolphins love them some tail. While the mating act typically takes only seconds, dolphins enjoy lots of foreplay. As a biological imperative, dolphins are polygamous, as this increases maintaining a strong, diverse bloodline and the continuation of the species. To achieve this goal, at times, dolphins form mating herds. Dicksee's pod, however, was a regular swimming orgy with little concern for the next generation.

"Hold that thought, baby! You know killing sharks always makes me wet," Dicksee clicks.

"Girl, what you mean? We dolphins, we always wet," Special clicks.

Dolphins are highly intelligent mammals. They solve complex problems. They utilize sonar to locate objects the size of a screw underwater with their eyes covered. In many ways, dolphin brain capacity far exceeds humans—except for Special. His Mom did way too much blowie when he was a calf, and he came out a few sardines short of the tin, hence his name. On the other hand, he was, as the girls liked to say, "exceptionally good in the waves." In fact, he was the only male who could last more than 30 seconds in the waves with Dicksee. He was, indeed, special.

Dicksee calls the pod to her with a series of clicks, whistles, and what clearly sounds like a low moan. The rest of the pod writhes into her, a mass of splashing gray flesh; slipping and a sliding.

"Yo, Dicks, we a little close in. Humans see us," Special says.

"I know. It excites me," Dicksee clicks as Lil Big Fin rubs his little big fin all over her.

"Yo, little ho, that's messed up," Special clicks.

"Not like that, bro. I just like to look at 'em. Sometimes I think we related," Dicksee whistles.

"Like you my cuz or something?" Special asks.

"No, dawg, I mean related to humans," Dicksee whistles.

"Yo, Dicksee, you gonna talk all day? We getting busy back here," Pixie asks, playfully poking Dicksee's tail with her snout. Pixie is the smallest dolphin in the pod, but she makes up for her size with her enthusiasm and her tight little blowhole, which can suck a conch shell off the seafloor at 10 fathoms.

"What wuz you sayin', Dicks?" Special clicks.

"There's something familiar about dem humans. We all know us dolphins supposed to save 'em if they get in trouble in the water," Dicksee clicks.

"Yeah, even my ho ass mama taught me that," Special clicks. "Here I thought you wuz a badass killing that tiger shark. You going soft, Dicks?"

"Mama told me there's a legend, dolphins and humans come from the same maker. You buy that shit, Special?" Dicksee asks in a fast series of clicks and whistles.

"I feel you, but don't get all deep on us now, Dicksee. You looked pretty fine killing that shark. Got me all tingly, you know? What you say, Dicksee?" Trixie clicks, nibbling on Dicksee's flipper.

"What I always say, girl. Party at my place, everyone, and you're always tingly, Trix!" Dicksee whistles as she flips on her back.

"Word!" Lil Big clicks as he prods Dicksee's belly with his snout.

"Yo, dawg, I'm all about the love," Dicksee whistles, "except when it comes to tiger sharks. Fuck them tiger sharks!"

"Yeah. Fuck them sharks," Pixie whistles. As she nuzzles Dicksee's belly, Pixie sees tiny beams of light fall onto Dicksee's glistening body. "Yo, Dicks, you glowing, girl,"

"Yeah, I'm feeling you too, girl. Keep nuzzling me right there, Pix. Yeah, baby, that's the spot," Dicksee whistles as she vanishes from the sea in a flash of amber light.

A group of tourists gaze at the mating pod, unaware of the unbridled passion beneath the waves, or Dicksee's disappearance.

"Look, Billy, dolphins!" an excited father points and yells to his teenage son who had just finished snorkeling off the beach. The teen gave up looking for shells in the murky water, unaware he narrowly escaped death by tiger shark a few moments ago. The teen doesn't bother to turn around to see the dolphins. He's too busy staring at the topless beach volleyball players to notice.

29

Good OCD

Before we continue, it's important to understand Good OCD versus Bad OCD. You see, Good OCD is one of my superpowers. Bad OCD is my kryptonite. Bad OCD is a disconcerted jazz band led by a skinny saxophone player who can't keep time. Good OCD is a symphony orchestra playing the Star Wars theme, conducted by yours truly, and it's brilliant—*like me!*

Bad OCD is a perpetual state of nerve-racking planning and preparation. Not Boy Scout prepared, I'm talking astronaut on a 2-decade mission to another galaxy prepared. Bad OCD forces me to *next*, like a kidnap victim with Stockholm syndrome. I wake up planning *next*. I fall asleep planning *next*. My *next*, your *next*, it's irrelevant; one of them will fill my brain, unless I'm with Grace, operating, in the water, or playing guitar.

There's always a Plan B, and the crazy part is even when Plan A is killing it, I'm thinking about Plan B. I have to force myself to sit in the room and just be in the meeting, the party, the restaurant, the walk along the beach. Just be in this moment, Freddy! I tell myself over and over again to stop imagining the future, but my message falls on deaf ears, and the sad part is, they're my ears, and they're not even pointy.

Next fills the empty space, because there can be no empty in my head. *Why? Again, I don't fucking know.* Use it or lose it, Freddy. I have to do something, anything, everything. It's like leading a double life, and being in 2 places at once is exhausting. I'm always nervous on the inside. Nervous, but not shaky. A shaky eye surgeon is the worst!

Now let's talk Good OCD. Good OCD is the perfectionist's dream. I do everything right away. Pay the bill that just arrived in the mail, Yelp dozens of restaurants to find the perfect new waterfront place to take Grace for dinner, spend 17 hours online researching our amazing trip to the Galapagos—which scored us a marine biologist guide with our own private catamaran—that was worthy OCD time! Oh, did I neglect to mention, I'm incredibly wealthy? Well, I am, so I bought out the entire boat for just Grace, me, and the crew.

I'm not sure where Mother acquired the money I inherited when she died, but suffice it to say, *she left me a shitload of moolah.* Understand, I didn't want for anything materially growing up, but we lived modestly. Fuck modest, being rich is da bomb!

Here're some other Good OCD things… Move too fast and knock a hole in the wall with a doorknob, well, OCD has me covered. Immediately go to the hardware store, buy 2 types of doorstops (just in case), install doorstop, get spackle, patch, and paint hole in said wall, return extra doorstop. Change the engine oil before the odometer hits another 5,000 miles. Answer all emails the day I receive them. Research my next surgery. None of this is rocket science, unless I'm operating, of course.

When I'm operating, my patients hit the Good OCD jackpot. This is very, very, very important. I never perform an operation I haven't researched and practiced dozens of times. Many eye surgeons practice technique on goat eyes. It's not so much about killing an animal that bothers me, because I figure someone in Miami will make themselves a nice curry out of the rest of the creature; it's just, goat eyes creep me out. Have you ever looked at one? The pupils are these freaky horizontal black lines conjuring images of the serpent of Eden—*apple, anyone?* While these pupils benefit grazing animals watching for predators, they creep me out big time—Eeeeeeeheheheee! No goat eyes for me. Good OCD to the rescue.

Remember the game Operation, where the buzzer goes off if your tweezer hits the wrong spot? Well, Hasbro's got nothing on me. I invented my own model of the eye I can operate on over and over again. It's made of liquid Kevlar. I practice my surgical techniques hundreds and hundreds of times when I'm not working—practice makes perfect. *To give you a better idea of what it's like to be inside my head, let's look at a day in the life of what I like to call Freddy's Good OCD, shall we?*

5:30 a.m. Pop awake, feel Grace's warm little butt cozied up to my loins like a peel around a banana. Brain goes directly into high gear. Kiss Grace. Determine if her reaction invites me in for an early morning visit to Graceland. An eyes shut kiss and a pat on my shoulder communicates *not today, Freddy, not today.*

5:31 a.m. Disappointed but not discouraged because looking at Grace's sleeping face brings me joy. Out of bed, and into the bathroom. Turn on lights. Already thinking about efficiencies, turn on shower to preheat water. Pee, brush whilst peeing, place shower mat on floor, right foot first into shower, look for sewer moths *(old habits die hard)*, check water for proper temperature, adjust if needed (*it's always perfect, because I set it*), rest of body goes in the shower.

5:32 a.m.-5:59 a.m. Breathe deeply as I dunk my head under the shower stream. Brain disengages. I am Buddha slow and it frikkin rocks, baby! My concept of time disintegrates in the shower.

6 a.m. Daily shower alarm sounds puppy barks 3 times to shake me from *now* and to force me to turn off the shower. *The alarm is a weak excuse for Mother calling me out 3 times. I miss her calm voice, but nonetheless the puppy alarm is effective and makes me smile, because who doesn't like puppies, right?*

6:01 a.m. Another *next* is calling me—surgery in 59 minutes.

6:02 a.m.-6:03 a.m. Dry off, put on scrubs.

6:04 a.m. Turn off bathroom light switch, only once. Think about flicking the switch another 14 times. *Not today, Bad OCD. Not today!*

6:05 a.m. Kiss Grace before I leave. Grace smiles, winks, and says, "Here's looking at you, kid!" *She says this every morning I perform surgery, and I chuckle every time.*

6:06 a.m. Grab a protein bar, run down 9 flights of stairs (without counting them as I do on Bad OCD days), think about today's procedure.

6:07 a.m. Jump in the Maserati, start it, and feel the car's vibrations all the way to the hospital.

6:11 a.m.-6:19 a.m. Park, turn off the engine, pat seat, bid car farewell. Run through every step of the corneal transplant procedure in my mind. Think about the kind of stiches I will use. Imagine the surgical outcome. Repeat. repeat, repeat until I enter the patient's room.

6:20 a.m.-6:29 a.m. Visit patient. This is critical to reinforce trust and put people going under the knife at ease. Make them feel like I give a damn, and I do. *Really.* Restoring people's vision is my life's work, and other than Grace, it's the most important part of my existence. Visiting patients used to be awkward for me, however, once I understood patients awaiting surgery are all petrified of their *next*, I grokked it. I have performed hundreds of operations and I can unequivocally say every single patient I visit before an operation is thinking only of *next*. Will I wake up? Will I be able to see again? I hope this idiot knows what he's doing. And of course, several patients are thinking about how handsome I am and my flickering eyes when I smile. *Honestly, can you blame them?* When I was a resident, I operated on a Buddhist monk. I expected him to bow and express his connection to the greatness of the Universe. He was about as Zen as a rabbit in a field full of foxes. I wanted to be relatable and told him I was more anxious than he was. *If you happen to be a doctor and think this is a good idea, it's not.* The monk pulled the IV tube and ran from the prep room, his open hospital gown flapping in the breeze, exposing all of his holiness behind him. *You would think a guy who spends his life in robes would look better in a gown?* Suffice it to say, now that I understand my patients' state of pre-surgical anxiety, it's easy to reassure them, because one thing I relate to, is overcoming my own anxiety. If not, I couldn't even hold a scalpel. Plus, once I flash them my charming smile, they float into the operating room seeing stars—the ones coming from my eyes.

6:30 a.m.-6:59 a.m. Review patient's chart with surgical team. We've established I don't like groups of people, or even most people, but my surgical team is not most people. They answered an ad I placed, *really*. The ad read: Seeking top-notch surgical team to support uber perfectionist eye surgeon. Qualifications: Ivy League college, 10 years of surgical experience at Bascom Palmer or similar, and most importantly, are you so OCD you make anal retentive people feel like they soiled themselves? Excellent pay, benefits, Maserati signing bonus. Stop overthinking and apply now. People who respond to an ad like this are just as messed up as me, without having to contend with everyone else's *next*, that is. They have enough problems keeping up with their own *nexts*. One of them, Bridgette, goes so far as to have a Plan A, B, C, D, and even DDs for every operation we've performed. Bridgette is my favorite, *and not because of her double D's*. You would think all of those *brilliant people's nexts* would get in my way. They don't. Why? *This one I know*. Because my team meets before every procedure and discusses all Plans. A, B, C, D, DD, E through Z if needed. By the time I've made my first incision, I've been through all the possible *nexts* they are thinking, and once I know their *next*, it becomes *now*. *Get it?*

7:00 a.m.-8:04 a.m. I cut into this eye as if I entered heaven. I perform the operation like a wizard with a scalpel wand, and I'm so *now* my head is floating. Time for my post-surgery compulsory mantra: this human will see the light. And they do, 'cause like I said, with Good OCD, I'm a fucking wizard.

8:05 a.m. Patient to recovery.

8:06 a.m.-3 p.m. Me and my team, high fiving, and wearing fresh gloves, of course. On to next patient. Same routine. Lather, rinse, repeat.

In between surgeries, I visit patients from previous procedures. Remarkably, after patients come out of anesthesia, *next* is non-existent and *now* barely has a pulse. Yeah, these anesthesiologists have one hell of a job. They basically almost kill every one of their patients and then resurrect them. *Neat trick.* I smile at the patient, tell them their surgery went exceptionally well, (*because, like I said, wizard here*), ask how they are feeling, ask for any questions as they numbly nod their heads. Unless a family member is there with them, whatever I say will be a fuzzy dream.

"The doctor told me the operation was Hell, and he's going to take me fishing for kangaroos," says the 84-year-old when her son comes in to check on her. What I really said was, "The operation went well, and her vision would be good as new." *Close enough.*

3:01 p.m. Throw scrubs into the laundry bin, take the stairs to the garage, hop in the Maserati, and the engine purrs me directly to now. *Ahhhhhhh.*

30

Grace

If your kid becomes a psychotherapist, assume they have childhood issues to resolve, some of which might possibly, kind of, sort of, all be your fault. If your kid becomes a psychiatrist, you really fucked up. Some psychiatrists, like other humans, are flawed. Despite this, they try their best to use science, medicine, empathy, and talk therapy to rid people of their demons. Some are good at it, some bad, and the rare few, have true grace. Even Grace's angry racist father and druggie mother couldn't steal her grace.

Everything Grace does is graceful. How she speaks, moves, looks, smiles. Grace doesn't enter a room; she floats in like Princess Di bestowing her royal wrist wave on her subjects; befriending all with her smile, warmly greeting each and every person, owning it with love, and being ever so present. The thing everyone admires most is how Grace shares her grace. It's as if just glancing at her, being in a room with her, fills one with grace. *You know the expression lit up a room? Grace lights up a room like ten thousand wax candles in a house of mirrors.*

Grace is Swedish. You know Swedes—blonde hair, blue eyes, excellent bone structure, flawless skin, great figures, and they're tall, basketball player tall. No wonder Swedes are depressed. They're humongous people and their parents feed them tiny meatballs and pickled fish! Not Grace, though. She hates pickled fish, stands 5'1" with the perpetual sunny disposition of a Hawaiian weathergirl. What's the weather today, Grace? Another 78-degree sunny January day on the Big Island with a light swell out of the north? Surf's up! Everything about her exudes grace. Grace is ladylike in all she is, except in her appetite for Freddy, which is cavernous.

Grace's grandparents moved to Miami Beach, from Sweden, by way of Minnesota. Her grandfather, Swen Lingonberry, spent his adulthood in America as a farmer. Swen loved riding high in his John Deere, the smell of rich black dirt churning under his tractor blades, how the corn caught the light of the warm sun. Summer in Minnesota was delightful. *Winter in Minnesota was colder than a penguin on a Popsicle.* Age was creeping up on him, and after years of vowing to move south before he found Valhalla, Swen sold the farm before he bought it. He made a bundle.

Swen, his wife Helga, and their 16-year-old daughter, Gretchen, all moved to Miami Beach and bought a waterfront house on North Bay Drive.

Gretchen was a delightful young girl in Minnesota. She was an excellent student, did her chores, drove the tractor, sang in the choir of the Holy Lutefisk Lutheran Church, and made a mean pickled herring casserole. *And, yes, it tastes as bad as it sounds.* Gretchen's junior year in Miami was overwhelming. Kids in Minnesota had weed and booze. Teens at Beach High had weed, cocaine, pills, shrooms, fast cars, and faster boys like Jim Whisperer.

Jim had a banana yellow Camaro, with white bucket seats, six stereo speakers, and an ashtray full of half-smoked joints. More importantly, Jim had quaaludes. *Quaaludes are small round white pills which induce a state of, let's call it, Valhalla.* These hypnotic sedatives were so dangerous and addictive they were eventually banned, but back in the day, they were the *'this will get you laid,'* drug of choice. Gretchen gobbled them like Swedish fish—*the candy, not the herring.*

Embarrassingly pregnant, Gretchen dropped out of senior year. Swen beat Jim to a bloody pulp and told him to do the right thing. Jim, being a cowardly a-hole, thought the right thing was to flee to his cousin's house in Tampa. A few weeks later, Swen tracked Jim down, thrashed him like a ragdoll, hogtied him, drove him to the woods, and placed him face down next to a blazing fire. Swen was a big Swede—Frankenstein's monster big, so Jim didn't struggle, or talk. Swen let Jim braise until he was covered in sweat and dirt. Then Swen brought out a funnel with a short hose attached, a noisy coffee tin, a compound bow, a quill of arrows, and a bottle of vodka.

Swen took a slug of vodka, grinned, and muttered something about *popincolon,* which Jim thought might be a word from Norse mythology, or The Hobbit? *Either way, Jim didn't like the sound of it.* Swen gulped a plate of pickled herring and meatballs, hoisted the vodka bottle to his lips and downed it. Herring and meatballs made Swen gassy. He bent over, picked up the compound bow, and let one rip right next to Jim's face—an arrow. The bow made a *thwanggg* sound, followed by a whizzing noise past Jim's ear, followed by a louder *thwanggg* in Jim's face, smelling of herring and meatballs, followed by a squeal.

Jim looked himself over for arrow holes and was relieved to know the squeal didn't emanate from him. Swen disappeared into the woods and returned with a bloody wild hog held aloft by its back legs. He grabbed a long spike, impaled the pig, and placed it on a spit over the fire. Sitting next to Jim, he opened the coffee tin labeled, *Minnesota popping corn*, written in thick black marker, and filled the funnel. Jim's eyes grew wide as Swen jammed the tube of the funnel up the pig's butt, at which point the word popincolon needed no translation. Then Swen opened another bottle of vodka, gulped some, and stared into the fire.

As the popcorn began popping, causing the pig's belly to twitch and swell, Swen refilled the funnel, took a huge gulp of vodka, kicked Jim's body close to the fire, and spoke. "Listen closely, swine, cauz some people dey have a hard time understanding my accent. Understand?"

Jim numbly nodded yes.

"Young men are pigs longing for corn. Bad ones escape da pigsty, root around in da forest making a mess of tings hoping for a morsel dat tastes better den vat dey got at home." Swen paused for dramatic effect, and to take another big swallow of vodka. "Good pigs stay on da farm and eat da corn dey have. Good pigs, bad pigs, dey both get a belly full of corn. Vel, are you a good piggie or a bad piggie?"

Jim sold his Camaro, bought a minivan with a car seat and a decent engagement ring, returned to Miami, and proposed to Gretchen. You could say his conscious got the best of him, or perhaps it was his newfound fear of popcorn. Either way, Gretchen could once again show her face at the Miami Beach Lutheran Church of the Mother of the Holy Sunscreen in time for the wedding.

After the wedding, Gretchen realized she married an idiot, racist bully. Gretchen hated Jim; how he looked, talked, walked, sat, snored, chewed his food, and how his face smelled of mildew, no matter how often she washed their towels. At least he was responsible, got a job, and supplied her with drugs. Just what the world needs, another racist cop.

This is not meant to imply all cops are racist. The vast majority of law enforcement officers are great people putting their lives on the line to protect and serve, yada yada yada, but a few cops, like a few doctors, plumbers, and politicians, are racists. Not the 'Confederate flag under the rifle rack in the truck rear window, you can see them coming' racists, they are the racists who live next door, take their trash cans in, and vote, kind.

Roughly 4 months of *Married-to-Jim-Hell* later, a baby came into the world, beaming such sunshine Gretchen had to pry her baby out of the hands of the obstetrician.

"Congratulations! I've never seen a more radiant child," the doctor said as the baby giggled. "I've never seen a newborn laugh like that. What's her name?"

"Ingeborg," Jim replied, "after my grandmother."

Gretchen held her baby to her breast and watched in amazement as the child gazed back at her and held her hand. Even on quaaludes, Gretchen never experienced such overwhelming love and peace. She smiled at her mesmerizing baby, who giggled and winked at her mother like they were old friends. "She's Grace. I'm not arguing, Jim." And Grace it was.

The doctor floated out of the room in the joy Grace imparted on everyone, and asked to no one in particular, "Ingeborg?"

Grace's early Catholic school education was pivotal in her development. It instilled a true goodness in her to help others. She learned lessons from the Old and New Testament, the seven sacraments, how to honor her parents (even her dick of a father and druggie mom), God's love for man, loving your neighbor, *yada yada.* It was Grace's early journey down this educational and spiritual path that led her to psychiatry—*remarkably, not as a patient*. Also, Grace looks super-hot in a plaid schoolgirl skirt.

After Jim died, Gretchen dated one fucked up guy after another. Gretchen had a proclivity for men with mental illness, and drugs up the wazoo. Grace observed and learned from her mother and her string of crazy and crazier boyfriends. Instead of resentment for being put in these dangerous circumstances, Grace swore to put an end to people suffering from mental illness and addiction.

Grace's grandparents played a huge part in her life, and despite Swen's palpable hate for her father and shame over Gretchen's addiction, Swen showered Grace with love and respect, and taught her how a man should treat a woman. Swen treated his wife, Helga, like every moment of every day was their first date.

Grace isn't brilliant. Grace is Sherlock Holmes, Leonardo DaVinci, Mr. Spock, off-the-charts brilliant. Clever, creative, fun, mischievous, get-'er-done fucking brilliant. Experiencing Grace, holding her hand, smiling with her, even listening to Grace discuss mental illness, was all a joyous adventure.

During her residency, her professors took note when Grace began a healing relationship with a man suffering from schizophrenia that nobody could reach. The man thought he was Jesus. In their first session, Grace asked the man what miracles he performed that day. The man got very quiet, started sobbing, and told her, "The miracle of someone finally hearing my voice, my child." In psychiatry, they call this "joining," but for Grace, it was just another day of being graceful.

By the time Jim died, Grace knew what kind of man her father was. It didn't matter. To Grace, as a psychiatrist and a human, there were no bad piggies, just other humans suffering humanity. Despite her parents' failed attempt at parenting, nobody fucked up Grace. That would be impossible. She is grace itself.

31

No way!

Back in the middle of the spaceship

"It can't be. Grace! Are you really here? You're made of light, too. Talk about lighting up a room! Crazy. It's like we're melded together?"

"Freddy? God, you're beautiful," slips from Grace's lips before she can consider her circumstances. "What the heck is going on, Freddy? I was just checking out of Trader Joe's. Hey! Where's my grocery basket? I got those dark chocolate peanut butter cups you love, and oh, yeah—where the fudge am I, my love?" *This is bad. For Grace this is cursing. Grace never curses.*

"You're here. By the way, you're beautiful too," I say, trying to act all cool.

"Thank you, babe. Great! I'm here. Now, Freddy Fluid, my love, where is here?"

"I was told it's not so much where as when."

"Okay, when am I? God, you're even beautiful from the inside," Grace says.

"Inside? Hey, knock it off!" Grace's head appears halfway inside and halfway outside of my neck.

"Your brain looks exceptionally complex, and of course it's the most beautiful brain I ever saw," Grace remarks, with a wink.

"Thanks, doc, but as I've been telling you for years, get out of my head," I say nervously.

"Yes, dear. It is quite a unique brain. Your neural pathways are simply stunning. A psychiatrist would know these things," Grace replies.

"Of course."

"I've seen thousands of them, but never one like this," Grace says, kissing my brain, causing my heart to skip several beats.

"Hey, knock it off! Please."

"You used to be much more fun, Freddy. This will loosen you up," Grace disappears into my belly, kissing it from the inside, causing me to laugh uncontrollably.

"Hey, you might hurt something."

"There's nothing here but light beams, Freddy. Neat trick. Where, I mean, *when* are we?"

"When indeed, Grace. Sorry to have kept you, #009. Just on time, Grace," #1 says.

"Uh, hello, talking orca?" Grace nudges me in the ribs from the inside. I giggle.

"Where were you? You only flashed away for a second. Wait! You're him. The sad dolphin I saw on the moon that night on Loop Road. Fuck me! I knew I wasn't imagining you."

"Come on, Freddy. You saw a sad dolphin on the moon? Let me in on the secret," Grace asks.

"I look like an orca, Freddy; or more correctly, orcas look like me. Let's get your cetacean life form identification correct, please," #1 says.

"Yeah, sure, call yourself an orca. I'm glad you clarified that, because I wouldn't want to think you were the saddest fucking dolphin I ever saw."

"About my appearance, Freddy, Grace, if you'll permit me?"

"Hey, get them off me," I say in a muted voice as my form becomes covered in glistening light beams.

"Right-o. It doesn't hurt, #009. They're light beams. They are our mode of, well, everything. Permit me to explain. I am #1, ruler of Rolexa. That's Rolexa, not to be confused with those twits on Timexa. While I appear in the form you see in front of you, I have the ability to transform into any matter I envision, real or imagined."

With that, #1 transforms into a dragon, followed by an eagle, then a human male who could be my twin, a tiny spaceship, a pomegranate, and finally a tin can filled with nails, then back to his orca form.

"And, as you have just witnessed, I also have the ability to shape matter into anything, and I mean, *anything*, I determine to be useful, such as this spacecraft. I created this ship with my thoughts. It has the capacity to travel any place in the Universe."

"This is all fascinating, #1, but what does this all have to do with me?" I ask like a failed game show announcer—tell us, space creature, what have we won?

"Or me. And why, may I ask, do you have a sexy British accent?" Grace chimes in.

"Ah, quite right. Actually, I like it. A proper British accent makes me sound more intelligent, if it were even possible, just a little sexy, and maybe a tad taller. It's a perfect combination. Chicks in every galaxy can't resist a Brit. Believe me, I've tried them all."

"Languages, or chicks? By the way, we don't like being called chicks anymore," Grace says like an adorable kindergarten teacher correcting a 5-year-old.

"Quite right. Apologies m'lady. Both."

#1 goes on to speak in German, Italian, Swedish, Aramaic, and several other languages composed of musical notes, whistles, clicks, and snortles. Then, back to English, like an Englishman.

"It is quite true, though, the English accent gets them every time, right, Grace?" #1 jokes.

"Not today, #1, not today!" Grace says.

"Ah. I'll get right to it, then. Once in every 10 generations since I planted my seed on this planet, the ruler of our land—Moi—visits Earth to determine its progress. To date, it has been mostly one disappointment after another.

First, the atmosphere froze off our original spawn. They were an exceptional combination of apex predators and prey. As your species refers to them, dinosaurs. I mean, who doesn't love a good triceratops, or those flying things—what did I call them again? Ah, pterodactyls, that was it. Did you know they could swim? Everyone looks at those big wings and thinks, great flying beasts. They were actually designed as underwater swimmers. The whole terrifying dinosaur thing went out the window when Earth's first taste of climate change came about. We tried a gentler approach next. We planted the seeds for cetaceans. Modeling them after me, of course. We almost got it perfect with them, you know. Especially dolphins. They look a lot like me, however, as you can plainly see, I am an orca. What jokesters those dolphins. By all rights, they should have ruled this planet. But do you know what went bloody wrong? Go on, ask me. Ask me, then," #1 says like a scared guy picking a fight.

"I give. What went wrong with dolphins? They seem like perfectly intelligent, happy creatures with perpetual smiles painted on their faces," I ask in return.

"Ah, the goofy smiles. That's a problem, #009. Not like my regal smile," #1 says, flashing us a practiced movie star smile that makes his teeth glisten, like he just finished brushing with Bon Ami. "You don't see a silly smile on my form, do you? Ask me why they're always smiling, like someone painted clown makeup on their snouts."

"I give. Why do dolphins smile like clowns?"

"Because, that nitwit #2 mixed the light spectrum formula wrong. He gave them crazy strong libidos. All they want to do is shag. All day, all night, Shaggyanne. Do you know there are wild mating herds of dolphins?"

"We saw them on an airboat in Ozello. Remember, Freddy? It was wild. We went back to our Airbnb and pretended to be dolphins. Remember, babe?" Grace asks, winking, and I flicker like a loose light bulb.

"Grace. Shhhh!!!!" I say in a muffled tone.

"Fascinating," Grace remarks.

"Sure, fascinating to you. To me, there goes another wasted attempt, and another 10 generations of experimentation. Earth is 70% water. Dolphins should have been Earth royalty, but instead, they spend so much time having dolphin orgies, they shag themselves silly. You know the original dolphin design didn't have a Cheshire Cat smile. I wanted them to have a regal smile, like me. Dolphins should be respected, but they are considered the clowns of the ocean. Jumping through hoops for fish at amusement parks. Damn that #2!"

"Why don't you just fire him?" I ask.

"He's my spawn," #1 says.

"I didn't realize there was nepotism in space?" Grace questions.

"My dear child, when your species begets entire galaxies, everyone's related."

"This is all very interesting, #1, but I still don't know why I'm here, or even why you're here? Since you are all about light, why don't you illuminate us?" I snark.

"Ah. Very good quip, #009. A regular quip off the old block, you might say?"

"Huh?" I ask.

"Yes. To that point. Yada yada yada, every 10 generations, we plant our seeds."

"Seeds?" Grace asks, like a PTA mother asking if the class snacks contain peanuts.

"Yes. Our DNA is strategically placed into Earth's DNA matrix via your water supply. Dinosaurs, dolphins, chimps. They were all very promising until those species discovered sex was fun. Did you know if you give a chimp a vibrator, they will literally shag themselves to death? And those triceratops, talk about being horny. What is it about this planet that makes everyone so horny?"

"Something in the water, perhaps?" Grace jokes.

"You got yourself a quick little bird here, Freddy."

"Hey, we're not birds either! Try to keep up with the times, #1," Grace says.

"Apologies again, m'lady. After the dinosaurs, dolphins, and chimps, we had our first go at humans, with a more targeted tracking approach. You know those fitness watches everyone wears?"

"Sure, I have mine right here."

"The watch is actually a tracking device. We planted the need for the device into the general consciousness of your species in this present generation," #1 explains.

"But everyone has one, in every country. How did you convince an entire planet to buy a watch?" I ask.

"Facebook!" #1 declares proudly.

"So, aliens are behind Facebook? That explains everything," Grace jokes.

"You don't really believe some college kid thought that app up?" #1 shoots back.

"Brilliant!" I remark.

"From there I was able to track all humans, especially my seeds," #1 says, beaming at me like I'm the last beer in the fridge.

"There you go again with the seeds. You don't mean? No way!" I say, like a guy who just found out he kissed his cousin.

"Way, #009! I am your father!"

32

Bad OCD

Yes, the day of the sewer moths was the start of it all, but there have been countless days of Bad OCD. To be fair, to welcome one even further into my insanity, let's take a look at a day of Bad OCD.

7:01 p.m.-7:14 p.m. Take the truck out for a cruise down the MacArthur Causeway. I need to drive her once a week, or she won't be happy. She's almost as old as me, and a girl has to get out and let her hair down, right? It's a beautiful evening, cruise ships in port, Coast Guard cutter cruising Government Cut to the Atlantic, windows down, the hum of the engine, and John Prine on the radio keeps me bathed in *now*. I love the hum of this engine. I think she's got another 250,000 miles in her. Wait! What the fuck is this noise? A squeak? Maybe it's the Porsche next to me. Sometimes they sound almost squealy. I'll slow down so they can pass. Nope. Still squeaking.

7:15 p.m. I pull onto the shoulder and check under her hood. Looks pristine, as always. I have the best mechanic. He keeps her tip top. I don't hear anything. Don't start this shit, Freddy. You know what will happen. Too late, Bad OCD has plans for me—*bad ones*. Back in the truck. Drive off cautiously, so as not to break anything which might already be broken—like this old beast of a truck would ever quit on me; neither will Bad OCD. There it goes again. *Squeak, squeak, squeal.* And here it fucking comes, creeping into my brain like mold on a loaf of bread you could have sworn was fine the last time you saw it on the kitchen counter.

The feeling of having OCD isn't what I imagine people with schizophrenia feel; at least they get to lose touch with reality. I empathize because I understand what it's like to hear voices with my mind full of *next*, but the thing is, OCD doesn't come out swinging like a psychotic break. No, OCD is subtle, like your mother's hot friend, let's call her Brandy (*even though her real name is Lois Applebaum*), asking you over to help her move. And before you know it, she takes her top off, because she's hot and sweaty from moving boxes, and you panic because you're only 16 and you have a wonderful girlfriend, let's call her Grace (*because, well, you know*), and you don't know what to do, and 23 minutes later you find yourself breathlessly running down the street in a cold sweat, but you have no idea how you got there or why you're on that street instead of with your wonderful girlfriend. Yeah, that's Bad OCD. And here it comes—*Squeak*. Fuck! "Siri, call JAY!" I yell my mechanic's name into my phone. "Hello, Jay, Freddy Fluid here. I'm good, thanks. My truck is squeaking. Yes, squeaking, well, maybe a squeal or 2 thrown in. No, no grinding sound. No, no gear slippage. Yes. I'll bring her in first thing Monday morning. Thank you, Jay." *Yeah, thanks for nothing.*

7:16 p.m.-11:53 p.m. Call everyone I know with a truck and ask about squeaks. Do 355 Google searches. Ignore Grace when she comes to kiss me goodnight. Go up and down stairs to garage 7 times, counting each step. Open and close truck's hood 7 times, starting engine and listening for sounds, 7 times. Do 77 more Google searches. (*I like the number 7, OK? And, if you haven't already noticed, I can't bring myself to write out numbers. It's 7, not seven, or my leg shakes like an old washing machine stuck in the spin cycle.*) Fall asleep with laptop on my chest on the couch.

2:04 a.m. Wake up in a cold sweat thinking about noise in the truck.

2:05 a.m.-3:59 a.m. Google Toyota truck squeaking and squealing, 458 results, some of which contain images of naked women squealing in a truck bed with baby pigs—*don't ask.* Search is inconclusive. Could be a belt, no, it doesn't sound like a belt. Fight sleep.

4:00 a.m. Fitfully back to sleep.

5:30 a.m. Wake up. My head pulses like a *techno dance floor.* Truck noises, truck noises, what could it be? Kiss Grace. See if invitation to Graceland awaits. Grace whispers, "Sorry, babe, Aunt Flow is visiting." (*You would think a doctor would simply say she was menstruating.*) I feel rejected and throw the covers back in a huff.

5:31 a.m. Dash to bathroom. Turn light switch on and off, insuring switch is facing up on the 15th flick. Whilst I'm peeing, grab toothbrush, thrust into my mouth, attacking my teeth, *like a drunken sailor scrubbing rust from the deck of an old ship.* Brush teeth until I finish humming the Star Trek theme—twice. Finish peeing. Wipe off the edge of toilet seat with toilet paper, because as careful as I am, a drop of urine lands on toilet rim—*Yuck.*

5.32 a.m. Turn on shower, step inside quickly—too quickly, and it jolts me like someone threw a bucket of ice water in my face. I retreat to the tile floor. I have no patience this morning and keep my hand in the shower, testing the cold water until it's barely warm enough, but I jump inside *like I'm trying to beat an Olympic runner by 0.000001 of a second.* My brain is racing and battles the watery *now.* Though my body relaxes, my brain is stuck on

Saturday's tasks. No surgery, no patients, and the thought of the squeaking, no, more of a squealing noise in my truck haunts me like a schizophrenic spirit. "Might be the front end?"

5:33 a.m.-5:59 a.m. Breathe deeply as I dunk my head under the shower stream. Brain disengages. I am Buddha slow and it frikkin rocks, baby, but the water pressure is low today, and my brain skips ahead to fill up every centimeter of *next*, and it sucks. What if my truck breaks down? Does Grace still love me? Was that a sewer moth going down the drain? No, it was belly button lint. Where does that lint come from anyway? *Next, next*, stupid, annoying, irritating, aggravating *next* makes my body tense from the inside, and I'm frightened. All of my cells have the creepy crawlies, *like I'm stuck in a haunted house, and not the Disney version.*

6 a.m. Daily shower alarm sounds soft puppy barks 3 times, and I scream at Alexa, "Shut the fuck up, Alexa, you stinking machine!!! Who do you think you are, my mother?"

6:01 a.m. Stare at my pitiful face in the mirror and think I might be coming down with something. I look gray. *Was it really belly button lint, or a worm? Fuck me.*

6:02 a.m. Dry off, put on shorts and a t-shirt.

6:03 a.m. Turn off bathroom light switch. Fight the urge, but Bad OCD wins out, that bitch, and I flick the light switch another 14 times, making sure it's facing up.

6:04 a.m.-9:36 a.m. Google Toyota truck squealing, and read every article, while calling every human I've ever known who's owned a truck, ask about truck noises, until Grace nuzzles my neck.

9:37 a.m. "You okay, babe?" she asks. I don't respond, or turn around, but reach back and pat the back of her calf. "Off to yoga, Freddy. I'll bring you breakfast," Grace says softly in my ear, as I perform another 83 Google searches until her return in 80 minutes.

10:57 a.m.-11:00 a.m. Grace sets a plate of eggs, fried potatoes, Cuban toast, and sliced, salted tomatoes in front of me. "Eat, Freddy! Your favorite. Manny's Café," Grace says, and spins me around in my desk chair. Our eyes meet, and Grace's *now* salvages me from the depths. She puts a forkful of eggs into my mouth, like she's feeding an old cat with no teeth. "Come on, Freddy, just a bite. You'll feel better." Despite my hunger, I fight the urge to chew, until Grace winks at me. Damn, the wink. I chew! "That's my big boy," Grace teases, and pinches my ass.

"Truck squeal," I mutter, motioning to the computer screen.

"Yes, Freddy, my love. Now, chew," Grace says, putting the toast in my mouth until I clamp down with my teeth, and Grace heads off for a shower.

11:01 a.m.-11:24 a.m. I can't stand it. My brain overloads with visions of broken-down trucks. My truck. The one Mother got me. I have to fix it. I'll just look under the hood. Run down 9 flights of stairs, counting all 135 steps to the bottom, whilst simultaneously thinking about my truck transmission.

11.25 a.m.-12:17 p.m. Jump in my truck, start it, open the hood. Nothing to see or hear. Close the hood, sit in the driver's seat, and feel the vibrations as I find myself driving to the Everglades, googling truck squeals and squeaks on my phone at every light, every stop, even moronically when I'm doing 60 on US 41, until I get to Loop Road. I should call Grace. She'll be worried. Instead, I google truck screech as I drive on under the majestic tree canopy.

12:18 p.m.-12:54 p.m. It's quiet in the Everglades. If I drive slowly, I'll be able to hear the truck noise here. It's nice out, too late for most creatures to be out in the open, but looky there! An 11-foot python splayed out, sunning itself across the road in the afternoon sun. Jackpot. I stop, turn off the engine, grab a burlap sack from under the seat, and slowly walk toward the snake. I always wanted to catch one of these big-ass snakes. Years ago, irresponsible pet owners released their snakes when they outgrew their cages and now pythons rule the 'Glades. Some are big enough to eat a gator. I cautiously make my way across the road, ready to grab the snake's neck from behind. Good. It's not moving. But then I hear a squeaking noise. Fuck! It's coming from my truck. WTF, the engine is off! All at once, the snake takes off straight at me. "YIKES!" I leap into the air, as the python whizzes under my airborne feet, darts under my truck, and lunges for the engine. A second later, the python is on the ground, holding a large possum in its bulging jaws. I examine the scene in wonder, as 3 baby possums fall to the ground from my truck's engine compartment, hissing and squeaking. No, it's more of a squeal. Fucking squealing possums, Freddy! Won't find this shit in a Google search. Bad OCD, you a-hole! I can't wait to tell Grace about this. Grace! Shit. I have to call her. "Siri, call Grace. Grace! Hello, Grace! It was a fucking possum with 3 babies, and a huge python ate her!!!"

"Freddy, I tried calling you a dozen times. Possums? Snake? Are you okay, babe?"

"You see, it was a squeaking, no, squealing noise."

"Where are you, Freddy? You left over an hour ago?"

"Loop Road, Grace."

"Loop Road? By yourself. Are you having another one of your Bad days?"

"I was, Grace. See, there was this possum."

"Okay, Freddy. Are you coming home? We had lunch plans with Bill and Susan, remember?"

"Bill and Susan? Fuck! Sorry, see the truck was—"

"Okay, Freddy, just come home and tell me all about it, my love. I worry about you when you get into one of your states."

"I'm sorry, Grace, it was a pos—"

"You'll have to tell me later, Freddy. I'm at lunch now. Let's go for a swim when you come home. That always relaxes you," Grace suggests.

"Yes, a swim sounds nice. Apologies to Bill and Susan. I'm so sorry, Grace," I say, as I step out of the truck, burlap sack in hand, grab the snake behind its possum-filled jaws, toss it into the sack, tie it up, and heave it in the truck bed. "Take that, fucker!" I say to the snake, as I drive off like I'm escaping a crime scene. The baby possums are on their own. I don't know how Grace puts up with me.

12:55 p.m. I make my way onto the highway, patting the truck's dashboard. "Nothing to see here," I say, until a flashing check engine light comes on. "FUCK!" I scream. I drive down the road doing 65, googling 1999 Toyota Tacoma, check engine light, all the way to South Beach.

Bad OCD never really goes away; it waits under the surface for a trigger to release it from its lair. Could be a squeal, a check engine light, sewer moths, or some other seemingly innocuous annoyance, and when she's done, *you feel like a shipwrecked sailor clinging to the last piece of flotsam in a stormy sea.*

33

A couple of dicks

Back in the bottom of the ship, #2 continues his struggle to locate Freddy.

"Hey, #2?"

"Shhhh! Don't bother me. I think I have it adjusted right this time, #3. Here he comes."

"Good job, #2. This might be him. Hey, Mister, execuseeeeee meeeee? Are you Freddy Fluid?" #3 asks.

"Freddy Fluid? No, I'm Sam. I was just checking the sewage outfall and, wait, are you a talking whale or an alien?" Sam asks.

"Both. I'm from the planet…Oh, sorry, Sam. Someone else is coming through. Hey, #2, you got another one. Are you Freddy Fluid?" #3 yells.

An agitated, slightly confused Max beams into the chamber in the bottom of the spacecraft.

"Freddy? The only fluid around here is this stuff I'm floating in. What is this? What the heck is going on! Wow! The DEA really have cranked up their tech. Did Dick send for me? Dick? Are you here? Where is that hunk?" Max asks.

Burt sneaks over to the chamber, and whispers to Max, "Hey, Buddy. I don't know who you are looking for, but these two are a couple of real dicks."

"Dicks? Oh, I get it. Good one, Burt. You sure were right, #2. We need a comedian around here," #3 says.

"Who are you, Earthling?" an agitated #2 asks.

"Hello, I'm Max, Mayor Max Roosevelt. Nice to meet you," Max says joyfully, like he's meeting a potential voter.

"Oh, God, not a politician, guys. Before we know it, he'll have us forming committees," Burt jokes.

"Committees. Good one, Burt! A politician, #2? #1 is not going to like this at all. Nope. This is almost worse than when you beamed up that lawyer," #3 says.

"Hey, #3?"

"Yes, #2?"

"Zalk you, and the light beams you rode in on," a discouraged #2 says as he swims off.

34

My father—the alien

Back with Freddy.

"My father? Bullshit!" I'm finally losing it. "GET OUT OF MY HEAD!!!" Aliens? There's no such thing as aliens, Freddy. Fucking OCD! This can't be happening. As I believe we've established, when OCD is good, it makes me pay my bills on time, when it's bad, I worry there're worms coming out my asshole.

This right here, my father the alien, definitely ain't the good one. This is Bad OCD! Very, very bad. Fucking aliens, sure, Freddy. Bad OCD is a slow asphyxiation of everything else. Nothing matters but the imaginary evil *next*. My perseverant thoughts tether me to an imagined hellish outcome, my entire being bobs in pain, like a sinking boat anchored in a sea of blood pudding—*Yuck!* Aliens. Aliens! Aliens!! I'm an alien? No fucking way! Way? Oh, God, this is the worst my OCD has ever been. It's usually day-to-day stuff that sets it off. Should I turn down this street or that? Will something bad happen if I don't?

To be clear, Good OCD is a superpower if I want to solve a problem using a methodical and well-researched approach, allowing me to completely focus on my work, my patients, my surgery, my Grace. When it's bad, I'm nervous buttering toast. *Get it?* I can't sit still like everyone else. That's what led to the rituals. Turn the light switch on and off exactly 15 times, check twice to verify the switch is facing up at the 15th flick of the switch. If not, crap, start over again. Put on my left sock, left shoe, right sock, right shoe. Never sock, sock, shoe, shoe. Why? Why, you may ask? *Again, I don't fucking know.* Psychiatrists say rituals provide a sense of perceived control for highly anxious people; calming the chaos that surrounds us. What the fuck is calming about frantically flicking a switch 15 times? *Because if I don't, something bad will happen, that's fucking why. Get it?* But I've never hallucinated before?

Usually, my mind races between 2 places at once—*now and a minute from now, next.* Rarely do I view the past, until this morning, but it's not every day a boy meets an alien claiming to be his father. I don't know why the past always seems unimportant. Maybe I'm moving too fast to have a reverse? But why can't I sense the future here? In this place it's no longer about *next* or about right *now, and it's very, very, very bad* because your father is an alien, Freddy! I'm so fucked!

"We prefer zalked, my boy, but you're not fucked or zalked, and for the record, you are not hallucinating. Back me up here, Grace," #1 says.

"I'm right here, Freddy. I heard everything you thought, and don't worry, I won't let you sink into the pudding. By the way, nice imagery, babe. Blood pudding—Yuck!" Grace says. *(I told you she was perfect.)*

"You both heard all of that? Really? I'll go along with it, sure. If you know everything, #1, how come I don't know what's going to happen *next* here?"

"It seems, Freddy, my dear boy, you finally caught up to yourself."

"Huh? Wait! You really are my father?" I question in a drained, broken voice.

"Dear boy, do you think a being like me goes around nicking people from random planets?" #1 asks.

"Freddy Fluid. You're an alien! So that explains it," Grace quips.

"Explains what?" I ask.

"Pretty much everything, Freddy. Nice job on this model, by the way, #1. He's gorgeous," Grace comments.

"Why, Freddy is a chip off the old block, if I do say so myself, but I think I have a stronger chin," #1 says, changing form to look identical to Freddy, with just a tad grayer hair.

"You're beautiful, #1!" Grace says without realizing it. "Whoops, sorry, Freddy. Don't get jealous, but look at him."

Holy shit. He looks just like me. I mean, I look just like him. I'm no biblical scholar, but I don't recall any mention of how God felt about having a son? Probably how #1 feels now. My son, the doctor. Probably a happy sigh until he realizes I'm an OCD mess who can read people's future thoughts. Even the OCD meds wouldn't have fixed this shit. My father. I have a father! Finally.

I wished for this moment my whole life, and here he is, my father—the fucking alien.

35

The producer

In The Big Blue Diner on South Beach, a bright, bustling restaurant, full of a mix of locals and tourists. In the 1950s-1970s, this area was a mecca for an older Jewish population escaping the brutality of northeast winters, longing for a sunny retirement. The streets were filled with open air produce stands, smelling of fresh, and not so fresh, fruit and vegetables from around the world. Delis, butcher shops, druggists, kosher bakeries, hotels, and apartment buildings lined the streets. Meanwhile, in the present day, a pancake breakfast costs $20.

"Yes, Ma'am. I'll have the pancakes and eggs, please."

"Okay, hon. You want toast with that?"

"Why, yes, Ma'am. Thank you kindly."

"White, rye, whole wheat, challah, sourdough, or gluten-free?"

"White will do just fine. Thank you, Ma'am."

"Do you want butter, margarine, vegan spread, or avocado?"

"Butter will do just fine, Ma'am. Can I ask you something, though?'

"Sure, hon."

"People in Miami put avocados on their toast?"

"Sorry, hon. That's avocado spread. They mash up an avocado, add some salt and garlic powder, and charge you $3.50 for a tiny scoop."

"Gosh darn, what will they think up next?"

"You're not from around here, are you, hon?"

"Why, no, Ma'am. I'm from Mt. Airy. Mt. Airy, North Carolina."

"Never heard of it."

"NEVER HEARD OF MT. AIRY? Why, Mt. Airy is the greatest little town in America. It's the birthplace of Andy Griffith."

"Who?"

"WHO? WHO? Ma'am? You never heard of Andy Griffith?"

"Can't say I have, hon. You want coffee before I put your order in?"

"Just a darn minute, Ma'am! Are you telling me you don't know who Andy Griffith was?"

"Nope. Hey, you want any bacon or sausage? We have pork sausage, turkey sausage, andouille sausage, chicken sausage, imposter sausage, pork bacon, turkey bacon, and tofu bacon."

"No, thank you, Ma'am. But, honest, you never heard of Andy Griffith? *Andy of Mayberry*? Opie Taylor? You know, little Sonny Flowers?"

"Nope. Hey, I gotta run. Those people have been flagging me down for more coffee for 5 minutes now, and I'm going to blow my tip."

"Sorry, Ma'am, I don't mean to hold you up. I just don't understand how you never heard of Sonny Flowers. After he played Andy Taylor's son on *Andy of Mayberry*, he had his own TV show, *Happy Days*."

"Oh, *Happy Days*."

"Good. Now weez connecting. I knew you watched him on TV."

"Oh no, hon. I never saw it. I think my grandmother told me about the show. The '50s, with Fonzie, right?"

"Why yes, Ma'am. Now we're talking."

"So Fonzie is from your hometown?"

"Dang. Just when I thought we wuz getting somewhere. That's okay, Ma'am. I don't know what I was thinking, coming here looking to cast someone in my new movie—Mayberry, The Next Generation."

"Oh, why didn't you tell me you produce movies?" the server asks, adjusting her apron and hiking up her short skirt.

"Oh, Miss! Can you pleaseeeee bring us some more coffee," comes a voice from another table.

"Sorry. HEY, JACKIE! Can you bring table four coffee? Thanks, Jackie. You're the best," the server bellows across the room.

"And it's too bad, Ma'am, because you're the spitting image of a young Helen Crump. You know, stern and pleasant. The kind of schoolteacher the kids respect, and the kid's father wants to take on a weekend trip," the man says, lost in his own imagery.

"Helen Crump. Count me in."

"Well, bless your heart. Maybe this could work. I've got Leon DeCapricorn playing Andy and directing, so I'll have to run this by him."

"Leon—fricking Decapricorn?" the server says, sitting down at the table across from him.

"Yes, Ma'am. Ole Lee, that's what his friends call him. Lee is a big Andy fan. Lee likes to screen everyone he works with. To make sure they have good chemistry."

"Chemistry, Biology, Geometry, whatever. Tell Lee I'm his girl."

"Well, let me just give you my card, Ma'am. I'm Andy, Andy Tyler. My parents thought it would be funny."

"Andy Tyler? Funny? I don't get it?"

"Oh, that's okay, Ma'am. I reckon I need to take a picture of you to send to Lee. I'll just get out my phone. Just look at you smiling. Why, you're as pretty as a peach."

"Are you kidding? I look like crap. Wait here a minute. I have head shots in my purse, 'cause my father told me you never know who you might bump into. I'm glad I finally listened to the old man. Oh geez. I'll be right back with those pictures," the server says as she grabs Andy Tyler's face and kisses him hard.

"Whooowheeee! Waitresses sure don't treat their customers like this at the Bluebird Diner in Mt. Airy. No, Ma'am! I guess that's why they call this the Magic City."

"You just wait right there, Mountain Man. I'll show you some real magic later," she says, dashing off to retrieve her purse. "Hey, Martin. I quit! I'm going to be a movie star. Leon DeCapricorn. I can't friggin believe it. Hey, Andy, you still want your breakfast, or I could whip you up a little something at my place?"

"HEY! Where are my manners? Hush my mouth. I don't even know your name," Andy says.

"I'm Thelma, Thelma Lou."

"Well, I'll be. Just like Barney's girl! They named you after her."

"I think my parents named me after that little girl in Dr. Suess."

"I think that's Cindy Lou?"

"Who?"

"Exactly! Cindy Lou Who," Andy says.

"Who?"

"Exactly."

"Huh?"

"That's okay, Thelma Lou. I'll explain later."

"Hey, Andy, your watch is blinking? I've heard rumors about this. NO WAY! NOT NOW!" Thelma Lou shouts.

"Huh? Well, would you look at my watc—" Andy says as he vanishes.

"Holy hamburgers! Don't take him. Not now!" Thelma Lou calls out as she slumps to the floor. "A MOVIE. I had a movie," Thelma sobs, then jumps to her feet, fists darting to the sky, as her hopes vanish with Andy Tyler. "A movie with Leon DeCapricorn! FRIGGIN ALIENS!! KISS MY FRIGGIN GRITS!"

36

Who's your daddy?

Back with Freddy.

"My father, huh?"

"Quite!" #1 says.

"So, where the fuck have you been all my life?!!!"

"Quite understandable, you would have questions. Allow me to elucidate, my dear boy. Every 10 generations, we come to earth to inspect our offspring and determine if we are on track."

"How colonial of you," I say.

"Ahh. Quite. However, our goal is not colonization, rather keeping this planet healthy. No matter what guidance we provide, you Earthlings have a way of… How do I say this kindly? Hmmmm. Well, I better just spit it out. You wankers make a bloody mess of this place! It's all we can do to maintain the ozone. It's not like we don't have thousands of other planets to attend, but you creatures have a unique gift for turning this place balls-up."

"Balls-up? I'm not sure I understand what it means, but I like the way it sounds. By the way, #1, if you designed humans, you could have done a much better job with those things," Grace says.

"Ah, quite right. Balls-up is British for fucking things up, and yes, just like we did with testicles. On our other planets, the dangly bits are on the inside, and pop out as needed, but the heat index here doesn't allow for it without killing off the swimmers," #1 retorts.

"Those things are disgusting. Ask anyone on the planet. You could probably ask any of the other species here too, none of them, not even the males think, *why I have beautiful balls*," Grace says with a wink.

"Can you communicate with other species, #1?" I ask.

"Indubitably! I'll teach you, Freddy. It's a simple technique," #1 says, like he's going to teach a caveman how to light a match.

"Really? Uh, great, but back to where I came from, if you don't mind, Dad. Is it okay if I call you dad?"

"Dad. Egad! You may call me Father."

"Yes, Father," I say as I feel specks of light dripping down my cheek. Grace gives me a hug—from the inside. "Cut it out, Grace!" I say, chuckling.

"Back to your origins, my son. You definitely resemble me in humanoid form. I would have expected no less. Your mother is the most exceptional, gorgeous being I ever encountered on any planet, anywhere. In addition, Fiona Fluid has a unique intellect. When I laid eyes on her, I knew I had to handle it myself," #1 says, winking.

"What do you mean, handle it yourself?" I ask, in a *you better not be talking about my mother like that* tone.

"You know, Freddy, handle it. Good one, #1!" Grace says with another wink.

"Ewwww!" I say, like a guy who just found a used condom floating in his soup.

"A gentleman never tells, but let's just say your mother and I are quite close. I've been quite close to Cleopatra, Marilyn Monroe, Joan of Arc—she was a hot little bird—Judy Garland, and countless other stunners. That Judy could really belt out a tune, especially when she was at her peak of pleasure. Sometimes she was so loud, I had to wear earmuffs… But, I digress. Fiona, your mother, why, she's the best shag of all. Why, just this mor—"

"HEY! That's my mother you're talking about! And why are you talking about her in the present tense?" I ask, like a flustered schoolgirl trying to find her cell phone.

A flash of lights bounds around the chamber, flitting from end to end in the shape of an owl. The bird stops on my shoulder and kisses me on the cheek, then flies to the ground and takes human form.

"Well, I'll be gobsmacked! You always could make an entrance, luv," #1 says with joy.

The owl transforms into Mother, and she is as beautiful, and ageless as the last time I saw her. Even in her casket, she was the most stunning person at her funeral. I try to speak, but my body will not respond to my orders. Instead, I stand petrified. The only detectable movement, thousands upon thousands of tear-shaped light particles streaming down my cheeks.

37

#1

A long time ago, on the very first planet, in the first galaxy, in the first universe, He came to be. It is unknown whether He created it, or it created Him, because there were lots of clouds and stardust and such floating about, so it was hard to see.

The planet was stunning, with crystal clear water which both absorbed and reflected the light of the six indigo moons, three silver suns, trillions of amber shooting stars, and countless violet clouds. The colors of the celestial bodies responded to His moods, with clouds turning red, suns turning aqua, and moons turning green when He laughed. His breath informed the orbit of the planet. His ears summoned soulful music, the envy of the finest fairy chorus, as stars shot past the clouds, moons, and suns. When He was happy, the planet gently swirled in an infinity loop around the entire Universe. *When He was unhappy, the place looked like a crime scene at the planetarium.*

What is it like to be the first sentient creature in the Universe? At first, it's fucking brilliant. A planet comprised entirely of water, to do with as one will. Go anywhere, do anything, but after a few thousand eons, been there, done that. It took a while before it hit Him, and He wasn't even sure what a while was, so He created a perpetual hourglass to track time across the Universe. It was powered by Rolexa stars, and unfortunately also served as a grave measure of His long period of loneliness. In fact, He was alone for 12,000 eons before He realized He was alone. Once He did, He realized something else—*He was as lonely as an omnipotent being on an empty planet.* So, He decided to craft Himself some company. There was just one problem, He didn't know how. He considered His dilemma for 1,135 years and had His answer.

He reached deep into His mind to conjure an image so appealing, just His thoughts brought it to life, and there before Him was the first life form; a shooting starfish, *and no, it didn't have little pistols and a cowboy hat.* The starfish reminded Him of the actual shooting stars of Rolexa, which were made of infinite energy and passed through the watery planet, and the Universe, without any change to course, speed, or trajectory. The shooting stars even passed through Him, and it tickled; *and He liked it very much.* He observed the starfish for 300 years. Being a starfish all alone on a water planet, it did very little, and it did not communicate, so He granted it the gift of telepathy. The first conversation went like this.

"Hello."

"Hi!"

"So, you new around here?"

The conversation went downhill from there.

He could access any area of the planet by just thinking about it, and He'd transport there. He blinked all around Rolexa, creating unique and beautiful life forms; coral gardens, seahorses, crabs, lobster, octopus, turtles, sea dragons, eels, anything His mind conjured came to be, *and He saw it was good, yada yada yada, but not quite good enough.*

After creating thousands of other life forms, He saw it fit to create His equal, *and He saw it was good, yada yada;* because there, before Him, was His seed, a whale type creature, a tad bit smaller, with a shorter snout, and clearly inferior. He was, after all, the most omnipotent creature in the Universe. Then the other creature spoke, and He knew He had screwed the pooch. (*Yes, even the omnipotent can screw up, sewer moths, olives, and George Smelt, being a few prime examples.*)

"You got anything to eat around here? I'm so hungry I could eat a… Hey, what do you eat around here anyway?" the new creature asked.

"Eat? I have no need for nutrition, and you were made in my image."

"Image, shimage, how about some grub?"

He didn't know what to make of this foul-natured creature. He had longed for the company of another, to share His thoughts, His planet, His existence, *but deep down, He was hoping for a girl.*

"Hey, what do I call you anyway. Mom, Dad, Bro?" the new creature asked.

He hadn't thought of naming Himself, or this creature. Up until now, He didn't really have a need for an identifier, but since He was first, He kept it simple. "You may call me #1, and you, Sir, are #2"

"#1, #2, huh? Did you just think those up now? I'm gonna say yes. Is that the best you can do? Geez! You know, why don't you put some effort into it?" #2 said. "So, how about some sashimi?"

"Sashimi?"

"Here, I'll show you," #2 said, as images of fish filled both of their minds.

"Seriously!?" #1 said.

"Come on. All you have to do is think some up, 'cause you're in charge around here, right?" #2 said, appealing to #1's ego.

"If I must," #1 conceded, blinking fish into existence. "Would you look at that! Little versions of me, but without the brain capacity, aren't they the cutest thi—" #1 gasped as #2 swallowed the tiny fish in one gulp.

"Delicious," #2 said.

"You, Sir, are an animal," #1 said.

"Animal, schmamaninal. That's what I call fresh fish. Could use a little soy sauce, though," #2 said.

"Soy sauce?" #1 asked.

"Hey, don't ask me. I just got here," #2 said.

While #2 could communicate telepathically, he could not teleport. #2 had to get around the old-fashioned way, swimming. This gave #1 the advantage of ditching His spawn as often as possible, because ironically, He couldn't stand being on the same planet with the very creature He created to keep Him company. Despite all of His brilliant creations, #1 was still lonely, and His failure with #2 haunted Him, so He reached for the stars with His mind, and what He found surprised Him. There were other planets, other galaxies, scattered about the Universe, all as empty as a shadow.

#1 decided to chance it again and created another clone-like replica. He was still hoping for a girl. This time, He got one. #3 popped into existence a free spirit. She was delightful, quirky, chatty, loving, had an enchanting singing voice, loved caviar, and was goofy as Barney the Dinosaur's sister. *(Barney had a sister, right?)*

Over the next several eons, #1 went about the Universe, creating every possible life form He could think up. To be honest,

#2's dour thoughts and #3's goofiness, served as templates for a few of #1's creations, such as hyaenas, dinosaurs, platypuses, pilot whales, and beluga whales; the latter of which were definitely inspired by #2 and #3. While #1 spent another few eons populating and grooming species from every galaxy, He was still lonely. When He came upon the planet Earth, it was a steaming, sputtering ball of molten lava. #1 sneezed on it, and it cooled, its surface covered in saltwater—*and a bit of orca snot.*

There was something about the place that called to Him. Perhaps it was all the water? #1 planted His creations on Earth, then left and returned every 10 generations thereafter to determine Earth's progress, as He did with thousands of other planets. However, on one visit, while enjoying a dip in His favorite saltwater pool—the Atlantic Ocean—He found the key to overcoming His timeless loneliness. Her name was Fiona Fluid.

38

Oh mother, where art thou?

This is the first, but not last occasion, I can't utter a single word, until— "Mother!"

"Hello, Freddy, my love," Fiona Fluid says in a comforting voice.

What the fuck is happening to me? First Grace. And now, Mother. She's alive? Impossible. This is maddening. And this shapeshifter claiming to be my father. I must be having a breakdown. Shit! All those years I thought I was going nuts, thinking about how fast I moved, breathing underwater, being able to predict *next*. I need one of Grace's psych evals. I'm going to wind up committed to a hospital as a danger to myself or others. Nobody will let me near their eyes.

Oh Freddy, you should have at least taken the OCD meds Grace prescribed. Now it's too late. But then again, there have been rumors of alien abductions, and just recently, people have been talking about flashing fitness watches and aliens. Oh, this is just a mind fuck. "I've gotta get out of here!"

"I told you, you were always free to come and go, my son. And, by the way, ouch! Shapeshifter indeed. Can a shapeshifter do this?" #1 asks as light beams fly in every direction.

What the fuck is happening now? I'm shrinking. Bright lights engulf me, like twinkling stars in the Milky Way. Clouds of light are all around, shining indigo globes, violet rings of light and gases, and amber stars flying in every direction. It's moving at a dizzying pace, surrounding me more quickly than I can comprehend. Simultaneously, I am frozen in place.

The light. Each light beam is alive, coming from all of the stars, planets, galaxies, and every being on them. I see them all, feel them, taste them in the back of my mouth and it startles me, *like licking a 9-volt battery*. The light is emanating from and being absorbed by each galaxy and every being in them. It's incredible. I see. I see…What the fuck? It's like being in the middle of a giant snow globe? Oh, crap, I've lost it!

"More like you've found it, my love. It's the Universe, Freddy," Fiona says.

"Mother. You heard my thoughts?"

"Yes, Freddy. Now you can hear mine. And this shapeshifter really is your father. By the way, I call him Eddie. Short for Edison, you know, like Thomas Edison. Another one of his bright kids," Fiona says.

"Edison indeed. You don't think that simpleton came up with the lightbulb idea on his own, do you?" #1 retorts.

"So, I'm not crazy?"

"Do I get to weigh in?" Grace quips.

"This being really is my father? Why didn't you tell me, Mother???!"

"We'll explain everything, Freddy," Mother says.

"Oh, this is going to be good. I wish I had some popcorn," Grace says, as a rain of little explosions surrounds her.

"As requested, m'lady," #1 says, handing a tub of buttered popcorn to Grace.

"You're making popcorn? You abandoned us—EDDIE!" I scream.

"Never! You are my most precious creation, and your mother is the only creature I ever truly loved. That is, until you were born."

"Seriously, an alien?"

"Indeed, my boy, but actually, you're all the aliens. I was here first. I can explain everything," #1 replies.

"Go ahead. Apparently, I have plenty of time."

"Actually, you don't," #1 says.

"Huh?"

"I'll explain—in time. Don't you want to know about me and your mother?"

"I'm listening."

"I was back on Earth for my every 10 generations check-up, as the last batch we planted was getting ripe. Of course, I was in the ocean, because look at me."

"Makes sense," Grace says.

"Quite! I was swimming through the waves, when I beheld the most beautiful creature I ever encountered. Skin as white as my favorite star, Proxima Centauri. Her eyes, like the planet Xipophereia, and a smile like an orca. I swam right up to her, nibbled her swimfin, and transformed into the best version of a human I could."

"Why did you pick brown skin, dark hair? I mean, I know I'm good looking, actually, very, very good looking, but why the Middle Eastern look?"

"I was modeling you after #007?"

"James Bond?" I ask.

"Ah, right-o. James Bond, secret agent. Alas, dear boy, you are much better looking than Sean Connery," #1 remarks.

"He really is, #1. You know you are, Freddy, but Daniel Craig, he's a looker, all right. A bit short for a secret agent, though?" Grace says.

"What a delightful sense of humor. I see why you like this one, #009. #007 was my creation in the year you Earthlings refer to as 1, in the Middle East. He was modeled after me, in human form, of course. Some say he was perfect, inspirational, even magical, but it didn't last."

"What happened to #007?" I ask.

"Romans," #1 answers, slowly shaking his head from side to side.

"Romans?"

"They killed him. You look a lot like him, Freddy. That Mary, she was quite the looker too. Her beauty pales in comparison to you, my love," #1 says.

"Nice save there, Eddie," Mother says.

"You expect me to believe I'm Jesus's brother?"

"Christ, no!" #1 says.

"Whew!"

"More of a distant cousin."

"Jesus Christ!" The words spill out of my mouth.

"Again, close, lad, but no cigar. #007 was John the Baptist," #1 says.

"You slept with John the Baptist's mother?" Grace asks.

"Heaven forbid. Did you ever see John's mother? She was a good soul, but she was 200 bloody years old. They didn't do facelifts back then, so she was a bit of a fright. I artificially inseminated her."

"I'm related to John the Baptist?" I question, like a kid who just found out the Easter Bunny is allergic to eggs.

"Why do you think he was always dunking everyone underwater? He thought since he could, all the rest could as well," #1 says.

"Could what, #1?" I ask.

"Why, breathe underwater, like you," #1 replies matter-of-factly.

39

The animator

In Normandy Isles, a bustling working-class residential neighborhood at the northern end of Miami Beach, Miami Sound Machine plays through a blue-tooth speaker, while an anime artist contemplates his next frame.

Geronimo Goldberg had a crayon, chalk, pencil, marker, or some other writing implement in his hands since before he could walk, and started doodling all over his highchair. Geronimo's father was an archeologist with a fascination for Native Americans. He thought it would be a great honor to name his son, Geronimo. His father, however, failed to consider just how many times a day, a shy, overweight, pimply-faced kid named Geronimo, who was forced to walk their yappy chihuahua around the neighborhood, would get his ass kicked.

Growing up an outcast, Geronimo fashioned his anime character as a misunderstood, powerful, and slightly vengeful underdog, who happened to appreciate a good meal. After many failed submissions to a variety of producers, Geronimo borrowed

$30,000 from Grandpa to produce and self-publish his anime characters, Bustella Beans and her dog, Chunka. To everyone's surprise, besides the artist and Grandpa, Bustella went as viral as Covid, with contracts coming in from Asia for a TV series, movie rights, and sequels. Geronimo moved Grandpa out of his nursing home to a cottage behind the house he bought with his huge advance check and hired a cute live-in nurse. *Grandpa was as happy as an old man with a cute nurse, which at 98 was very fucking happy.*

The inspiration for Bustella was based on Geronimo's two earliest loves; pastelitos and the 19-year-old friendly counter girl who served them to him. If you never had a pastelito—a Cuban puff pastry filled with deliciousness—you've wasted much of your life, or at least your tastebuds. Although Geronimo never got further than exchanging pleasantries with the yummy girl who served them and didn't even know her name, he fantasized about her every waking hour since the moment their hands touched over a greasy white bag of guava and cheese pastries; and thus, the anime version of Bustella Beans came to be.

Geronimo developed Bustella's character into a large, gregarious girl, with a dynamic personality, a strong libido, martial arts expertise, an anime artist boyfriend, and a healthy appetite (for food, justice, and her boyfriend). Along with her sidekick, Chunka, a Pitbull with a gaze that could wipe the smile off a politician running for re-election, they did their part to keep Miami safe.

In Geronimo's stories, Bustella was born in the kitchen of a Cuban coffee shop in Normandy Isles to Blanca, her waitress mother. Her father, the rapper, Grande Cojones, was absent in her life, but sent his latest CD every year and $10,000 cash on Bustella's birthday, which was Grande's version of child support.

Bustella grew up working in the coffee shop with Blanca, folding napkins, washing dishes, cleaning the counter, talking to customers, and breaking other child labor laws, until she turned 11 and graduated to making cafecito. At 12, Bustella was a skinny thing, which drove the kitchen staff crazy, so they stuffed her full of lechon, rice, beans, Cuban bread, and flan until she, let's say, filled out.

In her first adventure, Bustella who was particularly spry for a 19-year-old girl in a larger body, jumped the breakfast counter and gripped a robber's chest between her brawny thighs, while Chunka latched onto his nether regions, until the lack of oxygen and excruciating pain caused the robber to succumb. Bustella was promoted to security guard, then branched out into patrolling all of Miami-Dade County.

The first episode was so well received, Geronimo quickly gained a cult following, and Bustella's adventures erupted from his mind like Old Faithful. Over the years, the anime characters took on so much life, they became real while Geronimo drew.

"Geronimo! Conjo! This time, make my biceps bigger than my ass," Bustella says.

"Hey, leave some room in the frame for me," Chunka barks.

"There's plenty of room for both of you," Geronimo says.

"Come on, Hefe, look at these guns," Bustella says, in her best Hulk pose.

"Don't forget to make my teeth extra sharp and grungy, Geronimo," Chunka barks.

"Don't worry, I got you, dawg. *Dawg, see what I did there?* This episode, you two are going to mess up an evil lobbyist, and rescue a girl from an abusive foster home," Geronimo says.

"Cool, but don't forget my new outfit, Hefe," Bustella says.

"How's this?" Geronimo asks, drawing a pair of gold booty shorts, a white halter top, and red, white, and blue boots onto Bustella's body.

"Hefe, those shorts make my ass look good. Love the boots, same colors as the U.S. and Cuban flags, but they're so tight. You sure I can run in them?"

"You don't have to run, babe. Just push this," Geronimo says, as he draws a button onto the side of the boot's heel.

"No bueno, Geronimo. Last time I pushed a button like that, sparks flew right up my hooc—"

"Bustella! Babe, it's me. I got you covered, look," Geronimo interrupts and draws a frame with Bustella standing proud, her boots planted firmly on the ground and a villain floating in the air. "See, gravity boots. Push the button and everyone else loses their gravity, you stay grounded, walk over, and collect the trash."

Chunka growls.

"Don't worry, Chunka. I told you, dawg, I got you," Geronimo says, and draws Chunka with a red, white, and blue collar on his neck. "See, I got you a gravity collar, dawg." To which Chunka wags his tail in approval.

"Very, very bueno, Hefe," Bustella says, and kisses Geronimo hard. (*And yes, if you're wondering, they're in love, so it's not weird she's a cartoon or anything.*)

"I'll just draw this lobbyist making a deal with the mayor."

"Lobbyists taste bad, Geronimo," Chunka barks.

"That's why I made the gravity collar and boots. You don't even have to bite the guy. The lobbyist is going to try to get the mayor to approve a new development on endangered wetlands in exchange for Congressional votes on funding a suspended train track over the Everglades."

"Bastards! I don't care how he tastes, I'll bite him," Chunka threatens.

"Come on, Hefe, let me kill them," Bustella says.

"You know our motto, babe," Geronimo reminds, and they all repeat. "Mess 'em up! Don't kill 'em!"

"Here, look, guys, Chunka gets to maul his legs, so he can't get around so easy," Geronimo says.

"Conjo, Hefe, that's weak," Bustella says, in an emasculating fashion, causing Geronimo to draw something uncharacteristically mean.

"Don't do me like that, babe. Check this out!" Geronimo displays his drawing of Chunka hanging from the lobbyist's barbed tongue by his large brown teeth.

"Hefe, that shit's going to sell like churros," Bustella says.

"Money turns you on, huh?" Geronimo asks, grabbing Bustella's ample butt.

"You know money doesn't get me wet, Hefe," Bustella says, nuzzling Geronimo's neck.

"You know I can't draw when you do that."

"Then don't draw," Bustella says, then kisses him again.

Chunka barks uncontrollably

"Hey, boy, don't be jelly. We got some love for you, doggy. Hey, Bustella, your watch is blinking."

"What watch?" Bustella asks.

"Don't ask me, I didn't draw it? Must be those fucking alie—" Geronimo says as he, Bustella, and Chunka vanish in a flash of amber lights.

40

Father knows bloody best

"You know, I wanted to name you Frederic, but your mother insisted on Freddy," #1 states. "She asserted Frederic was too stuffy."

"Quite!" Grace says, in her best British accent.

"This one is quite the charmer. Why, if I hadn't met your mother…" #1 says, and I shoot Father an angry look.

"Joking. Only joking, lad. Now, do you want to know about breathing underwater?" #1 asks. "It's easy; like drinking Mother's milk."

"That's exactly how it feels," I say cautiously.

"Hey, keep my boobs out of this," Fiona jokes.

"Quite! But they really are magnificent, luv," #1 says.

"Again, Ewwwww!" I respond.

"Don't be so uptight, Freddy. Why, you drank from both of them. It was a beautiful sight to behold. The way you and your mother locked eyes, while your little hand wrapped around her index finger," #1 replies.

"You always were a breast man, Freddy," Grace quips.

"Wait! You were there? When I was a baby? You're telling me you were there?"

"I told you, I've always been with you, Freddy. Always," #1 states.

"Well, that would have been nice to know—for the last 29 years, 10 months, 30 days, 15 hours, 58 minutes, and 43 seconds of my entire life. Fuck!!!!!"

"Actually, it's 15 hours, 59 minutes and 42 seconds, Freddy," #1 says.

"Huh? You've been with me my entire life. A life of abandonment and pain, thinking Mother and I weren't worth your time, and now, now, all you can do is correct my math? Screw you!"

"Freddy Fluid. That's no way to talk to your father. He adores you, and he never left you, or me," Fiona says in a hushed tone. Fiona Fluid is the model of composure. Mother never raises her voice at me, or anyone. She always has a way of calming me, no matter what. "It will all make sense when Eddie explains. Give your father a chance, dear."

"Yes, Mother. You look great, by the way, for someone who's been dead for 4 years, AND LYING TO ME MY ENTIRE LIFE! What the fuck, Mother!??!"

Compose yourself, Freddy. Shut your eyes. Breathe. In and out. Shut your eyes. That always helps you concentrate. What's really happening to me? Am I supposed to believe I beamed aboard a spaceship, and Grace and Mother are here? Oh, and my father is an alien? And not just any alien. A shape-shifting orca alien who thinks he's a God. You've outdone yourself this time, Freddy.

All these years, living a moment ahead of myself, it's too much. I'm going to wake up from this nightmare, and everything will be back to normal. Well, normal for me. What if it's not a dream? I never dream. Maybe I finally cracked. OCD, thinking I know what happens next, delusions of grandeur, breathing underwater. I'm a raving lunatic. That's it. I'm going to wake up in a mental hospital, alone, sedated, strapped to a gurney. People will want to determine my competency. Go ahead, ask me, who is the President? Easy—the current moron. What country are you in? Easy—this one. What time is it? Time? I don't fucking know. See, nothing wrong with me, with the exception of my math skills, which up until now have been perfect. How do I know this? Why, because my alien orca father told me? Fuck me!

"Freddy Fluid, language. We can hear your thoughts," Fiona reminds calmly.

"I see how overwhelming this is for you, son. But go easy on yourself. They're not delusions of grandeur, my boy, because I am, after all, your father. And I wasn't correcting your math, lad, merely pointing out an inaccuracy in your time keeping," #1 says.

"I see where Freddy gets his healthy ego, Fiona," Grace says.

"Ya think?" Mother says.

"May I continue?" #1 asks in a gentler tone than he has up to this point; like he's speaking to a confused patient in a nursing home.

"I guess I'll go along with this charade until my keepers crank up the psych meds. I hope you have me on something good, Grace?"

"Yes, about that. All this dribble about your brain being cracked—rubbish! Between my and your mother's brilliance, our beauty and gifts, you are certainly not a padded cell dweller. I assure you, Freddy, my boy, this is all real," #1 says, patting my shoulder. "May I continue, old chap?"

"Might as well, because in a few minutes, I'll wake up, and you'll be gone."

"Have you ever dreamed before, Freddy?" Mother asks gingerly.

"No! So, it's a hallucination. All of you are," I say like a drunk talking to pink elephants.

"Have you ever had a hallucination, Freddy?" Mother asks.

"There's a first time for everything, Mother. I am disappointed, though."

"Why, son?" #1 asks.

"My lifetime without a father, and this is the best hallucination I can come up with? Really, Mother, you expect me to believe you're alive, my father looks like the only sad dolphin ever created, and, oh yeah, Grace is in a spaceship with us, and able to travel inside of me?"

"Hey, you spent plenty of time inside me," Grace says with a wink and disappears inside me, rapidly traveling the length of my body, head to toe and back again. Slow at first, then faster as I laugh uncontrollably.

"This one's a real firecracker, and, as we've established, Freddy, I am in orca form, not a bloody dolphin." #1 says.

"Fine. Sad orca, then."

"I am not SAD! I am regal," #1 says.

"Stop tickling, Grace. Please!"

"Not until you listen to your parents, Freddy. Your father wants to tell you about breathing underwater," Grace says, moving faster and faster until all I can do is laugh.

"Fine. Just please stop before I laugh myself out of my skin, Grace."

"Ah, that's it, my boy. You just keep laughing, and I'll tell you all about it. Your lovely caramel skin is just like mine," #1 says, transforming back into an orca. "And I do not have a sad dolphin face, more of a happy orca face, if you ask me. Orcas are the largest member of the dolphin family, you know. About the breathing underwater thing, see, no blowhole," #1 says, pointing to his forehead.

"Who cares about your blowhole? Why don't you blow thi—"

"Freddy Fluid, language," Fiona chimes in.

"Sorry, Mother."

"You're not hearing me, lad. I don't have a bloody blowhole. The cetaceans on Earth have to surface to breathe air from the atmosphere. That's why they have blowholes. I had to design whales that way because there's barely any oxygen in Earth's waters. You can blame that on #2 as well, the ninny! Rolexa's waters are like a bloody oxygen bar, compared to the meager offerings on Earth. So, instead of having a blowhole sucking surface oxygen, Rolexian have skin cells…How do I explain this? Hmmmm... My skin cells, and yours, extract oxygen from water, Freddy. That's why you breathe like Darth Vader when you don't get your 25 minutes-a-day of wetness, my boy."

"So, your skin works like gills?" Grace asks.

"I DO NOT HAVE BLOODY GILLS!!" #1 shouts.

"Gills?" I numbly ask.

"No wonder you swim like a mermaid, Freddy. All this time, I thought you had excellent lung capacity," Grace remarks, once again entering my body. "Whew, you do have beautiful lungs, Freddy. I knew you would, but there's an extra layer of something in here I can't identify, and it's blinking."

"Of course, it's blinking, Grace. This entire place is blinking."

"Yes, but these lights are different. They're amber, like your eyes, and his," Grace says, pointing to #1.

"He definitely got your eyes, Eddie, and your gills," Fiona says, giggling.

"Sure, laugh at a guy who just found out he's part fish," I say.

"I am not a BLOODY FISH!" #1 screams.

"Well, there's nothing fishy about this. At some point in the development of human embryos, we all have structures resembling gills," Grace says.

"I do not have bloody gills," #1 mutters.

"I'm sure you're happy to finally meet your father, right, Freddy?" Grace says, smushing my mouth from the inside. "I said, right, Freddy?"

"Yeah, I guess," I say like an airline passenger who just found out his flight got rerouted through Newark.

"Now we're making progress," Grace says.

"You're very good with him, dear. I knew I left him in good hands," Mother comments, and Grace curtsies.

"So, why show up now?" Grace asks.

"Yes, about that. You see, son, it's time," #1 says.

"Oh no, not the time crap again," I say.

"Now, now, dear boy, time is all there is, and we only have 8 hours," #1 says.

"8 hours until what?" I ask.

"8 hours until the Universe may just possibly go—kablooey," #1 says, and I shudder like a baby peeing into their diaper… on a cold day…*in Chicago*…in January.

41

The horologist (And no, it's not what you're thinking.)

In Miami's Coconut Grove, a bohemian community known for its offbeat charm, wild parades, and artsy residents, a long-haired loner looms.

Tick Tockington is a horologist. A proud tradition in the Tockington family. Tick comes from a long line of horologists, dating back to his Swiss, great-great-great-grandfather, Clock Tockington. *Unless you were one of those people who won the spelling bee, you might ask, so what's a horologist? (And, no, they are not scientists who study whores, although that might make for a popular college major.)* Horologists are clockmakers of the highest degree. Although, and not to be contradictory, the only thing Tick Tockington likes better than taking apart a watch and staring into its workings, as if lost in another galaxy, is, in fact, the company of a good whore. Tick spends his days tinkering in the sunny window of his Horology shop on Grand Avenue. It thrills Tick to be surrounded by ticking timepieces clicking away in synchronicity, interrupted here and there by a rambunctious cuckoo clock.

Tick repairs everything from wristwatches to pocket watches to complex grandfather clocks. Tick often dreams of shrinking himself so he could fit into each timepiece and repair it from the inside as if he were floating within the watch, as if Tick were immersed in some kind of fluid. Sometimes in his daydreams, Midge Minge, his favorite whore, joins Tick for an au jus romp through the gears and mainspring.

On this particular day, as has been the case every day for many, many years, Tick woke from his daydream, gazing at his reflection in the glowing hourglass across the room. At 67, Tick's eyes showed the same fear they did in kindergarten—the fear of pissing his pants. He pissed his pants the last time It showed up. It was Tick's first week in school. Tick had just turned 5. Tick was so humiliated, his parents sold their home and moved so Tick could change schools. Since then, Tick knew for certain, that It, the alien that is, would be back.

He knew what the alien would ask of him, for the alien had taught him the task. Tick knew how to perform the task, had trained his whole life for it. Tick could do the task in his sleep, blindfolded, standing on his head in a tropical storm in Coconut Grove. Tick would bet good money he could perform the task the alien taught him under any unforeseen circumstances, except, if and only if, Midge, or in her absence, one of his auxiliary whores, gave him crabs; and not the kind you get on South Beach for $85 a plate. These were the disgusting, crotch biting, itch like a mother, parasitic kind of crabs. This happened once before, courtesy of Midge. It was 21 years, 11 months, 3 days, 6 hours, and 22 seconds ago when Tick failed to perform the task as he was scratching his crab infested balls so intensely, he couldn't free up both hands simultaneously to perform the task—well, you get the point.

Tick knew he was the fail-safe against the end of the Universe, or what the alien referred to as "kablooey." The alien burdened the then tiny Tick with this huge responsibility over a half century ago. Tick counted every second since the alien's departure, which robbed him of a life, and concurrently gave him a purpose beyond that of any mortal man, or at least any horologist, which explains the whores. Tick couldn't commit to a relationship with any woman, man, or family, when at any moment he might be called upon to save the Universe from—kablooey. Plus, as we've established, Tick really liked whores.

Every day of his life since the alien visited, Tick readied himself. The alien told Tick, if he would be needed to perform the task, which was highly likely, it would be at precisely 4:20. Tick, being 5 years old in a kindergarten bathroom, alone with an alien, understandably neglected to ask: a.m. or p.m.? Since that day, 22,650 days ago, at precisely 4:20 a.m. and p.m., Tick takes a deep breath, smiles in wonder at the amber stardust whirling within the hourglass clock entrusted to his great-great-great-grandfather, grabs the hourglass's neck, and holds tight.

The alien instructed Tick to hold on to the hourglass for dear life for 1 second and release it. No big deal, unless and only unless, Tick hears the alien's acoustic signal, and the alien reappears, in which case Tick is to hold on to the hourglass for dear life, until otherwise instructed by the alien, or in the event it all went to shit—until kablooey. When Tick was 5, he could barely get his tiny hands around the neck of the hourglass to perform the task. At 67, his arthritic hands fit the hourglass's neck like O.J.'s glove.

No matter, Tick performed the task 45,300 times since the alien left. 45,299 times successfully, not counting the crab incident. He was ready. And he hoped he wouldn't piss himself—again.

42

Wound too tight

"Oh, Eddie, don't be such a drama queen. It's not that bad, Freddy. Your father just needs to adjust your clock," Mother says.

"My clock?" I ask.

"Freddy, my boy, you think your brain is buggers. It's not. Why, it's an exceptional brain," #1 says.

"I agree," I say, *because it's true.*

"Each being has their own clock, lad. Their sense of time and place in the Universe. Some people are in sync no matter what, not like those bloody slouchers on Timexa. Thanks to me, my boy, you are set on Rolexa time; 59 seconds ahead of Earth time. That's why you're always trodding off into everyone's *next.* You're not broken, my boy; you're just wound too tight!" #1 says. "You see, time is relative, and being my relative, your clock is just a bit off. Everyone needs a reference point, lad, and yours is from my home planet."

"Rolexa time? You knew about *next,* Father? And you, Mother? How could you leave without telling me any of this?"

"I knew, dear; that's one of the reasons I left. Well, that and the cancer, but Eddie fixed me up with just a few Rolexa moon beams. We thought taking care of me was getting in the way of your research. Eddie promised to adjust you once you completed your macular degeneration research. He said you needed *next* to complete it," Mother says.

"You finished your research, Freddy? Why didn't you tell me? Oh, Freddy, I'm so proud," Grace says as she runs her hands up and down my spinal cord, from the inside.

"Hey! Stop it, Grace! You're telling me Flipper here cured your cancer?" I ask like a kid who just learned his parents snuck off and replaced his dead goldfish—with an orca.

"FLIPPER! Shamu would have been a much better reference, lad," #1 says, then whispers to me, "You know, my boy, there were multiple Flippers, and most were played by females. They're typically less aggressive than males, except Squirt. She was a feisty little bird, all right. People think she got her name because she was little, but if you ask me, they called her squirt because in the heat of passion, when she was good and ready to pop, she squir—"

"Eddie!" Mother interrupts. That's quite enough reminiscing about your lost loves; especially when I was just crediting you with saving my life."

"Quite right, luv!"

"And yes, Freddy dear. I'm good as new, thanks to your father, so please take it easy on him," Mother says, blowing Eddie a kiss.

"Wait! You can cure cancer?" I ask, like a kid at a magic show.

"Simple technique, dear boy, but it doesn't work on Earth. I had to zap Fiona to Rolexa for a bit. The light from our moons destroys any known pathogens. That's why I've been around since before dirt. Actually, my boy, I created dirt."

"Did you create my OCD, because if you did, gee whiz, thanks, Pops! That's the best gift a father can give a boy."

"Oh no! Don't blame the OCD on me," #1 says, then whispers to me, "You get that from your mother's lot. Rumor has it her father accidently asphyxiated himself whilst cleaning a stubborn stain on the loo with bleach and ammonia."

"You knew about *next* too, Mother?"

"I knew, dear; and nobody could clean a bathroom like your Grandfather—rest his soul. OCD runs in the family, Freddy. I'm sorry, dear. Oh, Grace, Rolexa is so romantic, you would love it there. Both of you would. You haven't lived until you've taken a moonlit swim under indigo moons with a gorgeous man," Mother says.

"Oh, Freddy, let's go visit Rolexa when this is over. You're going to stop so many people from losing their vision. It's miraculous, Freddy! I'm so excited! Is anyone else excited about Freddy's research?" Grace says, kissing me all over, and under.

"I am," Fiona says.

"I think it's safe to say your mother and I are very proud of you, Freddy. I would expect nothing less of you, my boy!" #1 says.

"I'm so close," I say, like a guy who lost his car keys on the beach and thinks that shiny thing in the sand 50 yards away might be them; but probably not.

"Ah, but your research *IS* finished, my boy. It will be perfectly clear. Now, let's get busy resetting you."

"Reset me?"

"More of a soft reboot, lad. We all have internal timekeepers, a clock, if you will. In your case, you were lucky enough to inherit my settings," #1 says.

"Settings, settings?" I question numbly.

"We'll have you right as rain soon enough, lad. And, Grace, we'll be needing your help," #1 says.

"Count me in!" Grace dives into my chest.

"I told you I fancy this one, Fiona. That's what I call throwing yourself into your work. Bravo, Grace," #1 remarks.

"So, what can I do to help?" Grace asks, like a princess visiting a disaster site.

"Just work your magic, Grace, and I'll work mine. This might help your quest," #1 says, and sends a mass of light waves hurtling into Grace's head.

"I understand, #1," Grace says, like a teenager who's just been baptized.

"You have 8 hours, Grace, which should be more than ample time."

"Ample time? Ample time!!!???" I shriek.

"Yes, 8 hours to work her magic, until we have to do the reset," #1 says. "The girl's bloody brilliant, lad. You're in good hands. Besides, if it doesn't work, I'll go with a hard reboot."

"Hard reboot? Hard reboot?" I wail, like Frankenstein's monster seeing fire.

"You see, dear, a hard reboot might cause you to forget some things," Mother says.

"What kind of things?" I ask.

"Well, everything, but don't worry. Grace is going to get the job done," #1 assures.

"And what happens in 8 hours?" I ask, like a failed politician waiting to concede the election.

And in one quick auctioneer breath, my father, the alien, announces, "8 hours from now, Grace will be pregnant, because you two boinked last night, and if we don't reset you before your little swimmer penetrates her egg in precisely 8 hours, 13 minutes, and 6 seconds, Rolexa Standard Time, Grace's *now* egg and your *next* sperm will collide, thus vaporizing the entire Universe I spent a bloody lonnggggg time creating, so may we please get on with it. Capisce?"

"Boink, *now*, *next*, collide, vaporize the Universe. Baby! Got it," Grace says, unconsciously patting her belly and grinning, like a woman who just found out she's about to be pregnant.

"I need to sit down?" I say shakily, and *next* hits me like a shovel of love to the face, and a very father-to-be voice escapes my light beam lips. "Sorry, Grace. You're the one who should be sitting. Want to sit?"

"I'm good, babe," Grace says, beaming.

"We're going to have a baby!" Grace joins light beams with me and flashes them on and off, not saying a word, and I feel the grace she is in my life and will be in our child's, sparkling through the lights. Oh, God, I'm going to be a parent, a dad, not like this guy who abandoned me, abandoned us.

"I am truly sorry, son," #1 says.

"Crap! I keep forgetting my thoughts are in the public domain here."

"I kept an eye on you all along, Freddy, but meanwhile, time to save the Universe, tick, tick, tock. You take it from here, Grace, and congratulations," #1 says in a grandfatherly voice, *as if the guy doesn't already have a trillion grandkids in hundreds of galaxies.*

Grace pats her tummy, winks her light beams, and we're off—*and, we're going to have a baby!*

43

Oh, baby

You might be wondering how I feel about babies? You must understand, being with a baby or toddler is the closest I come to being with God, and I don't mean #1. Sit with a baby, until they are about 2 years old. Just sit there. I dare you. And no cootchie-cootchie-coo shit either.

Sit quietly and look into their eyes, for God's sake. Anyone with a hint of emotion will see all of the beauty in the Universe in a baby's eyes. Spend time with a baby when they are in a good mood and want to play. Nothing is more present than a human infant or toddler. Until they turn 3 or so, then they're a regular trifecta of bratty, dirty, and snotty; always thinking about *next*, and it's mostly things they want. I want ice cream, gimme that toy, read me a book. And it all comes out as the 3-year-olds thinks it— and it's all *next*.

When I want to be *now*, I do pro bono work with infants and toddlers with rare eye disorders. Unfortunately, there are lots of them. Babies keep me in *now*, because it's where they live. When your mother, father, grandparent, sibling, girlfriend, boyfriend, even your dog, when they love you, you can see it in their eyes. It's true. Their eyes sparkle. Not like mine, because, well, you know, I'm special, but you can see it, nonetheless. Baby eyes cast sparkly little fishhooks which capture your heart—and I can't wait for ours to reel me in.

44

#2

If #2 were a drink, he would be a dark and smelly. He was a nearly attractive creature, looking very much like a pilot whale, but his off-putting scowl made others untrustworthy of him, and rightfully so. He rarely told the truth, cheated, stole, was crass, and had no respect for time, as he was perpetually late. #2 was small-minded. He was selfish, scarfed down anything resembling food before anyone else had eaten, and had a downright miserable demeanor.

Beyond that, he had a gift for making everyone around him unhappy. Just looking at him made one flinch, as if he were a leper. If #2 were human, he would be one of those guys who sits on the couch all day in his dirty underwear, eating blocks of cheese, drinking warm orange soda, scratching himself, and watching sports. #2 didn't see himself this way at all, though. In #2's eyes, he was a misunderstood God. A great inventor of technology. It was, after all, his idea to create their bubble spaceship in the shape of their home planet, and he invented the transportation devices they use for beaming.

He never got any credit from #1. #1 had gone so far as to tell #2 that he wound up with all of his bad qualities. #2 felt shunned, especially by his creator. And that led him to wanting recognition. He thought everyone else in every galaxy was an idiot. He hated everyone and everything in the entire Universe, except one being—#3.

45

The tech sorcerer

In Miami's upper east side, an area formerly home to cheap hotels, and cheaper women, a one-man computer repair shop opens for business and welcomes the first customer of the day.

"Good morning, I am Chip. Chip Fixer. Welcome to my store. How may I be of service?"

"When I turn on my computer, I get a black screen and a spinning wheel."

"Yes. Let me take a look."

"Sure."

"I'll plug in the keyboard. Can you enter your password, please?"

"Sure."

"Has it ever done this before?"

"Not the black screen, but the wheel spins a lot, and it's slow."

"It's your RAM. I can replace it for $200. It will be ready Tuesday."

"Umm, okay, I guess. Hey, how long have you been in business?"

"Over 4 years."

"Good. I guess I can trust you."

"YOU MAY CERTAINLY NOT!" a British voice booms into the shop, preceding the entrance of two very handsome fellows that, if not for a bit of gray on one of their heads, could be twins.

"This man is a scoundrel! Oh, he'll fix your computer, all right, but it will leave here with a special bug, implanted by this criminal genius of a WANKER! Now piss off!" #1 says, as the customer takes his computer and bolts for the door.

"What are we doing here anyway, Father? Where's Mother and Grace? We only have 8 hours, remember? Who the hell are you?" I ask the computer guy.

"I'm Chip Fixer!"

"I didn't ask what you did. I asked your name," I say, because *tick, tick.*

"I get that a lot. My name is Chip Fixer. My parents were computer engineers. They thought it would be funny—*assholes, may they rest in peace.*"

"What the fuck are you doing here, Chip, and where is here?"

"Here is my store, Sir. Welcome! And I do not know to what your brother is referring to. I am an ace technician, Sir. I can fix anything with a chip. What can I do for you?"

"First off, he's not my brother, he's my father," I say to Chip, and then give my father, the alien, a good orca ass-reaming. (*Orcas have asses, right?*) "I can't believe you're my father! You're supposedly a God. Can't you just blink yourself a new computer? In fact, why would a God even need a computer? And, only 8 hours until kablooey!"

"How dare you make an ethnic slur! There is no kablooey here. I must insist you leave my store. Get out, you bloody bigots," Chip says.

"I'll stop you right there, old chap. First, look at us, you ninny! We're browner and more Middle Eastern looking than you. Second, the kablooey reference has nothing to do with YOU blowing up anything. It's actually him we need to keep an eye on," #1 says, pointing to me. "Although, you may have played an unwitting, but meddling part in all of this. You're bloody clever, for a wanker," #1 says.

"YOU ARE THE BLOODY WANKER! To what are you referring, wanker?" Chip asks.

"You bloody well know. You've been tracking my signal for 26 weeks, 2 days, 14 minutes, and 16 seconds," #1 says.

"It's you! Your technology is crazy advanced. British? Russian? German? Everyone I've told about this thinks I'm as mad as a bag of ferrets. Please tell me, Sir. I have never seen such brilliance," Chip remarks.

"If it was so bloody brilliant, you wouldn't have found it, you ninny."

"Father. Remember, 8 hours, tick, tick," I say, because come on already, the world is ending, and this guy wants to spend our last hours talking to a genius bar dropout.

"Yes, about that. Fiona, Grace, please join us," #1 says, and out of thin air, Fiona and Grace's photonic forms appear and turn humanoid.

"I knew it! Aliens! Fucking aliens!" Chip shouts, then passes out.

"Eddie dear. What are we doing here? Can't you just blink yourself a new computer? In fact, why would you even need a computer?"

"I said the same exact thing, Mother," I say, *because I'm a lot like Mother, you know.*

"Ahhhhhh. Permit me to explain," Eddie says.

"Not the permit me to explain bit. Sit down, kids. We're going to be here a while, and 8 hours, Eddie, remember!" Fiona says, tapping on her wrist.

"Yes, dear. Actually, 7 hours, 51 minutes, 2 seconds. I realize I make being a God look easy, but it's hard to be everywhere, even for a God, so I invented a few shortcuts, and this bloke has stumbled upon a weak point."

"Shortcuts? You?" Fiona asks.

"There are over 7 billion humans on Earth alone, my dear, and I needed some extra eyes on things," #1 replies.

"What kind of eyes?" Grace asks.

"Electronic eyes, luv. Video doorbells, robo vacuums, electric cars, baby monitors, automatic pet feeders, drones, laptops, tablets, phones, fitness watches, anything techy," #1 answers.

"We love our robot vacuum. Freddy's so cute, he named the vacuum 'Sucky'," Grace says.

"They're all the rage these days. I wish I had one when Freddy was growing up. His OCD made vacuuming a full-time job. The kid couldn't stand a speck of dust," Fiona says.

"Ladies! Please! Tick, tick!" *Geez! What is wrong with these people? And Sucky is a perfectly logical name for a vacuum.* "You watch everyone though their appliances?" I ask.

"Yes, but when you say it that way, it's kind of creepy," #1 says.

"It is kind of creepy, Eddie dear. Why are we here?" Fiona asks.

"This Chip bloke was fixing a fitness watch 26 weeks ago and happened to discover one of my little transponders. They were barely perceptible. He's a regular computer sorcerer, this one," #1 says.

"He looks so peaceful passed out like that. Maybe we should turn him over. His face is mashed against that printer cartridge. He's going to wake up with one hell of a tattoo," Fiona says.

"Quite! This place is a bit dodgy," #1 remarks, and Chip's body gently turns over onto a mattress and pillow, which magically appear.

"Nice touch!" Grace says.

"'Twas nothing. Once Chip found the transponder, he started searching for them on every device he repaired and attempted to track my monitoring frequency. He planted a signal tracker in every device he's fixed since, but instead of tracking our location, Chip's tracker melded with the Rolexium used to make my transponders and it opened a series of small vision bubbles in the Universe. They've been popping up randomly all over your planet for months. Nothing we can't fix now that we've located their source," #1 says.

"Vision bubble? Wait a minute, is your ship shaped like a bubble? Is that what I saw every time I thought I was going bonkers?" I ask.

"Of course it was me in the spaceship, lad. I've been monitoring you all along. Remember all those soap bubbles floating in your bath, Freddy?" #1 asks.

"You saw me take a bath?" I say, *and not in a creepy way.*

"I smiled every time you washed the shampoo from your hair with the duck, my boy," #1 says. "I created ducklings too, you know. Adorable little creatures. Makes you smile just thinking of them."

"Hey, #1, remember, 7 hours, and whatever. Oh, just keep explaining. You were right about the *permit me to explain* bit, Fiona. Geez!" Grace says.

"Told you. It's this way every time he says, '*permit me.*' Tick, tick, Eddie," Fiona says.

"You were precious, Freddy, but back to business. A vision bubble is a transmission point in a vast network of starlight, emanating from Rolexa. A vision bubble opens and closes within milliseconds when we transport, and during this time, beings on the Rolexa side of the bubble get a wee glimpse of the other side. The bubbles are meant to appear when we're beaming things here and there, but they shouldn't just pop up on their own, and they should never allow any being to see Rolexa. It's all this Chip Fixer's fault—clever little wanker! We've only had a few accidental occurrences prior to this. The last was in the time of the Pharaohs. All those plagues. Frogs weren't dropping from the bloody sky. The Egyptians were witnessing the annual tadpole graduation ceremony on Rolexa through a vision bubble. We blamed it on that poor chap, Moses. Not to fret, we took care of him in the end. The story of Moses never making it to the Promised Land was a cover-up. I blinked Moses to Rolexa thousands of years ago. Talk about the Promised Land. He has a harem of gorgeous woman, his own vineyard, and all the bloody matzoh he can eat. The bastard still beats me at gin rummy. I think old Mo's cheating, you know. Where was I again?"

"Vision bubbles, transponders," I say, hoping to move things along, because *tick, tick, tock.*

"Ah, transponders! That's the problem, my boy. My transponders fused with Chip's tracker, causing our fitness watches to become two-way vision bubbles linked to my transponder monitoring stations on Rolexa and this ship. Thanks to Chip, every time a vision bubble opens on Earth, you Earthlings see a glimpse of Rolexa, or our ship and inhabitants, get scared shitless, and scream something along the lines of, FUCKING ALIENS! Then your fellow humans forget the entire thing; mostly," #1 says in one quick breath.

"Mostly?" I question, because I can't keep listening to him drone on. "Does he always go on like this, Mother?"

"I warned you," Fiona says.

"So, mostly?" I ask again. Will he ever get to the point?

"Yes, mostly. As soon as I discovered the vision bubbles opening, I had #2 and #3 pop down and trace their source. They had to beam up some humans on the Earth side of the vision bubbles to determine the source of the transmissions, which led us to Chip. They were supposed to wipe the humans' memories, but #2 being the wanker he is, screwed that up too. It seems a few people that were beamed aboard remember seeing #2 and #3, when they're in an altered state, like when they are drunk or high, and aforementioned people have been drawing pictures of them, telling their friends, etc., thus, those nincompoops, #2 and #3 have become urban legends," #1 says.

"#2 and #3?" Grace asks.

"They're what Eddie considers inferior beings made in his image," Fiona replies, and #1 gives her a stern look. "Just speeding things along, Eddie dear."

"Thank you, luv. Yes, quite inferior. You can meet them once we deactivate you," #1 says.

"Deactivate me?" I ask, like I'm really screwed.

"Poor choice of words, my boy," #1 says. "But first, I need to deactivate Chip's surveillance system and wipe his memory."

"His computer or his mind?" Grace asks.

"Just the equipment, Grace. I wouldn't dream of hurting Chip's magnificent brain. In fact, he'll be jizzing his geeky megabytes all over the place after we save the Universe, and he wakes up on Rolexa in his dream job—tech sorcerer. Now, not to be a nag, humanoids, but back to the ship before you know, tick—kablooey."

"Fucking kablooey! Wait!! There really are fucking aliens, and I'm one of them? FUCKING ME!" I say, like a guy who just realized he's from another planet!

"Freddy Fluid, language." Mother admonishes.

46

Cliff Hanger

In downtown Miami, in a concrete state office building with slits for windows, a social worker struggles to see the light.

"I don't care what the judge ordered, Ann, we can't give Twan to his mother," Cliff Hanger says.

"You looking for a contempt of court charge?" Ann asks.

"Won't be the first. Let's go back to court. Isn't that why we pay you attorneys the big bucks?"

"Yeah, sure! I bought a tank of gas with my last check. We presented our case, Cliff. It's over."

"Jane can barely take care of herself. Doesn't the judge see it?"

"Look, after what happened to Jane in foster care, there's no way the judge leaves her kid with us. You've got to see the optics, Cliff?"

"Screw optics! And you look, Ann, I was a caseworker, not Jane's caseworker—the piece of crud, but I worked here when Jane's parents lost custody for burning and starving her, only for her to be assaulted by her bigger piece of crud foster father. We all agonized over what happened to her, and how the system, our system, failed her. Nobody should have to endure that pain, especially a child. All that trauma, Ann. You can't tell me you don't see it when you're with her? Three psychiatrists diagnosed Jane with bipolar disorder, and they all missed her underlying personality disorder."

"She covers it up with the meds and street drugs, Cliff. You're a psychotherapist. You know all about medication."

"Exactly! And she goes off her meds whenever nobody's watching. Come on, Ann, she can't handle a 3-year-old."

"Let's say you're right, which you always are. That's why you're running the foster care system, Cliff. What can we do about it now?"

"I was the only one stupid enough to take the job, and I'm right about this. The hairs on the back of my neck are tingling, Ann. It only happens when something crazy is about to go down."

"I've got something right here to quell your spidey senses," Ann says, reaching into her desk drawer.

"It better be a radioactive spider or Kentucky Bourbon."

"Why, Cliff Hanger, are you insinuating an officer of the court, such as myself, would dare drink on the job? But this might help," Ann says, lifting a can of bug spray out of her desk drawer. "Guaranteed to get rid of pesky spiders, but it doesn't do shit for these sugar ants who made my top drawer their lair. Come on, Spidey, let's go see Twan. Jane and her attorney are coming to get him at 3 p.m." Ann stands up and walks toward her office door. "Let's say our goodbyes to Twan. I'll even turn the other way when you do one of your little blessings over him."

"Okay, counselor, but mark my words, some weird stuff is about to go down. Besides, they're not blessings, they are aspirational thoughts released to the Universe," Cliff says as they walk down the hallway to the visitation room, and he opens the door for Ann. "After you, counselor." Cliff looks into the room to see Jane frantically bouncing Twan on her lap like a shopping mall Santa on crack.

"Hello, Jane. Mrs. Longtooth. At this morning's hearing, we agreed you would be here at 3 p.m.? It's only 1:35 p.m.," Cliff says.

"You people kept me away from my baby long enough, Cliff!" Jane says, clearly in an agitated state, causing her to launch the wide-eyed Twan high into the air like a terrified chick at an Easter egg hunt.

"My client has every right to retrieve her child now, Mr. Hanger," Drucella Longtooth says.

"Yes, of course. It might not be as hard to retrieve him if you didn't bounce him so high, Jane," Cliff comments.

"Shut up, Cliff! I don't have to listen to you anymore. Besides, Twan likes me to bounce him high. And where's my $20 million?"

"That's not how settlement agreements work, Jane. I'm sure Mrs. Longtooth has explained the process," Ann says.

"Shut up, mouthpiece. You're just jealous. You can't even have kids. That's why you're trying so hard to keep mine," Jane taunts.

Cliff watches his typically stoic attorney tear up. This isn't the first time Jane has lashed out at his staff members, and while Jane had just cause to be angry at the system, it wasn't fair to take it out on Ann, who had several miscarriages in the last few years and bent over backwards to accommodate Jane's unpredictable behavior.

"Don't worry, Jane. You'll have the money in your account before I can say contempt of court, right, Ann?"

"It's up to…" Ann attempts to say.

"Sorry, Mrs. Longtooth. This isn't a courtroom. Let's concentrate on what we are here for; Twan's and Jane's well-being," Cliff interjects.

"Yes, of course," Mrs. Longtooth says.

"I'd like to say goodbye to Twan. We've spent a lot of time together. Okay, Jane?"

"Yeah, I guess," Jane says, bouncing Twan faster and faster on her lap.

Cliff times his grab just right and reaches out for Twan on an up bounce. The petrified Twan stretches out his little arms and clenches them around Cliff's neck like Velcro.

"Hey there, little buddy," Cliff says in a calming voice. "I'll miss you, Twan. May the Force of the Universe watch over you."

"Yeah, just like they watched over me. Right, Cliff? Don't fill my kid's mind with your wanna-be Jedi bullshit," Jane says.

"Sure, Jane. Just saying goodbye to Twan. You are a bright, wonderful child," Cliff says, hugging Twan.

"Cliff, your watch is flashing," Ann says.

"Well, would you look at that," Cliff says, smiling as his watch flashes faster, and faster until it blurs out of sight. Cliff shoots Ann a farewell smile as he and Twan transform into light beams and vanish in a flash of tiny stars.

"Goodbye, Spideyyyyyy!!!!" Ann yells.

"I'll see you in court!" Longtooth yells.

"FUCKING ALIENS!!! Do I still get my 20 mil?" Jane asks.

47

Darkness into light

"Where to next, Grace?" I ask.

"Let's finish your research, Freddy, before you get distracted," Grace says.

"Brilliant. I knew you were just the right human for the job, Grace," #1 remarks.

"All right, for all the good it will do. And what could possibly distract me?" I ask, as we flash off to my research laboratory.

"Oh, I don't know," Grace says, patting her belly and winking.

"Our baby," I say, like the idiot who forgot we're going to have a baby—or end the Universe.

"Tell us about your cure, dear," Mother asks.

"As you know, Mother, macular degeneration is a progressive disease destroying the central part of the retina. My patients say they feel like they go through life watching a squiggly solar eclipse. This wretched illness is one of the world's major causes of blindness. I'm so close to curing it. I've been working on this for 6 years, 7 months, 22 days, 7 hours, and 48 seconds. Father, you claim I need *next* to complete my work. Well, tick, ti—" *Oh, you know.*

"You have it all laid out in front of you, lad. He's quite clever, you know, Grace," #1 says.

"So he's been telling me; since we were 6," Grace says.

"Perhaps if you tuned in on your *next*," #1 suggests.

"*Next* has been gone since you kidnapped me," I say, and he smiles at me.

"Kidnap is rather a strong term, don't you think? I see what you've done here. Very clever, my boy. Quite promising, indeed, and using stem cells derived from each patient's own blood negates the transplant rejection issues typically seen. The only thing stopping you is the life span issue," #1 says, and I feel like a kid whose father finally came to the science fair, only to see them screw up the experiment.

"Exactly. I've tried everything, but the stem cells degenerate after a year. If only I could find a way to stabilize them," I say.

"Quite. If only there were a perpetual source of energy you could imbue those cells with," #1 says, and I smile, because he gets it, and so do I, as *next* fills me with visions of stardust.

"I've been such a moron. It's been right in front of me all along, but as usual, I'm overthinking." #1's eyes fill with flickering lights, and they're not coming from his eyes, they are reflecting from mine, and the room fills with so many flickers, nothing else is visible, because finally, I see the light—starlight.

"My flickers!" I say, grinning from ear to ear.

"Exactly, my boy. Like the stars on Rolexa, the starlight within you is infinite. All you have to do is smile,' #1 says.

Next visions fill my head like the 4th of July, and the fireworks are directing the show. Rolexa stars are perpetual. The stardust in my eyes is the same matter. Freddy, you idiot! All I need to do is bind my stardust to the patient's stem cells, but how to do it?

"All you need to do is ask them, my boy," #1 says and smiles at me. I smile back, *because, hey, we're having a moment here.*

I never thought of the lights as living beings. "Oh, lights, a little help here," I say aloud feeling foolish, which makes me grin, and the lights from my eyes swirl all around and flitter down my microscope eyepiece and bind to the stem cells which are glowing like tiny comets. I smile because it's working, and my smile releases a multitude of flickers filling my entire lab, and everything is lit up like Times Square on New Year's Eve. Grace, Mother, and Father smile at me, and I know I've done it. "We've done it. All of us. The cure for macular degeneration, *and we're going to have a baby!!!!*"

"Not to overstate the obvious, but you had it in you all along, my boy. I'm proud of you indeed. Very proud," #1 says.

Grace kisses me, winks, and pats her tummy. "I'll thank you properly later."

"Brilliant. You're curing their eyes with yours, and with your Rolexa stardust, those stem cells will regenerate the atrophied retinal cells and stop the leaky blood vessels in perpetuity. I'm so delighted, I could cry, but I don't think there's room for any more lights in here," Mother says, and kisses me on the cheek.

"Wait!" I say, *because I like to say "wait" a lot. Gives me a chance to catch up to myself.* "This biotechnology could be used to cure so many diseases."

"Bravo, lad. If you put your smile to it, there's nothing you can't cure, but in the meantime, tick, tick, tock. If we don't re-sync you, this will all be for naught."

"Yep, naught, nix, zero, zilch. Let's get on with it, because we have some babying to do, Freddy," Grace says.

I smile at her. *And we're going to have a baby.* I know I said we're going to have a baby before, and trust me, I will say it again. People with OCD perseverate and repeat things, OKAY?! Repeating things puts the C in OCD all right. I do this to make sure you understand me. It's not that I'm self-obsessed, even though Grace and Mother might argue differently. I repeat myself so you'll understand me, because it's important I'm understood. Fuck! I am self-obsessed. *And, we're going to have a baby.*

48

The author

In Miami Shores, a village of 10,000 humans, 20,000 squirrels, and a decent smattering of peacocks, an author stares at his computer, praying for its transformation into an Ouija Board, guiding his fingers to literary greatness.

Ernest Hamingway lives most of his life inside his head. Thankfully, he isn't alone in there. The cast of characters inhabiting Ernest's mind are the low-life scum who live in the shadows of Miami. We're talking drug dealers, gang members, crooked politicians, car salesmen, and the absolute lowest of the low—podiatrists. There's also a good guy in Ernest's mind, and his novels; Flip Flysalot, based on a self-actualized version of Ernest. In Ernest's novels, Flip is always the hero; *and oh yeah, he can fly*.

Ernest's first memory was of flying. He was being pushed in a swing. No matter. In Ernest's 3-year-old brain, with his arms held out to catch the wind just right, he was flying, and from that point on, besides writing, flying was his favorite thing to do. Ernest got his pilot's license at 18. He spent every last penny he had on plane rentals, but what he adored was gliding. In the summer, Ernest headed to Maine to pilot for a buddy who owned a glider company, specializing in giving tourists a thrill. Ernest loved the solitude and quiet of gliding. It was, he thought, the closest thing to being a bird. It was during one of these flighty moments Flip Flysalot soared to life.

Ernest's novels were kooky, unpretentious, funny, self-obsessed, chock full of wild characters and set in South Florida; all the ingredients for a small cult following in Miami. Although his ego was huge, in the literary world, Ernest was relegated to the bottom of the stack of pancakes—*you know, that first one you make when the pan isn't really hot and it turns out funky, so you hide it on the bottom.* Still, his books made bank, so damn the critics.

Ernest's personal life was, as they say in Miami, a caliente mess. He had no friends and was unlucky in love. As such, in Ernest's books, Flip was portrayed as a hero who claimed to have a learning disability when it came to relationships.

Flip's first marriage to Franny, a biker chic he met when he was going through his Harley phase, ended in Flip's near death by heart attack when he returned from a motorcycle ride to find Franny on a ride of her own with five of his biker friends—*by ride of her own, to put it delicately, well, we're all adults here.*

Flip's next marriage was more of a disaster than his first. Flip got the point it was over when his second wife, Beth, bought them a fencing set for their anniversary. It only came with one safety vest, and Beth wore it. In Ernest's third novel, That Whore from Miami, Flip finally thought he hit the jackpot with his third wife, Beverly, until he found out—*wait for it—she was a whore, from Miami.*

Ernest was a prolific writer with over fifteen novels to date. Writing came easily to Ernest. He told his friends words flowed through him like liquid gold, until two months ago when the gold rush came to an abrupt halt. Ernest caught the most dreaded disease to afflict an author—writer's block. He sat for days staring at the picture on his wall. The painting of a medieval town had been his grandmother's. It always inspired him and filled his novels with color, and yet now, Ernest couldn't conjure one lousy word—not even in black and white. To make things worse, it wasn't just Ernest's lack of inspiration which was turning his well-endowed creativity into an impotent heap of mush. Something, or someone, was stopping his words from coming.

Ernest was challenged by self-published authors overtaking the book industry, and one in particular was driving him bonkers. When Ernie started writing 22 years ago, if you wanted to get a book published, you slaved over your keyboard, printed hundreds of manuscript copies, sent them all around, got a few hundred rejection letters, and if you were lucky, persistent, and talented, someone gave you a shot. Ernest had that shot with Frog's Leg Publishing two decades ago, and he never looked back.

Nowadays, any jerk with a computer, or even a phone, can write and publish a book. And they do. One particular jerk is Dan Johnson, who writes silly, sexy, cozy crime novels set in Miami, and people eat them up like medianoches after a night of drinking. One book reviewer called Dan the savoir of Miami's parched literary scene.

"Parched! They called it parched, Henry. You're my publisher. What are you going to do about it?" Ernest asks, shouting into his computer.

"Hang on, Ernest. I can't hear you. I keep getting this unstable internet connection message on Zoom," Henry says.

"I'll show you unstable. I took two Valiums just to get out of bed today. Henry, I'm so depressed, I had my carpenter make a new bookcase for me. It turns into a coffin. Should give new meaning to I'm dying to read that. I swear, this will be the end of me, Henry!"

"Calm down. It was one lousy review."

"One review. It was The Times! The Times, Henry. You don't know what it's like to bare your imagination to the world and have it met with ridicule, or worse, silence."

"Ernest, baby, your books are part of Miami, man. You're a cultural icon. I read The Times this morning. I didn't see the review?"

"It's right here," Ernest says, holding the paper up to the camera.

"A little closer, Ernest. My internet connection is unstable, and I can't see anything past the fold of the paper. That doesn't even look like The Times, Ernest. Is that a cut-out pizza coupon?"

"Yes. Buy one, get one free," Ernest says.

"The New York Times doesn't have pizza coupons. That's the Coconut Grove Times, Ernest."

"They have a circulation of over 800."

"Ernest. What's this really about? Did Dan get your delicate ego out of whack?"

"It's not my ego, Henry. I read Dan Johnson's latest book, Miami, Love it like a Grapefruit, and I have to say—"

"Ernest, buddy, let me stop you right there. He's a talentless hack who got lucky."

"If only that were the case. Dan's writing is dazzling, fun, romantic, and he captures the spirit of Miami like no one else. I'm afraid I'm the hack here, Henry. I don't think I can write anoth—"

"Ernest, baby, your watch."

"Watch, watch what? I can't hear you, Henry. Your internet connection is more unstable than me."

"Ernest, your watch is sparkling!!!"

"What? Bad connection, Henry. Yes, Dan's writing is sparkly as well. Thanks for rubbing it in." It is at this moment, Ernest sees his reflection all lit up in his computer screen, and he knows he is going on an adventure. Not Flip Flysalot this time around, baby! Ernest Hamingway is finally off on a journey of his own. "Goodbye, Henry! I'M OFF ON AN ADVENTU—" Ernie happily shouts, as he watches himself flash off into light beams.

"What, Ernest? The internet connection is unstable again. Damn internet! Ernest? Ernest, you still there?"

As Ernest flashes out of sight, Henry gets a glimpse of #2 and #3 through a vision bubble and yells, "Fucking aliens! Hey, Sally, get me Dan Johnson on the phone. I think we have an opening for a Miami author on our team."

49

Meditating Mel-low

Back in the ship, for a beat.

"Let's start with meditating. Remember when I tried to teach you how to meditate, Freddy?"

"You know that Jedi mind control stuff won't work on me, Grace," I say.

"I know, Freddy, my love, but this time is different. You can transform to light beams at any time, and we have help from your not-so-dead mother, and your father, the alien God orca thingy. Besides, *these are not the droids you're looking for*," Grace says in her best Jedi voice.

"She's a real pistol this one," #1 says.

"Hang on just a second. Before we go on, what exactly are you resetting me to?"

"Good question, lad. We need to reset you to *now*, but we can only do it when you're in the *null*. Grace's job is to get you to *null*, long enough for the reset to take hold," #1 answers.

"The *null*?" I ask, because this is starting to sound unbelievably stupid.

"Freddy, lad, I told you earlier it was a matter of when you were."

"Yes, yes, Rolexa time, Earth time, I get it. Please, just get on with it—Father!" I say, like an umpire chucking a belligerent parent from a little league game—youuurrrr outta theeerrree!

"Righto. There are three elements of time that, while they don't tell you when it's bedtime, or dinnertime, are critical to our existence. You're quite familiar with *now* and *next*," #1 says.

"Ya think?"

"Freddy, be nice," Grace says.

"Quite understandable for you to be frustrated, lad. *Now* puts you right smack in the moment, good, bad, or ugly, you're in the midst of it all. *Next* for you, son, is 59 seconds ahead of *now*, and as you well know, can be good or bad. However, dear boy, you have yet to experience the most powerful and concurrently delicate, unpredictable unit of time, because *null* is, in fact, the absence of time. Get it?" #1 says.

"Sure. You're resetting me to nothing. Clear as mud."

"Freddy dear, the *null* is the magical space between *now* and *next*. It's a moment so beatific, it's frozen in time. It's the top of a snowy summer mountain, the bottom of an aqua blue ocean, the Rolexa moons during an eclipse. A baby's first step. *Null* takes you completely outside yourself, dear. It's been said in *null* space you can hear the songs of the Universe," Mother says.

"You mean, like the voice of God, Mother? If I were to believe all this hooey, God is already here. Right, Dad?" I snark.

"God is everywhere, son. Most Earthlings are such self-obsessed nobs, they fail to hear or see God in their everyday lives. If you're paying attention, God is always in the *now*. A flower blooming in the sunshine, a hummingbird in flight, a baby laughing. *Now* is magical. And *next*, dear boy, what a gift you have, to know the future."

"Some gift. I hope you kept the receipt, Father, because I'd like to exchange my *next* for something less painful, *like a root canal*," I say.

"It will all be worth it when you experience *null*, my boy. *Null* leaves you breathless; and not in that I need my inhaler way of yours, lad. *Null*, Freddy, is the split second you see your baby born and you hold your breath until it takes its first. It's a magical millisecond, forever frozen in time. Understand?"

"Sounds more like *now* to me; and for the record, thank God, Mother never gave me an inhaler. That would have gone over big in elementary school. Know what today is, kids? Beat Up the Handsome Little Brown Boy With Asthma Day. No, thank you! Tell him, Mother," I say, "because what a load of shi—"

"Freddy, language!" Mother says.

"I got this," Grace says. "Freddy, my love, this is *now*." Grace winks at me, flashes the elf ears, and gives me a slow, sexy kiss that transports me to *now*.

"Wow!" I say, because I'm feeling very *now* from that kiss. "Not that I'm complaining, Grace, but this feels very much like *now*."

"Hold that thought, Freddy. Follow me to *null*." And just like that, Grace and I are in human form in a yoga studio in Buena Vista, an upcoming bohemian area of Miami. A red-headed woman in yoga clothes bounces into the room and hits us with a grin that looks like she's doing a toothpaste commercial.

"Freddy, this is my friend and colleague, Dr. Melissa Mellow."

"Very nice to meet you, Dr. Fluid, or may I call you Freddy?"

"Sure," I say, because I don't want to be a dick.

"I'm Mel. I've heard so much about you, Freddy. Grace wasn't kidding, you're absolutely gorgeous. Step into what I like to call

Mellowville," Mel says, leading me into a cinnamon-colored room full of yoga mats, smelling of incense and patchouli—*I might puke.*

"We're going to start with progressive relaxation, Freddy, Grace. Lie down on a mat and make yourselves comfortable."

I lie down, but who can get comfortable on a thin, clammy yoga mat, that who knows how many people have sweated on. Where's the disinfectant spray when you need it?

"Contract your toes, then relax them, and now your feet. Good, Freddy. Now your legs, pelvis, abdomen, spine. Work it, Freddy. Like this," Mel prompts, as she demonstrates. "Relax every muscle fully, Freddy. If it helps, pretend you're going to the bathroom."

Well, that's a disgusting image, but I'll give it a try. I look over, and even though we appear human, my body and Grace's tingle, contract and relax at an incredible speed. My cells are moving in concert with Grace's. We are one. When Grace first taught me this relaxation technique, I didn't think I could sit still long enough to perform it. But now, it's working. I feel the energy pacing through my body with such intensity, it feels like I'll explode, sending energy throughout the Universe, like an atomic bomb.

"About that, lad," #1 interrupts. "That's not the outcome we're going for."

"Still here?" I ask.

"Quite. We are only visible to you and Grace. We can communicate telepathically, lad," #1 says.

"Good. So, since you're here, let me ask a dumb question?"

"Anything, son."

"Is this power I'm feeling part of the vaporization dilemma, or as you call it, kablooey?" I ask, like a guy who just found out he was a human bomb.

"Quite! I knew you were a quick study, my boy. Now let's try to rein this in. 7 hours, 2 minutes, 3 seconds left. Tick, tick, tock, lad."

I feel the energy flow through the length and width of my body, like I'm plugged into a wall outlet. My brain buzzes with *now*. I'm joyfully pulsing.

"Great, you can do this, Freddy. God, you really are beautiful," Mel says.

"I know," I say.

"Remember, contract your neck, your head, your face. Good, Freddy. You're almost there. Last but not least, your eyes. Close them, feel them quiver," Mel coaches, and despite her incense's assault to my olfactory senses, I'm starting to like her.

"Wonderful, Freddy. Can you feel the energy flow? Some of my patients call it the Force. Being a surgeon, I'm not sure if you believe in outer space stuff, aliens, and all, but I do. In fact, my entire spiritual philosophy is based on the Force," Mel says.

If Mel had asked me this question a week ago, I would have told her she was preposterous. In fact, a week ago, I wouldn't be caught dead in this patchouli laden pit that reminds me of Jabba the Hutt's pleasure palace, so in as cool a tone as possible I say, "Aliens? I imagine it's statistically and scientifically possible, given the vastness of the Universe, number of galaxies, and planets, that other life exists. As you said, as a surgeon, I would need proof," I say, hoping I can push Father's buttons—*jackpot*.

"Proof. I'll give you BLOODY PROOF, all right," #1 says.

"Boys! Stop it. Freddy's just trying to get your goat, Eddie," Mother says, knowing goats creep me out.

"Only if you stop saying goat," I say.

"Freddy Fluid, play nice. Stop communicating with your parents and talk to yourself," Grace says.

"Don't you think I spend enough time talking to myself, Grace?"

"Good point! This time, listen."

"Concentrate on contracting and relaxing, Freddy. If you have any thoughts, don't fight them. Let them come and go. Eventually, there will be more going than coming," Mel says.

"I prefer coming," Grace says and winks, to break the tension. "Great, Freddy, your nose is twitching like an adorable bunny. Perfect. Don't forget to breathe. You don't want to explode, do you? Too soon?" Grace says like a wisecracking priest giving last rights, and I shrug like a guy on death row.

"You should feel the energy flow, Freddy," Mel says, *and remarkably, I do feel it.*

My body vibrates. I feel my cells, my molecules flowing up and down my body. It's very *now*. Everything is starting to slow down. Maybe this is what *null* feels like? The sensation is invigorating, primal, as if I were dehydrated and someone inserted an IV into my arm. It's not an IV. They're light beams! It feels like fluids are rushing throughout my body. Fluids! That's it, Freddy. You must be in the hospital.

I long to panic, but something is keeping me tethered to a calmness I never before experienced. Tethered! Yep, that's it. Fucking Bad OCD shatters my *now*, with an end of the world *next, and null is nowhere in sight. Now, next, null, aliens!* What the fuck are you thinking, Freddy? I'm in the psych ward, they have me strapped down, and are pumping me full of Thorazine. Yeah. That's what's happening. Get out of my head, fuckers!!!!

"I'm going to open my eyes, and I'll be where I belong, in a hospital. Okay. I'm opening them now. Just warning youuuu," I say in a sing-song voice, like a lunatic playing Russian roulette.

Breathe, like Grace taught you. In for 5 seconds, hold for 5 seconds, exhale for 5 seconds. Good, Freddy, good, you're doing it. Open your eyes, and they'll all be gone. Now, Freddy!

50

Nobody likes a little prick

Back with Freddy.

"Fuck! You're still here," I say, *because they're all still here. Fuck!*

"Language, Freddy," Mother says in a soft voice.

"Good meditating, Freddy, just like I taught you," Grace says, kissing me softly on the mouth—from the inside, *and I giggle like a tickled toddler.*

"What now, dear girl?" #1 asks.

"Human pincushion time!" Grace replies, holding my shaking hand.

"You know I hate needles, Grace."

"You'll hardly feel it, Freddy. The needles are tiny, and very sharp."

"Sharp isn't helping Grace," I say.

"A doctor, scared of needles?" #1 asks.

"I have nothing against needles. I use them all the time, in fact. I just don't want anyone sticking me with them, okay?"

"Here we go, Freddy," Grace says, and we appear in human form outside the North Miami Beach acupuncture office of Dr. Phineas Prick. The office is in a strip mall with a Chinese restaurant, an Asian grocery, a Cuban bakery, a quick oil change bay, a microbrewery, a fish market, a karate dojo, and a Botanica, sort of an all you can eat, gastronomical, spiritual wonderland that smells like a stadium bathroom at halftime.

"Dr. Fluid. Grace told me all about you. May I call you Freddy?" Dr. Prick says as we walk through the office door.

"Sure," I say, because, well, we've been through this before.

"Please call me Fin," he says, and I'm relieved because I don't want to call this little guy with big glasses who's about to stick me with needles a prick. "Would you mind answering a few questions?"

"Sure, like I have a choice," I say, because it's true, and *tick, tick, tock.*

"Fine, fine. How are your bowels?"

"Bowels?" I ask, like this is the stupidest question in the Universe, especially when it might end in 7 hours, and this prick, excuse me, Dr. Prick is asking me about my bowels.

"Okay," I say, like a guy who's been constipated since 1938.

"Don't be embarrassed, Freddy, it's a natural bodily function," Fin says, and I want to put my foot right up his—

"Freddy Fluid!" Fiona flashes in.

"Mother, he'll see you!" I say.

"Nobody can see or hear us but you and Grace, my boy," #1 flashes.

"Fine. Sorry, Mother."

"Good. Answer Dr. Prick's question," Mother flashes.

"Fine, Mother. I will. However, Grace and I are doctors. This man is a glorified tailor," I say, and answer Fin. "Yes, once in a great while, I am constipated."

"For someone who spends so much time in the shower, you need to drink more water. Good water intake is key to bowel health, Freddy," Grace says.

"Fine," I say, like a guy who could use an enema.

"How about your neck? Any neck or lower back pain?" Fin asks, and he's a real pain in my a—

"Freddy!" Fiona admonishes.

"Neck pain, no. Back pain, yes," I say.

"Good! Now we are getting somewhere," Fin says. "Take off your shirt and shoes, please. I'm only going to examine you." *And he eyes me like the dessert tray at a Weight Watchers convention.*

"It's okay, Freddy. I'll be right here," Grace says, and winks as I remove my shirt and wink back. *Two can play at this winking game, you know.*

"Stand up straight, Freddy. Does this hurt?" Fin asks as he pushes a spot on my shoulders.

"Shit!" I scream, as my temples throb like snare drums.

"Sorry, Fred. Do you mind if I call you Fred?" he asks.

"Yes, I mind." *Because, nobody calls me Fred. Nobody!*

"Okay, Freddy, I see exactly where your qi is blocked. Lie face down on this table, and we will begin," Fin says.

"My qi is blocked! I hate when that happens," I snark.

"In eastern medicine, the qi is the energy flow in your body. It connects along pathways in the body, which can become blocked, like yours, Freddy. The needles stimulate points along the pathways and unblock the flow," Grace explains.

"Rubbish," #1 says.

"There's a great deal of research showing the efficacy of acupuncture for a variety of—"

"No, no, dear girl, not rubbish to acupuncture, rubbish to all of this mystical pathway stuff. It's really the fascia, the connective tissue around everything that is stimulated by the needles," #1 says, and as he does, I realize there's about 30 needles in me.

"Hey, guys? Guys? You still here? He's sticking me!!! Am I bleeding? Grace, you never lie to me. Am I bleeding?" I flash.

"Not yet, my love," Grace says, like a battlefield nurse to a guy who's bleeding out.

"You're doing great, Freddy. I'm going to put this heat lamp over your chest. How does it feel?" Fin asks.

"It feels pretty good," I say, because the lamp is all cozy, and then, "Ouch!" he sticks my foot.

"Sorry, lots of bones in the foot. Tender tootsies. All done with this side. That wasn't so bad, was it?" Fin asks.

"I guess not. How long do I have to lie here?" I ask, because, you know, *tick, tick, tock.*

"About 45 minutes on this side, and then we turn you over, baste you a bit, and then do your front," Fin says, *and I hope he's kidding about the basting.*

"Sorry, Fin, you think you can do this more quickly?" Grace asks.

"We can't rush the qi, Grace. It's as fickle as an old man at a brothel," Fin says.

"He's witty, this one, Grace," #1 flashes. "6 hours, 12 minutes, and 52 seconds left. You sure you want to spend all this time here?"

"I'm sure," Grace says, like, she's sure. *Very, very sure.*

As I lie here, I feel the energy moving through my body like I did with Meditating Mel. It's moving up and down me. I'm not thinking about anything. No *now*, no *next.*

"How are you doing, Freddy?" Fin asks.

"Fine. Well, good, actually," I say.

"Good," Fin says, pulling the needles from my body, then wiping away the blood from a few needle spots. *I look at Grace like, 'I told you there would be blood.'*

"Sorry, babe. Just a little blood," Grace says.

"Let's flip you over and put this side under the broiler," Fin jokes.

Fin sticks me in the head, arms, chest, along my happy trail, feet *(again, ouch!)*, and puts the heat lamp on. I feel the energy whirling up and down my body so fast it's like I'm spinning, and I am. Not actually spinning. The energy is spinning. It moves up and down, and around my waist, circling like a counterclockwise cyclone, faster and faster. I see purple clouds, blue moons, and a silver sun. My mind is happy, *like I'm floating in the greatest science fiction galaxy ever created*, and all around me is bliss, and Grace is floating with me, holding my hand.

Nursing women call it the let-down. Although I don't have breasts, I am a life-long admirer. I'm told it's an odd sensation, when a mother's milk comes in. I feel as such. The back of my shoulders spasm upwards and fall like an angel shrugging its wings. From there, my lower back yields to my pelvis, my legs, toes, all in harmony. My body feels young, supple, like when I was 4 in the tub. Time seems very still. *I'm having a moment here.*

"Is this the *null*?"

"You'll know when you find the *null*, my boy. We'll all know," #1 says.

Fuck. I nearly feel time stop. Yet, from the neck up, I'm still a churning OCD mess. My brain won't fucking stop. I'm thinking about what's happening to me, but my head's not in the game. It's nice to finally have a relaxed body, but my brain is the real culprit here. How come it's not chill? Maybe I'm not ready to give up knowing the future, even if it's just 59 seconds?

Fin approaches. What a kind smile he has, and I smile back, shooting flickers everywhere. "Those lights are miraculous, Freddy! Looks like you found your qi." Just as I'm thinking I like him, he's pulling needles from my body, and yells, "Spouter!" Fin puts his thumb over the blood gushing from a pinprick on my head. "Sorry, it happens sometimes with the scalp. Lots of blood vessels. You're doctors. You know."

"Thank you, Fin. Oh, Freddy, you did great. We'll get you re-synched soon enough," Grace says.

"Before you leave, Freddy, I have something for you that should help," Fin says, tossing me a bottle of pills.

"Serrapeptase. The Japanese and Germans have been using them for years for a variety of issues. They're enzymes made from bacteria found in silkworms. Helps the worms break out of their tough cocoons. They have very strong anti-inflammatory properties," Fin says.

"Sorry, Dr. Prick. Nothing personal. I have an aversion to worms," I say, tossing the bottle back to him, without going into further detail about my myiasis fiasco.

"They were sewer moths," Fiona flashes.

"Oh, God, you knew?" I flash, as mortified as a guy whose mother caught him thinking he had worms in his ass.

"Yes, dear," Mother flashes in an, *it's okay, dear, everything will be all right* tone.

"You know, my boy; we all have our version of worms," #1 says. "Now, 4 hours, 48 minutes, 8 seconds, until, you know, tick, tick, tock," and just like that, the little Prick is gone, and we're back in the spaceship.

51

Drugs, sex, and rock and roll—*well, maybe not the sex part*

In the middle of the spaceship, Mother, Dad, and Grace, continue their quest to deactivate. I mean, reset me.

"Oh, not the band idea again, Grace, please," I say.

"Work with me, Freddy. We're trying to save the Universe, and our baby," Grace says.

"Sorry," I say to keep her happy, because she's carrying our baby starter kit in her fallopian tubes; and she hates it when I'm snarky, *although she is Grace, so she usually gives me a pass.*

"Here's your chance to join a band again, Freddy. You'll like this one; I promise," and just like that, I appear on a small outdoor stage, holding my vintage 1981 Gibson Hummingbird Guitar, surrounded by 4 other musicians. A tall, thin, ghostly platinum-haired blonde on upright bass, her twin on fiddle looking like a

Winter Brother's reunion, an ancient, bearded banjo player, and a blissful gray-haired mandolin player, who taps his foot, smiles at me like a hobbit leaving the Shire, nods at Grace, and starts playing and singing 'I'll Fly Away.'

His voice mirrors the expression on his face, sincere, imperfect, a bit scratchy, yet as charming and inviting as a glass of cool lemonade on a front porch swing in Savannah. The bass and fiddle are delightful. The bearded one is not much bigger than his banjo and plays like his fingers are inhabited by the ghosts of the Foggy Mountain Boys, and no *nexts*. Nope. Not one *next* from any of them; only music. I realize at this moment, I am playing, and singing the chorus. And even though I dread the whir of *nexts* that must be coming, the Miami sun reflecting off the mandolin puts me deep in *now*, and I slow down like I'm in water.

"Freddy, you're doing it. I knew you could. You guys sound great, by the way," Grace says, as the band transitions to 'Stardust'—the song, *not the particle remnants of celestial bodies, a.k.a. the stuff in my eyes.* The music is haunting. I look closely at the beatific mandolin player, his fingers magically moving over the strings of his instrument, as if they are making love. The sounds, the sounds are—wonderful.

"Sorry about the last band, Freddy. My bad on Billie and the Baby catchers. Constantina threw in that gypsy jazz to show off. Plus, I think she had the hots for you, the little hussy," Grace says.

"You're telling me. I barely made it out of her band unscathed, by Billie and her bass player," I say, and a feeling of capturing this moment in a forever place in my mind takes over. "This must be *null.*"

"You're almost there, Freddy. You sound great. I'm so proud of you. Doesn't he sound great, Eddie?" Fiona flashes, and the mandolin player is replaced by #1.

"Quite! You're a regular Beatle, my boy," #1 says and starts playing 'Rocky Racoon.' "Jump in, lad. I heard you practicing this one hundreds of times in your room."

I stop playing and give #1 a WTF look—*because WTF!* Almost *null* vanishes, and *now* is sent tumbling into an abyss. "Really? You couldn't let me do this on my own, Dad!" I say, *because he hates it when I call him Dad.* "I was this close," I say, shining light from my eyes into side-by-side laser beams less than a micron apart.

"Sorry, lad. You dipped your toes in the *null* waters, though. That's why I showed up. Had to be ready for the old reset. We're down to 3 hours, 42 minutes, and 1 second, before, you know— kablooey. Just need to get you *into the null* and keep you there long enough to align our clocks. Good job, Grace. What's next?" #1 asks.

"Take a deep breath, Freddy" Grace says, and once again, we're a bunch of tiny lights, flying off to who knows where.

52

Don't hold your breath!

I know where we are, and I don't like it.

"Time for breathing. This is going to be a hoot!" Grace says, and I am starting to think hoot is an expression best left for owls.

"Ahhh. Perfect timing, Grace. We may get you re-synced yet, m'boy. It's all about the breath, son," #1 says. "All about the breath."

Entering the North Miami office, the cultlike intake worker strikes me as a man who should be chanting and banging a drum on the street. He introduces himself as Izzy, *probably short for Intake Zombie, with that empty smile on his face.* Izzy asks me to sit, then asks me some questions. When he gets to the one about my absent father, Izzy shoots me a sympathetic look, like I'm a lost puppy. *Daddy issues. Paydirt for Dr. Gaspand Wheeze, the breathing guru.*

"Are you all still here?" I ask out loud to #1.

"Right by your side, my boy. You'll be able to hear all our thoughts, and we can hear yours," #1 flashes.

"I'm here too, dear," Mother flashes as well.

"And I'm right here, Freddy, my love. Don't worry, this is going to be a ho—"

"Don't say it, Grace, and please don't leave me alone."

"Never," Grace says and kisses me tenderly.

Iz, as I have taken to call him, leads us into a slightly larger office full of people in overstuffed, reclining chairs. The chairpeople are lying face up, on top of other face up chairpeople, who are holding them tight. They seem comfy based on their lack of movement, but I'm too nervous to actually look around and *next* is mysteriously absent from this place, so no clues for me. The intake worker guides me to a recliner, and flops down on his back, pulling me along with him, my new chair cushion. I fall onto him, and he wraps his arms around me from below, cuddling me tight like he's restraining a burrito who might make a break from the plate before the mariachis arrive.

I try to surrender, but Iz is much bonier than he appears. "Would you mind getting the fuck out from under me!?" I yell, pulling loose from Iz. *Did I mention I'm very strong?* I push Iz away and he slumps to the ground, laughing. The guy in the chair next to me laughs, and it hits me like a ton of rotting lunchmeat.

"Oh, no, Freddy. Sorry, my love!" Grace says.

"Stiff upper lip, m'boy," #1 flashes.

"Remember, Freddy dear, he's just a fellow human on a journey like you," Mother flashes.

"Hardly!" #1 flashes.

Did you know the sense of smell is one of the strongest connections to memory? As a physician, I could explain the privilege granted to olfactory nerves by the limbic system, but suffice it to say, the smell of ham and cheese will forever be associated with one person, *and he's in the recliner next to me.* "George Smelt!" I shout, almost happy to see him.

"Freddy Fluid! I'll be damned. What are you doing here? You didn't have a father either, right?"

It struck me at this moment, even though I sat across from him in science class for 2 years, I didn't know anything about George's childhood, that his father wasn't around. Maybe I could have been kinder to him. NAHHHH!!

"Hey, Porky." The nickname given to George by a cruel classmate spills from my mouth. *Okay, I was the cruel classmate. In my defense, almost 17 years later, George still smells of ham and cheese.*

"Ouch!" says Iz from the floor below me. "No size shaming here, please,"

"It's okay, Izzy. We're old friends," George says and smiles. "Besides, look at me, I'm built like a scarecrow," George adds, laughing and patting his flat belly.

I should feel bad. I don't. A 13-year-old can defend smelling of lunch meat, but a guy nearing his 30s?

A voice like a TV golf announcer wafts into the room from above one of the recliners. "We'll have none of that, Dr. Fluid." *I search for the speaker, for next, for any grounding signal. It's quieter than a lamb in a wolf's den.*

"Deep breath, Freddy. In through the nose, deep into your belly, feel it rise." Iz reaches from the floor and puts one hand on my belly and the other on my chest. "Feel it rise, Freddy," the unknown voice commands.

"Keep your hands off me, Izzy!" I shout, as Izzy's hand is awfully close to my privates, and he better not try to get anything else to rise. Iz slinks back to the floor, but is lurking, like a disobedient housecat. "What kind of place did you bring me to, Grace?"

"It's okay, Freddy. If you do this right, only your belly will rise, not your chest. Izzy's hands were only providing feedback. You can use your own appendages. Place one hand on your chest and the other on your belly. Good, good. Close your eyes, Freddy, Breathe," the golf announcer says, and I comply. "Everyone, breathe. Show the new guy how it's done, George," the golf announcer commands, *and I'm hoping he doesn't start handing out Kool-Aid because these people already drank it.*

"It's okay, Freddy, I send all of my anxiety patients here," Grace says, and I try to relax. I breathe in and out 8 times, with the rest of the recliner herd. I feel calm. Not Buddha slow, but quiet. It's nice. I keep breathing. Nobody is talking. I open my eyes and recognize the man from a picture in the front office—Dr. Gaspand Wheeze, a slight, shirtless man, with wild gray eyes, a gray goatee, a bird's nest of matching gray hair, and gold lame pants. *I think I found Aladdin's crazy uncle.* I fight my urge to bolt as Grace and my parents (did I just say parents?) are here, trying to reset me, so I breathe like Uncle Aladdin says.

I admit I do feel better. Everyone, even Uncle Aladdin and Iz, are puffing away in this room full of choo choos, so I close my eyes and breathe deep breaths in and out. I am feeling very *now.*

"Excellent, everyone. Excellent! Take a slow, deep breath into your belly and feel it rise. Good. Exhale slowly, like a 100-year-old man trying to blow out all of the candles on his birthday cake," Dr. Gaspand Wheeze says. This isn't as easy as it seems. My OCD jumps in and is already counting to 38 candles.

"This will never work, Grace," I say in desperation.

"This is the hard part," Grace says. "Stop thinking, Freddy, and visualize the birthday cake. Good. Don't worry about counting candles, Freddy. Focus on your breath, babe. Slowly try to blow out the candles. Don't think about how many there are. Watch the flames extinguish as you blow."

"Oh, I'm going to blow all right," I say, because tick, tick, tock. I try to make a break for it. Something is holding me in place. Fucking Izzy. "Hey! Let go!" I yell as Izzy reaches around my waist from the floor and tries to hold me to the recliner. "Fuck you, Izzy!" I yell as I break free. (*Like I said, I'm really strong!*) As I stand, Dr. Gaspand Wheeze gently takes my wrists, and slowly exhales.

"This can be very overwhelming, Freddy. Breathwork takes one deep inside themselves. Take a breath with me," Uncle Aladdin says while holding my wrists. For such a small guy, he's exceptionally strong and guides me back to my recliner. "Excellent, Freddy. Watch your belly rise. Now exhale slowly. Visualize those candles. Don't count them. Good. Fight your urges. Blow them out slowly, like you're cooling down food to feed a baby."

Baby. We're going to have a baby! Get it together, Freddy. Just blow out the damn candles. Slowly, I see the cake aglow in my mind. The candles are pink. Pink! Maybe this is a sign. Are we having a girl? Oh, I hope she's just like Grace, with none of my weird shit. My thoughts rush back into my mind like an incoming tide. With each birthday candle I extinguish, my thoughts wash away like seafoam. My head is clear. I'm breathing. I feel the oxygen saturate my body. I'm floating. Really floating. Actually, I'm hovering 4 feet over the recliner. It's wonderful. Maybe this is *null*?

"Grace, is this null?" *I know I'm not supposed to ask, but OCD, remember.*

"Almost, Freddy," Grace says.

"Neat trick, Freddy. Can you teach me to hover?" George Smelt asks.

"Sure, George. It's easy. Just think about having a baby," I say.

"Babies! That's why I'm here. Flora and I have three kids, Freddy. Babies are great, although our house looks like a Category 5 hurricane hit it, and it's noisy, smelly, and—I'm sorry, Freddy.

Didn't mean to drone on. I needed to have some quiet time, and this breathwork is great. When the kids get crazy, I take a few deep breaths and it really resets things."

"Reset! Shit!" My OCD races in. *Now* and *null* sneak off like teenagers doing a dine and dash at Denny's. "Sorry, George. No time to catch up. Wait! So, you and Flora from middle school?"

"You remember Flora?"

"Sure. She wanted to kiss you."

"She told you?" George asks.

"Sort of. Got to fly, George," I say, taking Grace's hand, turning to light beams, and flying into the air.

"Bye, Freddy. Goodbye, Grace, and congratulations," George says like he means it.

"Hey, George, I forgot to ask, what do you do for work?" I ask, *because come on, he still smells like ham and cheese.*

"I started my own genetics farm, specializing in the production of pig's milk. The milk makes an excellent cheddar, Freddy. Stop by the house. You can try some. It's great for bringing in breast milk, Grace."

"Breast milk—*Ewwww*. Nice seeing you, George. Say hi to Flora, and good luck with those kids of yours," I say. *It really is good seeing him.*

"Bye, George!" Grace says.

"How are you feeling, babe?"

"Happy. Relaxed. Thanks, Grace. Do you think all of this will reset me in time?"

"Keep the faith, babe. Just a few more therapies to try."

"Pig cheese. Told you!" I laugh as we flash off.

53

#3

If #1's cetacean form resembles a killer whale, and #2 looks like a pilot whale, #3 is a dead ringer for the goofiest, most lovable member of the toothed whale family—the beluga whale.

With their white skin, supple scalloped tails, and playful heads that turn almost 360 degrees when they pop out of the water for a quick look about, belugas are disarming, intelligent, mythical looking creatures, often mistaken for mermaids.

While #3 wasn't exactly a mermaid, she swam like one, peering at the surface from below. #3 loved watching everything from below. All cetaceans swim upside down on occasion. #3 did it all the time. Swimming upside down fit #3's positive attitude, as from below, everything was always looking up. This gave #3 unique perspective; the ability to see the foundation of all things, as well as the showy parts that bob to the surface. #1 told #3 she got all of his fun, positive qualities, and although he didn't say it, #3 knew she was his favorite. If #3 had been human, she would have been the high school cheerleader, prom queen who sang the national anthem at the Friday night football game, fed the starving children, voluptuous, Miss Universe type.

On planet Earth, beluga whales' frequent and verbose vocalizations give them the nickname "canaries of the sea," and just like belugas on Earth, #3 was quite the yenta. She made a point of communicating with every life form on Rolexa, from the smallest algae to the largest whale.

#3 had a constant smile, a friendly ear, and a kind thought to share with everyone. She listened to her fellow creatures' life stories, their problems, their challenges, their aspirations. #3 had a way about her that made everyone smile at the mention of her name. Every being was glad to see her coming and sad to see her leave, although when she left, every creature felt fuller from interacting with her. In short, #3 gave a fuck.

After many, many eons, #3 had spoken to every creature on the water planet of Rolexa, so she popped her enchanting head through the surface waters, rotated it a full 360 degrees, and chattered away to the Universe, hoping someone, anyone, would respond. After all, #1 was always nipping off to some other planet or galaxy and sharing his adventures about other life forms with #2 and #3.

It wasn't that #3 was jealous of #1's travels and encounters with diverse beings, for she possessed no negative emotions; she simply longed to experience more. As #3 bobbed on the surface, she heard them. Voices. They were coming through her sonar, which carried her chirps, whistles, and songs throughout all of the galaxies via Rolexa's stars. She heard fanciful stories from different worlds. She communicated with fiery crawly critters living in molten lava on Volcanix. She communicated with flying creatures made of precious metal and feathers orbiting the planet Dronex. She communicated with enormous sneezing paper trees on the planet, Cleanex. It was a yenta's dream.

Finally, even though it forced her to break #1's cardinal rule, which was to never interact with them, as they were, "a bunch of BLOODY WANKERS AND SLOUCHERS," #3 communicated with the residents of the planet Timexa. Time Moochers, it turned out, were the only residents of Timexa. Time Moochers were frightful looking creatures resembling tiny brown ticks and communicated with tones and whistles. #3 was intoxicated by the Time Moochers' musical language which was reminiscent of whale songs. The Time Moochers were equally enchanted by #3's calliope songs which sounded like a day at the circus. The most fascinating thing #3 learned about Time Moochers was they had no concept of time, therefore, they could not be constrained by it, and they had some really juicy information for #3; and it had to do with—kablooey!

54

What's it all about, Ralphie

Back on the ship with Freddy, Grace, Fiona, and #1.

"Are we there yet?" I ask.

"How are you feeling, my love?" Grace asks.

"Like an unexploded grenade," I say.

"What's next, doc?" Fiona asks.

"Don't ask me. Grace is in charge," I say.

"Ego, Freddy, ego! I was asking Grace," Fiona says. "Well, Dr. Whisperer?"

"A little walk back in time?" #1 asks.

"Exactly. Here we go, Freddy. Time for somatic therapy. Let's get to the root of your trauma," Grace says.

"I don't think you'll have to go very far. It's all his fault," I say, pointing to #1, as we flash off to an innocuous beige office in Aventura. "Oh no, Grace, you know I hate Aventorture."

"It's okay, Freddy, Aventura is great, unless you have to drive there. Thankfully, we're flying. You're going to love Dr. Angst. He's amaz-zing!" Grace says.

A 60-something year-old man with a reddish beard greets us and opens the door, inviting us in. "Grace! How lovely to see you. You must be the boyfriend. I'm glad you decided to come in. I'm Ralphie Angst. Please, sit down. Has Grace told you about somatic work? Perhaps on the way over here?"

"It was a quick trip," Grace says. "I thought I would leave the explaining to you, Ralphie."

"Quick trip through Aventura? You must have found a shortcut you'll have to tell me about. Permit me to tell you about somatic therapy," Ralphie Angst says.

"Oh no, not the *permit me* routine. If his explanations are anything like your father's, Freddy, you better sit down," Fiona flashes in.

"Nonsense!" #1 flashes as Grace and I sit on the couch.

"Somatic therapy came about, in part, by watching predator-prey behavior. Imagine yourself a sea lion splashing about in the kelp, catching fish. There you are, happily eating, when a pod of orcas swims by looking for their breakfast; and it's you," Ralphie Angst says.

"Couldn't he have used a different example? Wanker!" #1 flashes.

"Sorry, #1. I thought it would be more impactful this way," Grace says.

"Brilliant!" Fiona flashes.

"Let's get on with it. What do we have, 2 hours left? Tick, tick," I ask.

"We have 2 hours, 12 minutes, 0 seconds, but who's counting?" #1 flashes.

"I'M COUNTING!"

"What an enthusiastic patient you brought me, Grace. How wonderful!" Dr. Angst says.

"Let's continue. You're a sea lion, and orcas are hunting you. What happens?"

"I shit myself, so I'll taste bad?" I say, *because* that's the likely outcome, and *what the hell, it could work.*

"Very funny, Freddy. What happens to the sea lion is the same thing that happens to all animals, when they're hunted. Remember your basic psychology, Freddy? The fight-or-flight mechanism kicks in. The sea lion either braces for a fight, freezes in place, or swims away fast, escaping the orcas," Ralphie says.

"Great! What the fuck does this have to do with me, other than the orca reference?" I ask.

"What's this about orcas?" Ralphie asks.

"Nothing," I say.

"Daddy issues," Grace whispers to Ralphie.

"HEY!" #1 flashes, and I yell!

"Good. Good. We hit a nerve. Stay with me, Freddy. You're a sea lion; you escaped the orcas, by either your fight-or-flight response. The act of being preyed upon is a traumatic event, producing physiological responses in the body's sympathetic nervous system. When threatened, the sea lion experiences acute stress and its body releases hormones, resulting in increased heart rate, elevated blood pressure, rapid breathing and muscle tension. Under normal circumstances, once the orcas, in this case, representing the trauma in your life, depart, the sea lion's body resumes it's normal operation of eating, resting, and digesting."

"So?" I ask, *because, so?*

"So, Freddy, what would happen if the sea lion stayed scared?" Ralphie asks.

"Who cares about a sea lion? This is nonsense. Can we go, Grace?" I say, feeling like a broken-down Tesla, until Grace holds my hand and fills me like an electric car charging station of *now*.

"All animals, even humans, exhibit the same physiological responses, Freddy. The difference is the sea lion's body will typically return to its normal state of digesting and resting within an hour or so of the orcas departure. Some humans who experience trauma never fully process or release the trauma. Instead, the fear remains forever lodged in their body, causing the human to carry the trauma with them in the form of anxiety, hypervigilance, obsessive thoughts, compulsive behaviors, aggression, and shame. What we do in somatic work is train you to recognize what is occurring in your body, when, for lack of a better term, the orcas show up. Does this all make sense, Freddy?" Ralphie asks.

"Orcas! This is eerie. You sure he can't see you, #1?" I ask.

"Of course not. Your Mother and I are invisible to everyone but you and Grace," #1 flashes.

"Sure, Ralphie. Makes sense until the orca shows up," I say, shooting #1 an angry look. "Now what?"

"The most important thing to know about somatic work, Freddy, is we don't want to re-traumatize you. You're in charge of your journey here," Ralphie says, *and I'm tired of people telling me that lie today.* "I'll ask questions about what you are experiencing in your body while we dip our toes into discussing traumatic events. This allows you to become aware of what is happening in your body and self-regulate. Would you like to give it a crack, Freddy?"

"Sure, but can we stop talking about orcas? I've had my fill of them," I say.

"Hey!" #1 flashes.

"How are you feeling sitting on the couch, Freddy, right now?" Ralphie asks.

"Your couch is lumpy and has bad lumbar support."

"Good. Feel your body, Freddy. Tell me about your childhood. What are your earliest memories? Picture yourself in that moment. What are you doing?"

"Playing in the bathtub."

"Good. How's the water? Is it warm?" Ralphie asks.

"It was," I answer.

"Was?"

"It was when I got in the tub an hour ago," I say.

"How does your body feel?" Ralphie Angst asks.

"Cold, happy, lonely."

"Good. What's going on in your body in the tub, Freddy?"

"I'm shivering. Anxious. Like I'm supposed to be there, but I'm not supposed to be alone," I say.

"Good. What is your little body doing, Freddy?"

"I just told you, Ralphie. I'm shivering. Geez. You're not a very good listener for a shrink."

"It's perfectly natural to attack your therapist as a defense mechanism. What else, Freddy? Tell me about your breathing?" Ralphie says.

"Breathing, huh? This might be complicated. I can stay under water for hours. You see, when I'm the water, Ralphie, I breathe like I've got gills."

"You were right, Grace, Freddy's a hoot. I understand it's challenging to confront your past, Freddy, and humor can help. However, honesty in the therapeutic process is paramount to success. Let's try this again, and leave out the gills this time," Ralphie says.

"He is telling the truth, Ralphie," Grace says.

"Okay, I'll play along, you have gills. What else is going on for you in the bathtub, Freddy?" Ralphie asks.

"YOU DO NOT HAVE BLOODY GILLS!" #1 flashes in.

"The orca is watching me from his tiny bubble shaped spaceship," I say.

"Is this a joke, Grace? Are you filming this for the psychiatric convention in Vegas? Ha! This is genius."

"No, Ralphie. This is important. You might even say Earth-shattering. Please, continue," Grace implores.

"Um, okay, Grace, but only because it's you. What happens when you see the orca in the spaceship, Freddy?" Ralphie asks.

"I didn't notice him when I was in the tub, Ralphie. Turns out the orca is my father. He's an alien, and I was just a small, shivering fatherless boy in a bathtub, who was scared, cold, and lonely."

"Oh, Freddy dear, why didn't you tell me? Mother flashes in.

"It's not your fault, Mother. It's HIS!" I yell, pointing at #1.

"Excellent, Freddy. Let it all out. Keep pretending your parents are in the room with us. Did you prep him for this, Grace?"

"Nope. He's a quick learner, right?" Grace says and winks at me. I shiver.

"Wonderful, Freddy. I see you shivering. What's going on in your little body in the tub?" Ralphie asks again.

"I don't want to leave. Everything outside the tub makes me jumpy. I want to, need to, stay in the water," I say.

"Good, Freddy. And what will happen if you get out of the water?"

"Out of the water? Oh, that's easy. I can't breathe. I'm awkward and clumsy, and *next* will be all over me, like latex on a 90's pornstar."

"You really are a hoot, Freddy. Tell me about *next*?" Ralphie says.

"*Next* fills my head with the future, and robs me of now."

"Good, and how does your body feel when it's in *next*, Freddy," Ralphie asks.

"Like I belong in another place, another time."

"Wonderful, Freddy. Let's get you out of that tub. I'm going to teach you a simple breathing technique, known as Voo," Ralphie says.

"Voo, like Voodoo? Come on, Grace, let's go. Tick, tick, remember?" I say.

"I know it sounds silly. Please give it a try, Freddy, my love," Grace says, squeezing my hand, winking and whispering in my ear. "I'll wear the ears later if you do."

A wink and the ears. "That's not fair, Grace."

"All's fair in love, war, and kablooey," Grace whispers.

"Ready, Freddy?" Ralphie asks.

"Like my life depends on it!"

"Good, good. Sit back and take notice of your breathing. Don't do anything different, just be aware of it. Take a deep slow breath in through your nose filling your belly," Ralphie says.

"Come on, Grace, we already tried breathing," I say. Grace flashes pointy ears on her adorable face, and I succumb. "Okay, Doc. Deep breath in."

"Good, Freddy. Now, very, very slowly exhale, making the sound voooooooooooo for as long as you can," Ralphie says.

"Voo? Really?" I say.

"I understand it sounds ridiculous. I assure you; it's based in science. The voo sound calms the vagus nerve, which connects the brain to the gut. The theory is when we experience trauma, like the orcas coming for you," Ralphie says.

"HEY!" #1 flashes.

"The vagus nerve becomes stuck in fear mode and stops sending messages to your body to rest and digest. Basically, the voo sound resets the nerve," Ralphie says.

"Reset, huh? This could be just what the doctor ordered," #1 flashes.

"Ya think?" Grace says, winking at #1.

"Okay, Ralphie, here goes." I take a deep breath in through my nose, fill my belly, and exhale, slowly chanting, "voo." I feel silly, but my throat, chest, and back vibrate like a purring kitten. I repeat "voo" 7 times, and I'm more totally *now* than ever. I see something that looks more beautiful than anything I've ever seen before. Time is slowing down. "Hey, it's working!"

"I never had a doubt," Ralphie says. "Let's get to the heart of things, Freddy. Tell me about your father, the alien," Ralphie says, and *next* is all over me like the neighborhood bully, devouring *now* and sending *null* into hiding.

"Way to ruin a moment there, Ralphie Angst!" I say, shaking like a ragdoll in the hands of a rambunctious toddler, as Grace flashes us back to the ship.

55

The gang's all here

It's getting pretty crowded on the bottom of the spaceship as Andy Tyler, Cliff, and Twan beam aboard.

"Look, #2, a trifecta!" #3 says.

"Triple zalk me!" #2 says.

"Oh, #2uuuuuuuuuu! There's a few more over there," #3 says, pointing at Ernest, Geronimo, Bustella, and Chunka, who join all the other abductees in the chamber.

"What the hell are you supposed to be?" #2 says, swimming to Bustella and Chunka.

"They're with me," Geronimo says, jumping in front of Bustella. Chunka growls.

"Coño Geronimo! You don't have to protect me. I'm the badass here, remember?" Bustella says.

"I don't know about bad, but that's quite the ass you have there, Miss. Nicest one I've seen in all the galaxies," #3 says.

"Hey! That's my girlfriend you're talking about," Geronimo says. Chunka growls louder.

"It's cool, baby. You can't blame a fish for looking," Bustella says.

"She's not a fish. She's a whale. A beluga. Mystical creatures often mistaken by sailors as mermaids, and from the looks of this one, you can see why. A cetacean of the family monodontidae. The only other member is the tusked narwhal, which is believed to have started the legend of unicorns. If you don't mind my saying, you are a most striking specimen," Sam says to #3.

"I don't mind at all, cutie pie," #3 says, adjusting her flippers.

"What are you, some kind of whale-ologist kid?" Burt quips.

"An environmental scientist. I'm Sam. Sam Centrifuge. I've always been fascinated by sea mammals. They are extremely intelligent creatures, smarter than us, in my opinion, and they must be because this one has its own spaceship."

"Aww shucks, Sammy, you really know how to make a beluga blush. You finally beamed up a bright one, #2. And look at you, Sammy. Why, you're cute as a button with all that curly hair. Isn't he cute as a button, #2?" #3 asks.

"We're on a spaceship? I've imagined this moment ever since I learned to fly. I knew there was life on other planets. This is going to make a great next book. I'll show Dan Johnson," Ernest Hamingway says.

"Aliens! For real? I have to call Leon DeCapricorn. We'll use this for our next movie. I can see it now, Aliens of Mayberry," Andy says.

"I'm scared, Cliff," Twan says.

"Don't worry, Twan. The beluga appears to be friendly, but the other whale looks like he has hemorrhoids," Cliff says, pointing at #2.

"Good one. Can I use it in my act?" Burt asks.

"Sure. Hey, you, sad whale guy?" Cliff says to #2.

"He's a pilot whale. A magnificent specimen," Sam says.

#2 slowly swims past Sam, to Cliff, and Twan. "Yes?"

"Why'd you take us?" Cliff asks.

Twan smiles at #2. Nobody ever smiles at #2, except #3, and it causes him to experience a momentary lapse in meanness. "It was a mistake, okay? I didn't mean to take any of you."

"A mistake? I got it from here, people, or whatever we are," Max says. "It's time to assert our rights. Send us back! Send us back!! Everyone, SEND US BACK!"

"Fuck off, Mayor. I'm the boss here, capisce?" Al says, taking a swing at Max. Leif Netter races forward, and captures Al's head in his pool net.

"Let me out of here, idiot. I'll kick everyone's asses," Al says.

"STOP IT!" #2 yells, and flashes paralyzing lights at everyone in the chamber. "We were trying to find Freddy Fluid, and everything went to shit."

"Not quite shit, but you did make a real #2 of this," #3 jokes, as #2 swims off to face the music, *and the music's going to be bad—like opera!*

56

Trippin Ballz

Back in the middle of the ship

"Of all the predators on Earth, he had to pick orcas," I say.

"Quite the unfortunate selection, lad. The somatic stuff almost reset you, my boy. I'm sorry, Freddy, for everything," #1 flashes.

"Freddy, he apologized," Grace says.

"Pretty lame apology, if you ask me," I say.

"Freddy," Mother says.

"Fine! I forgive you," I say, like a guy with a grudge.

"How are we doing on time, #1?" Grace asks.

"Only 58 minutes, 13 seconds remain, Grace."

"Come on, Freddy, time to take a little trip," Grace says as we flash off to a farm in the Redlands, an agricultural community in southern Miami-Dade County.

"Doesn't seem like the time to pick produce, Grace," I say, arriving at a cornfield. A petite woman who looks to be 100, wearing nothing but a flowered sarong, pops her head through the stalks and greets us with a bellowing voice.

"Grace! It's about time you visited. Who's this hunk of gorgeousness?"

"Dr. Freddy Fluid. Charmed, I'm sure."

"Trippishunda Ballzacki. Nice to meet you, gorgeous. My friends call me Trippin, Trippin Ballz."

"Apologies, I just remembered a patient I need to check on. Let's go, Grace."

"Oh no, you don't, Freddy. You have to do it for us," Grace says, patting her belly.

"Us? Mazel Tov, you two! With your and Freddy's looks, your kid's going to have to fight them off with a club," Trippin says.

"Hahaha." I laugh and relax because she reminds me of Grandmother. *I miss Grandmother.*

"Follow me to another dimension, kids, and mind your step," Trippin says, as we enter a cluttered, musty log cabin, its walls covered with African masks. "Anyone ever tell you, you're a dead ringer for Jesus?"

"Yes," I say, *because, well, you know.*

"Nice to be working with you again, Doc. This one looks like he's wound as tight as a teenager at a strip club. He's going to need the whole enchilada," Trippin says.

"Throw everything you got at him, Trippin, and whatever you use needs to be fast acting," Grace says.

"I'll take good care of you, gorgeous," Trippin says, eyeing me like she's famished and I'm a hunk of chocolate cake.

"I don't like this," I say, because I don't fucking like this.

"It's fine, Freddy. People have been using hallucinogens for self-enlightenment for centuries. Just what the doctor ordered, right, Grace?" #1 flashes.

"Yeah, what the orca said is true, Freddy. You should listen to him. That's one sexy cetacean you got there, Grace. Another patient?" Trippin asks.

"Am I to understand you can see me, Madame?" #1 flashes.

"With all the drugs I've taken, baby, I exist on many dimensions. I can see you, hear you, feel you, whatever floats your boat. I guess you don't need a boat to get around with a tail like that? Hubba hubba!" Trippin says.

"Eyes off his tail, Trippin. He's mine," Fiona flashes in.

"Fiona Fluid, you enchanting creature," Trippin says, whistling at Mother.

"Rein it in, Trippin. That's Freddy's Mom and Dad," Grace says.

"Fiona and I are old friends. Remember that time you took me diving on shrooms?" Trippin asks.

"How could I forget? What you did to that poor moray eel!" Fiona laughs.

"Yeah," Trippin says, laughing. "I still feel bad about that. You can't blame an old broad for trying."

"Mother, you know this woman?" I ask.

"Yes, dear. Trippin and I used to date. The things she taught me," Fiona flashes.

"Ewwww!" I say, because *Ewwww.*

"Freddy dear, be more open-minded. That's why you're here, to expand your consciousness," Mother flashes.

"Exactamundo, Fiona. Here you go, kid. Over the lips and down those gorgeous gums of yours, Freddy," Trippin says, handing me a mason jar full of what looks like finger paint and smells of rotting mushrooms and olives. *(Yuck!)*

"Really, Grace? Olives!"

"*Whoops!*" Grace says, winking at me. I guzzle the drink. I'm gagging. I'm going to puke.

"Freddy Fluid, don't you dare spit that up," Mother flashes.

"Fine!" I say, forcing myself to keep this smoothy from Hell in my belly.

"How you doing, gorgeous?" Trippin asks.

"Trippin Ballz," I say.

"Yes?" Trippin asks.

"That's how I'm doing. I'm trippin balls."

"Makes two of us. Tell us what you are experiencing, gorgeous?" Trippin asks.

"Nausea, dizziness, bliss, pain," I answer.

"Good. Let's focus on the bliss, Freddy. What's making you blissful?"

"Grace, our baby, Mother being alive again," I say, and I'm sooooo *now*. My vision fills with rainbow marshmallow bunnies, baby dolphins frolicking in a crystal-clear sea, stars forming a circuitous route through colorful planets. I follow the stars, flying past galaxies to a clear orb of a planet, immersed in shooting stars. Cool! I can fly! I'm floating, eating the bunnies, who laugh as I swallow them.

"Good, Freddy. Now for the hard part. What's causing you pain?" Trippin asks.

"My father, the alien, orca thingy," I say.

"Good, good. Hey, sexy tail? You! Talking orca?" Trippin says.

"Yes, Madame?" #1 flashes.

"Alien, huh?"

"Yes, Madame," #1 flashes.

"We should talk. We could make a killing with a talking orca at our monthly drum circles. Love the accent. Obviously, you and handsome here have some unfinished business," Trippin says.

"I apologized, and he forgave me," #1 flashes.

"Did not," I say.

"Did too," #1 flashes.

"Boys. There's literally no time for this. Remember, kablooey?" Mother flashes.

"Fine, I fucking hate you!" I say to #1. *Now* shatters and *next*, mixed with a huge ass dose of hallucinogens attack. It smells awful in this cabin, like rotting fruit and bong water. I run out the door and stumble into a damp room smelling worse than George Smelt. The room is full of drums of leaking chemicals. A machine that looks like someone crossed a generator with a garbage scow spews. Noxious fumes bombard me. A giant worm that looks like a cobra gives me the once-over and retrieves a disgusting lump of yellow flesh from a slot in the machine.

I exit to a shockingly lovely garden. Worms dressed like construction workers dig away at perfectly round holes. The cobra worm with the flesh in its mouth follows me, eats some flesh, drops the rest of it in one of the holes, buries it, and taps it in real good, like it might sprout wings and escape. *It does.* The ground shakes and out flies a single chicken wing, battered and fried, no less, followed by dozens of flying wings from the rest of the holes. A truck pulls up. My Tacoma! The driver gets out. A fucking orca. He opens the truck bed, which is lined with big screen TVs all playing commercials for pig cheddar. The truck is full of olives and martinis. The wings fly in. The orca slams the truck bed shut. The logo on the truck door; the sports bar with the cute girls—*you know the one.*

Next and the drugs aren't finished with me. I panic, running until I find myself in an old stone prison. #1 in orca form is strapped into the electric chair, playing lead guitar. It sounds like Jimi Hendrix's funeral dirge. I look at #1's smileless face. My asshole meter flashes at warp speed. I let loose a blood-curdling scream, "ASSHOLE! YOU LEFT ME!"

I try to run, but something is holding me in place. Fucking Izzy. I'm back in the recliner. What the hell is happening? Dr. Wheezer appears in the form of a pilot whale, telling me to breathe. Mellow Mel materializes, in the form of a beluga whale, chattering away, directing me to contract and relax my muscles. Dr. Prick pops in, dressed in a pincushion, chasing me with bloody needles. Finally, Ralphie shows up, looking like an orca, asking about my childhood and making voo sounds. Jim Whisperer, Joe from middle school, and every other racist idiot who ever bullied me for my appearance or personality chase me with fiery clubs until I stumble again into a cornfield, terrified and alone.

"People don't usually make it this far, Freddy. Now we'll have to kill you," Trippin says.

"WHAT??!!" I yell.

"Just fucking with you, gorgeous. You're doing great, kid," Trippin says.

"GREAT? GREAT!? I'm Trippin Ballz!"

"No, I am. Never gets old!" Trippin laughs.

"Get me out of here, Grace," I say, squeezing my eyes shut tighter than a virgin's legs at a porno audition.

"You're facing your fears, Freddy. Stay in the moment, in the *now*. Breathe! I know you're terrified, Freddy. Let it all go. You're not alone. Open your eyes, and breathe, babe. Release your pain, Freddy. You got this," Grace says.

The images in my brain flash nonstop; orcas, belugas, pilot whales, dolphins, stardust, worms, racists, buried flesh, nuclear power plants growing chicken wings, George Smelt. He must be in league with the sports bar! I bet George is trying to get a sandwich named for him. I'm turning into a sea lion. I slip into the ocean. Well, this is nice. The water is cool. Fuck! An orca is chasing me. Good thing I breathe underwater. Hide in the kelp, Freddy.

The orca is circling. His teeth are huge and grungy. *Don't alien orcas have toothbrushes? A little floss wouldn't kill you either!* I'm tangled in the kelp stalks. I feel the orca's warm breath on my face. (Yuck!)

"Freddy! Don't be scared. Do it for me. For us. Find *null!*" Grace says, tapping her belly.

Come on, Freddy. Do this! Be *null* for Grace, and your baby. You can breathe underwater. Big deal. Plenty of alien orcas can bre—Wait! I'm part alien orca? Dammit! Don't go there, Freddy. Go away, Bad OCD! Focus on Grace, and the baby. Our baby. What will we name it? Oh, I hope it's a girl, and she's just like Grace, because nobody would wish my shit on their kid. Do it for them, Freddy. So, you can see *next*? Big deal. Besides, what you see doesn't always happen. Breathe, Freddy.

A final scary image crams my mind. I'm as petrified as a frozen margarita in that sports bar's drink machine. The image is vibrant; I would describe it as full of life, except it's the complete opposite. Clouds of amber stardust surround me in an indigo sky. There is nothing else. It's, it's, it's—total annihilation.

57

Womansplaining

Back in the bottom of the ship.

"Oh, hello, everyone. Now that #2 has gone off to see #1, I owe all of you an explanation. But first, oh, this is so wonderful. I can't believe you're all here! I've waited over half a century for today, and now you're here!" #3 says, in a happy, whistling voice.

"Half a century? Well, I may not be the brightest bulb in the box, Miss Whale Ma'am, but I'm only 32," Andy Tyler says.

"Sorry, we haven't been properly introduced. I'm #3. #2 just left to see #1. Understand?" #3 says.

"Enough with the math quiz. What gives, whale?" Al asks.

"Do you want to know why you're here? Oh, I can answer that," #3 says.

"Well? Share with the rest of the class," Burt says.

#3 snorts a little laugh. "Oh Burt, you crack me up. #2 was right when he said we needed a comedian. Speaking of #2, poor dear, and why you're here."

"Coño girl, spit it out already," Bustella says.

"Sorry, I'm nervous. It's because you're all here. So anyways, here's the story. #2 thinks he's missing his beam up target, Freddy Fluid. Dr. Freddy Fluid. Jokes on him, Freddy's been here all day. Do any of you know Freddy? Oh, sorry, I already asked that. I'm so nervous. Anyways, Freddy is with #1, his father. #1 is sort of everyone's father. Well, not so much your father as your great-great-great-whatever-grandfather," #3 says.

"I'd love to meet him," Ernest Hamingway says.

"I'd like to stick my foot up his ass," Al says.

"Maybe I can arrange for you to meet him one day. And no foot up the ass, please. We're all family here. Speaking of here, do you want to know why you're here?" #3 asks.

"Ya think?" Max says.

"Please continue, #3," Sam says, in an *I think I'm falling in love with you* tone that #3 has heard many, many times from a multitude of life forms in every galaxy.

"Well, aren't you a little ray of sunshine, Sammy," #3 says, winking at Sam and adjusting her flippers. "All of you are gifted with a healthy dose of your ancestor's, that is #1's, DNA."

"Hey, whale! Me and my pooch Chunka are anime. No way we're related," Bustella says.

"You would think, right, hon? See, back in the day, #1 had a fling with Petunia Pig; she was quite the looker. Well, #1 left her with child, so he's in your ink, hon, and your little dog, too. Hehe, hehe. Sorry, I saw it in a movie. I love movies. Don't you just love movies, hon? You don't mind if I call you hon, because we're the only girls in this place?" #3 says.

"We're cool, chica," Bustella says.

"Thanks, hon," #3 says, blowing Bustella a kiss. "Oh, I still can't believe I'm talking to all of you. I've been waiting for today for the longessssstttt, and, and. Sorry, I'm verklempt. See, I'm #1's creation too, so we're all related. I can't believe I'm meeting my family. *Sniff, sniff.*"

"Who, or what, exactly is #1?" Cliff asks.

"I can answer that. #1 is the Creator and Creation of all things, at least in this Universe."

"So, God?" Cliff asks.

"God, Buddha, Yoda, #1, whatever floats your boat," #3 says.

"Yoda, huh? I can live with that," Cliff says.

"I figured as much. Love those little incantations of yours, by the way, Cliffy—big fan!" #3 says.

"I want to play with Baby Yoda, Cliff," Twan says.

"Oh, aren't you the cutest little thing, Twan. Maybe later," #3 says.

"Holy shit! I'm the son of God. And Dad said I'd never amount to anything," Leif says.

"Please cut to the chase, #3. Why are we here?" Harvey asks.

"Well, if everyone would please stop interrupting me," #3 says.

"Sorry," Cliff, Leif, Twan, and Harvey say in unison.

"No worries," #3 says, winking. "See, being the direct genetic spawn of #1, you all have unique personality traits, and highly elevated degrees of *next.*"

"What's *next*?" Sam asks.

"I'm so glad you asked, Sammy. Aren't you glad he asked, everyone? Well, I am. *Next* is the future. Everyone's future. All of you experience variations of *next.* You might call it clairvoyance. A feeling of knowing what happens next. Sound familiar, Max, Cliff?" Max and Cliff both nod. "By the way, Max, those solar panels wouldn't have blocked us. We can see right through them. Where was I again?" #3 asks.

"*Next!*" everyone yells.

"Anyways, getting back to *next*, see, Freddy Fluid, #1's son, he's mostly stuck in *next*, 59 seconds from *now*. The problem is, #1 doesn't realize the full power of Grace's *now*," #3 says.

"Who's Grace?" Harvey asks.

"Whoops. Grace is Freddy's girlfriend. She's the most *now* being in this galaxy. She's beeaauutifulllll, to the point of distraction, and believe me, #1 is plenty distracted. See, #1 is so busy trying to win the love and approval of his son, who, he sort of, but not quite abandoned almost 30 years ago, he neglected to comprehend how powerful Grace's *now* is. See, in a few minutes, on account of them having sex last night, Freddy's fabulous *next* sperm is going to penetrate Grace's graceful *now* egg, and if Freddy's *next* meets Grace's *now* before we fix things, there won't be nothing left to fix. Get it?" #3 says.

"Wait just a darn minute, #3, Ma'am. What's *now*?" Andy Tyler asks.

"*Now, next*. What the fuck is this, Abbott and Costello? Get to your fucking point, whale," Al demands.

"You can't tell me I'm related to this buffoon?" Ernest says.

"People, people!" Max says.

"Hey!" Bustella shouts, and Chunka growls.

"Pardon me," Max says, bowing to Bustella. "People and Toons, please, let her continue."

"Thank you, Max. *Now* is easy to understand. It's simple. Just be," #3 says.

"Just be? Sorry, Ma'am, I'm losing you," Andy Tyler says.

"Oh, Andy, you smooth talker, you. It's simple. Pretend we're in Mayberry. Be totally present. You know, like Andy Taylor; he's very *now, and quite the country hunk*. Whereas his deputy, Barney Fife, is totally *next*; jumpy, nervous, always worrying about some bizarre version of the future. Get it? I love old TV shows. Don't you love old TV shows?"

"Yes, Ma'am. As we say in Mt. Airy, North Carolina, WWAD?" Andy Tyler says with a zen smile.

"WWAD?" Cliff asks.

"What Would Andy Do?" Andy Tyler says.

"See, he gets it. *Now* is easy peasy. I'll show you. Close your eyes, everyone, and no peeking. That means you, Al. Good. Everyone, take a deep breath into your belly and exhale slowly," #3 says, emitting a siren's symphony of soothing vocalizations, whistles, and clicks so captivating it could lure sailors to the rocks.

"Wow!" Cliff, Leif, Harvey, Geronimo, Andy, and Bustella say simultaneously.

"Looks like I've found my meditators and stoners! You guys are always the first to find *now*, and of course, the pooches. Pups are always in the *now*, right, Chunka?" #3 asks.

Chunka barks.

"Hey, #3. *Now* is better than blow. We could make a killing off this *now* shit. Let's talk distribution," Al says.

"This is better than flying," Ernest says.

"Good. Everyone with me *now*? Now, get it, because I explained *now*. It's funny, right, Burt?" #3 asks.

"Meh?" Burt says. "But this *now* stuff rocks, #3."

"Excellent. I'm so excited. Oh, I knew you all would help once you understood," #3 says.

"Help?" Cliff asks.

"See, it's simple. I need to borrow your *nexts*," #3 says.

"Borrow?" Cliff asks.

"And what if we don't want to give up our *nexts*?" Max asks.

"Oh, I can answer that," #3 says.

"Well, whale?" Al asks.

"Kablooey!" #3 says.

58

She blew it (Again, it's not what you're thinking.)

Oh, God. I blew up everything. All I had to do was find *null* for Grace and the baby. FUCK!!!!!!! I blew it. Graceeeeeee!"

"Freddy! Chill. You didn't blow it, I did. Too much LSD, not enough ayahuasca. What an ego on this guy. Imagining you're powerful enough to destroy the Universe, Freddy. Geez!" Trippin says.

"He gets his ego from his father," Fiona flashes.

"Does not!" #1 flashes.

"Let's not go there, Eddie. Trust me, Trippin, Eddie's ego is so big, it takes up an entire galaxy. He even named it—Egoastan." Fiona laughs.

"Earth presidents get museums, and nobody bats a bloody eye," #1 flashes.

"Point and match to Fiona," Grace says.

"Anyone ever tell you your father's a dick, Freddy?" Trippin says.

"I wouldn't know. I just met him today!" I say like a kid about to throw a tantrum in the grocery store line.

"Today! No wonder you're jumpier than my drug dealer at an FBI convention. All your bottled-up anger will make you sprain your sphincter, kid. Listen, Freddy, yeah, yeah, your father abandoned you. No child support, I assume, Fiona?"

"Child support?!! Madame, I am a God!" #1 flashes.

"A God, huh? So, no child support. Look, kid, you got every right to hate this guy. I mean, look at him. He's a killer whale, for God's sake, and with his humongous tongue, huge dorsal fin, glistening black and white skin, and a tail that gets me as hot as—"

"Eyes off the tail please, Trippin," Mother interrupts.

"Ewwww!" I say.

"Sorry, Fiona, you lucky girl you. Listen, Freddy, you're a grown ass man and it looks like you turned out okay," Trippin says.

"Well, I am a brilliant surgeon," I say because, well, you know.

"Yeah, yeah, whatever. Look, gorgeous, after all these years, I've slowed down. Believe it or not, these days I'm more of a voyeur, kid. Some people would say, and by some, I mean me, watching crap like this go down with all kinds of people who come here to trip and get their acts together makes we wise. Some people's journeys are happy vacations in Hawaii. Some people's journeys bring out their inner monsters. But the shit I've seen here today makes my privates pucker. Listen, smart guy, grow a set, forgive your old man, and stop obsessing and compulsing your life away. You're going to be a father. So, get your gorgeous shit together before you blow it. And by blow it, I mean life. Your life, the whale's, your mother's, Grace's, the baby's, the fucking

Universe, and most importantly, mine. Listen closely, kid. I got a hot date with an acupuncturist tonight, and I haven't been pricked, if you know what I mean, since the last full moon, so fix this. Do it for the people you love. Think about others for a change, Freddy," Trippin says, and pours more ayahuasca into my mouth. "Here, kid, this will balance out your trip."

"Grace, are you sure I can ingest this?" I ask like a chicken shit coward.

"Yes, anything can be eaten once, Freddy," Grace laughs. "Kidding, babe! Go ahead."

Here goes, Freddy. Stop thinking about how bad you had it without a father, your OCD, breathing underwater, *next*. Put it all aside and focus on Grace, and the baby. I didn't grow up with a father. Big deal. Plenty of kids grow up fatherless. I have OCD. Big deal. Lots of people have OCD, even Leon Decapricorn. That's it, Freddy. Find *null!*

It's at this point in time, moments from the conception of our baby, I understand my problem with crystal clarity. I'm an infantile fucking narcissist. Everything I do is about me, and if I don't grow the fuck up, I'm going to destroy the Universe and everyone I care about, even Grace and our baby. I don't know about #1? He claims to be a God. He probably won't die. Good riddance if he does. Then I'll be all alone. I don't want to be all alone. Fuck, Freddy, you just blew the top off your asshole meter. Still thinking about yourself. Get to *null!*

"You got some serious Daddy shit happening, Freddy. Hey, orca, swim that fine tail over here and make things right with your kid. Now, buddy!" Trippin says.

"Freddy Fluid, you daft wanker, I'm sorry. Okay."

"Whoa, there! I've heard better apologies from a serial killer. Geez! What should we expect from a killer whale?" Trippin says.

"Madame, I've never killed anyone," #1 flashes.

"There's been a whole lot of killing in your name. Tell me you never read the Old Testament? Lots of smiting there," Trippin says.

"Madame, man was created with free will, and I did not write the Bible," #1 flashes.

"Listen, Free Willy, don't give me that created shit. I guess you never read Darwin either. But what do I know, I'm just an old lady who likes to get high. Speaking of which, I think we better get back to your kid," Trippin says.

"Indubitably, Madame," #1 flashes.

"You're here! Oh, thank God, I mean, #1, whoever, or whatever the fuck you are, Father. Where's Grace? Mother? Grace? Grace!!! GRACE!! Is our almost baby okay?"

"We're here, babe. Everything is fine. It's the ayahuasca. And the acid and shrooms. I know it's a lot, Freddy. I'm sorry, this is the only way," Grace says.

"NO! I'm the one who's sorry. I'm sorry, Grace. I'm sorry, Mother, for everything. I'm intolerable. I'm a self-absorbed juvenile asshole. Please forgive me, Grace, Mother. I'm such a selfish pig, George Smelt could milk me. How could you stand living with me all these years, Grace?"

"Because I love you, Freddy," Grace says.

"I'm sorry too, Freddy. For lying to you, for everything. We're here now, and your father and I aren't going anywhere, unless the Universe explodes, in which case, I imagine we'll all be together, albeit in bits and pieces. Now, Eddie, apologize, and, Freddy dear, forgive your father before it's too late," Mother says.

"Very comforting, Mother!"

"Freddy lad. I really mean it. Please forgive me for not being there in a traditional manner. Only 2 minutes, 13 seconds left," #1 says.

"Don't be an a-hole, your Holiness. None of this qualifying, in a traditional manner shit. Tell your son how sorry you are and mean it this time!" Trippin demands.

"Quite right. I'm not accustomed to apologizing. Freddy, my boy. I've been a terrible father. I should have been there for you, explained why you are so marvelously unique, and guided you on how to use your gifts. I'm truly sorry. Please, Freddy. Forgive me, son."

"Fine. I really forgive you," I say.

"Whew, just in the nick of—" #1 says.

Hey, where did everyone go? I'm all wet. Where the fuck am I? "Trippin? Grace? Mother? #1?"

I'm on the bottom of the ocean. Geez! It's fucking cold. It's not as dark as I imagined it would be. There're light beams everywhere. The water is crystal clear. The lights are flying by. They're stars! Glorious stars, leaving trails of stardust, the same color as my flickers. Perpetual stars! Rolexa! I'm on Rolexa.

"Grace! Grace!! Are you seeing this?" I feel like sparks are jumping through me, like current flows through wire. My mind and body are racing between Buddha slow and breathlessly fast, like the time I drank a six-pack of Redbull and a half bottle of tequila *(don't ask)*. You're in the water, Freddy. Breathe slowly. That's it! I feel the qi moving across me like someone with wet feet plugged me into a socket, only I'm the socket. I'm Buddha slow. Good. You're in the *now*. Now—get to *null*. For Grace, for the baby, for the Universe! There's a stardust map pointing me toward the surface. Wooohoooo! I'm sailing through the water like Aquaman, guided by a path of perpetual stars. I'm fucking faster than ever! This is better than my Maserati. I'm exhilarated, as if I just had my first kiss with Grace. Grace! Where the fuck is she?? Whew! There she is, above the surface.

"Grace! I'm almost there, Grace. Isn't this amazing?" Why can't she hear me? "Trippin? Are you here?" Fuck, Grace is moving off planet. She's in the clouds. She's being sucked off *(not like that—get your mind out of the gutter at a time like this!)* into space. "Hang on, Grace. I'm coming, Grace!" I breach the surface.

I've never seen such colors. Violet clouds, indigo moons, silver suns, and amber shooting stars. Mother was right. Rolexa is stunning. "Grace!" She's reaching out for me. I'm trying to yell for Grace to grab my hands. Nothing comes out of my mouth. I must get to Grace. Something is in my way. What the fuck are these things? Low-flying constellations. Looks like a time-lapse scene from the Galapagos. Algae, fish, dinosaurs, whales, monkeys, alligators, and cave people floating past.

I wish #1 was here to see this. Evolution, baby! He's so full of shit with his *I created the Universe* thing. I have to find Grace. Where's Grace, and our soon to be baby? If anything happens to her, I won't be able to go on. I wish I could speak. Wait!! Maybe I can flash? Father, Mother, please, please save Grace and the baby. I don't care what happens to me. No use flashing, my light beams are frozen.

Here comes a cloud of stardust the size of the Sahara. The Rolexa stars. Cool! They're filling my eyes. I see a black path, with purple lights traveling so fast, they don't appear to be moving at all, rather the path is changing, vibrating, transcending time and space. I feel calm, peaceful. The path, it's leading to Grace. There she is. Reaching out to me from space. She's dressed in an animal print dress, like Wilma Flintstone, only with pointy ears. *That's hot!* Mind out of the gutter, Freddy. Remember—tick, tick! I try again to call Grace's name. Nothing comes out, and then the craziest thing happens; at least for today. The purple lights meld with my light beams, with Grace's. We grab each other's outstretched arms; hers from the galaxy above and mine from the sea's surface.

I'm calm, truly at peace. I see the outline of a tiny orb in Grace's abdomen, as radiant as Chernobyl. Grace's egg. It's magnificent. There's my sperm, flickering stardust on its way to her egg. If only I could speak, there's so much I have to tell Grace. What a selfish moron I've been. How I treasure her and our love, and I think I found *null—or kablooey!*

59

I gave at the orifice

In the bottom of the spaceship, #3 takes up a collection.

"Even I understand kablooey!" Leif says. "You can have my *next*, #3."

"Oh, I knew you would help. I only need to borrow your *nexts*, though. When we're through, you'll get them back, with an upgrade," #3 says.

"What's the catch, fish?" Al asks.

"Catch fish. Funny, Al. I get it because I'm a whale, right? He's funny, right, Burt?"

"Meh," Burt says.

"There's no catch, Al. I'll use a simple extraction method, involving placing my mouth over yours and sucking. Your *nexts* will pop right out. I'll store your *nexts* in my frontal lobe, then using my sonar, and stars from Rolexa as transportation devices, I'll direct all of your *nexts* into Freddy at the precise nanosecond his sperm, which is traveling in Grace's fallopian tube, needs to enter the *now* of Grace's egg, thus balancing the power of *now* and *next*—kablooey free. Easy peasy. Anyone want to volunteer to be first?" #3 asks.

"ME, ME!!!" Sam shouts.

"Aren't you the eager beaver? But first, I need everyone to sign this consent form," #3 says, and flashes a document into everyone's hands. "It's a simple hold, harmless form. No need to study it. Just sign it, and line up for the transfer," #3 instructs.

"Hey, #3, the second paragraph says in the event of kablooey, all terms and conditions are null and void," Max says.

"True, but that will only happen if we fail our mission and don't get Freddy to *null*, and if that happens, everyone and everything will be void. Take my word for it."

"Word, schmerd," Al says. "I'm not signing nothing."

"Fine, but if you don't sign it, I can't do your transfer," #3 says.

"What exactly are you transferring, #3?" Cliff asks.

"I can answer that," #3 replies.

"Not again, whale!" Al says.

"All of you were chosen for a specific reason. Besides your *nexts*, you have qualities Freddy is, how do I put this delicately? Dr. Freddy Fluid is a prince among men. He is the son of #1 and Fiona Fluid. He's the most perfect being ever created. It's just that he's, well, he's—"

"Spit it out, whale!" Al yells.

"Freddy is missing a few human traits, which you have in abundance, and... How do I say this?"

"Take your time, #3. We're here for you," Sam says.

"Thanks, Sammy, but time is the only thing I can't take. Here goes. All of you have some human quality Freddy needs to balance his somewhat fixed personality, and all of you are missing something in your lives, which I will happily provide, as soon as we stop—kablooey."

"Do you really expect us to believe this, #3? What, for example, could I give Freddy, and what am I missing?" Cliff asks.

"I'm glad you asked, Cliff. In your case, it's easy," #3 says as the gang chatters away disrespectfully. "Uh, excuse me! Uh, hello, everyone!" #3 whistles and shouts, "LISTEN UP!" And the gang settles. "Cliff, you are the most spiritual human here, and God knows Freddy Fluid needs him something to believe in. And, Cliff, you know exactly what you're lacking in your life," #3 says.

"I know," Cliff says, hugging Twan close.

"Exactly. So, who's ready for that transfer?" #3 says, and Cliff thrusts his eager mouth under #3's toothy maw, and sucks like a breast-feeding baby.

"Whew! Was it good for you, Cliff? Next! See what I did there, because I need your *nexts* and, never mind," #3 says.

"Leave the comedy to a professional from now on, #3," Burt says, rushing to be next in line, only to be cut off by Sam.

"Me! Me! Kiss me," Sam says, locking lips with #3.

"Whew! That's quite the face sucking technique you got there. You're going to need to stick around after class, Sammy. If there's an after class," #3 whispers.

"Okay, everyone, line up. Just 1 minute, 57 seconds left," #3 says.

"Hey! Aren't you going to tell us about our traits you're taking and what we get like you did for Cliff?" Harvey asks.

"Sorry, Harvey, no time. I'll rattle off the kind of trait you're giving Freddy when we do the transfer, but you're going to have to trust me until later about what you're getting."

"That's a sucker's deal. Screw off, whale," Al says.

"Too bad, Al, because I heard through the girlie grapevine, you could really use some help with that short fuse of yours," #3 says.

"Big deal. I get angry real quick. In my line of work, it's an asset," Al says.

"That's not the short fuse I'm talking about," #3 says.

"Hey! Fuck you, whale," Al says.

"Talk to me after we help you with your little problem," #3 says, winking.

"Ahh, fuck it!" Al says, signing the consent form and lining up for a kiss with the rest.

"Now we're talking," #3 says, transferring Al's *next* through her mouth. "Al, Freddy is going to get your bravado, and Sammy, Freddy's getting your passion to advocate for the environment."

"Me. Me!" Ernest yells and kisses #3 with all his might.

"Whew! It's always the little ones who surprise you. Ernest, Freddy is getting your love of flying."

"Here you go, #3. You don't even have to tell me what you're taking, but I hope I can count on your vote," Max says, laughing.

"Thank you, Max. From you, Freddy will get your ability to understand other points of view and compromise for the greater good," #3 says.

"That's a mouthful. If only you could give that to all elected officials," Max says.

"I figure Andy Taylor would help, so count me in, Ma'am," Andy says, kissing #3 gently.

"Nice touch, Andy. Freddy gets your WWAD meter. NEXT!" #3 shouts.

"I'll go, but I don't know what the hell you could get from me. I cheated on my wife with my best friend's wife, broke up two families, and left my kids," Harvey says, kissing #3.

"You, my friend, have fucked up like the rest of humanity, but you admit it and you have a horribly realistic ego, a trait more humans, especially Freddy, could use. *Next!*" #3 says.

"Did I ever tell you the one about the comedian who kissed a whale?" Burt asks, kissing #3 gently on the mouth.

"No, what happened?"

"Nobody whaley knows," Burt says.

"Good thing I wasn't giving Freddy your sense of humor, but Freddy is getting your most important comedic trait. Do you know the most important thing in comedy?" #3 asks.

"TIMING!" everyone yells.

"Never gets old," #3 says, snorting. "Next!"

"I guess I'll go. Not sure what Freddy could possibly need from me?" Bob says.

"Just a few inches," #3 kids, and Bob grabs his crotch. "At ease, fella! Didn't anyone ever tell you, you're freakishly tall? Chill, Bob. Freddy is getting your compassion," #3 says, kisses Bob, and yells, "Next!"

"I'll go next, but leave them out of it," Geronimo says, pushing Bustella and Chunka aside.

"Screw that, Papi!" Bustella says, pushing past Geronimo and kissing #3 tenderly on the lips.

"Holy *nexts*, Batgirl!" #3 says, then whispers to Bustella, "You should give these guys smooching lessons. Thanks, hon. As badass as you seem on the outside, Freddy gets your tenderness."

"Don't let that get around, chica. Bad for my image."

"Woof!" Chunka says, jumping up, doing a backflip, and licking #3's mouth.

"Whew! And I thought fish breath was bad. Somebody give Chunka a mint. Kidding, dog, from you Freddy gets your playfulness."

"Don't forget me," Geronimo says, planting a gentle kiss on #3's lips.

"Nicely done. Bustella must be rubbing off on you."

"Not cool, whale!' Bustella yells.

"Whoops! Not that kind of rubbing off, Bustella. English is such a nuanced language, isn't it, hon? Geronimo, Freddy gets your artistic nature. I think that does it, except for you, Leif," #3 says.

"Sure, but I don't think I have anything of value to give anyone #3," Leif says.

"Dude! You have the most valuable *next* of all," #3 says.

"Really, man! Could you put that in writing, and send it to my dad?" Leif asks.

"Oh, we won't have to once this is over, Leif. Your dad will see you for what you truly are."

"Oh, what's that, man?"

"You, Leif, have the unique ability to be totally present. In other words, you have the most *now next* of all to pass onto Freddy," #3 says.

"Cool! It's the drugs, but whatever, man!" Leif says, kissing #3.

"Thanks, everyone. Wish me luck! And, oh yeah, you won't be seeing me again for a while, or maybe never. See, as soon as I leave, the transporter will deposit you back on solid land. You'll be better than new, unless, ya know—kablooey, in which case, nice knowing you, especially you, Sammy." #3 says, as shooting stars pass through and around her head. She adjusts her flippers, smiles and sways, releasing a hauntingly beautiful series of whistles, clicks, and melody that sounds like—a day at the circus.

60

Tick, Tick, Tock

In the Horology shop of Tick Tockington

At 4:19 a.m., as he does twice every day, Tick sits down in front of the star-filled hourglass, waiting. At precisely 4:20 a.m., Tick reaches out his hands, and doing exactly as the alien instructed 62 years ago, grabs the neck of the hourglass, and holds on as if his life depends on it. Other than the ticking of the other timepieces, it's night-time quiet in his shop, until Tick hears it. Sounds from his childhood evoking memories of elephants, lions, clowns, and aliens—calliope music! And Tick pisses himself—again.

"Now!" the alien yells, waving her flippers.

When Tick practiced this task for the last 6 decades, the alien wasn't present. The alien promised Tick long ago to return at 4:20 one day and together they would save the Universe. Tick was instructed when the alien returned, he was to hold the hourglass in place by its neck until the alien told him to let go, no matter what. This morning, practice was over. The task was real, as remarkably, was the alien, as surprisingly, were a gazillion parasitic crabs, scampering through the hourglass. The lead crab making a beeline, or in this case, a crab line, all the way to Tick's hands.

"Crabs! Damn that Midge!" Tick calls out.

61

Yabba Dabba Who?

In the not so dull null.

So, this is *null*? Cool! I made it to *null*, holding Grace's hands. She's floating in space and I'm on the surface of the ocean, but we're together, and there's no place I'd rather be. Time is frozen. This is pure joy. Soak it all in, Freddy. The blissed-out look on Grace's face. Grace is still wearing the Wilma Flintstone leopard pattern dress, and pointy ears. *Damn!* Freddy Flintstone was one lucky caveman. *Mind out of the gutter, Freddy! Be null, idiot. Flintstones! It must be the fucking ayahuasca. This is null on drugs, kids. What the fuck is happening? I can't breathe; and it's fucking glorious.*

Mother was right. I'm breathless, like a vacuum is sucking all the air out of my cells. It's a splendid feeling, until a burst of *nexts* pound their way into my head *like nails from a nail gun, wielded by a burly lady roofer.* What the fuck was that? It's okay. Precious *null* is holding me still. I'm not scared or anxious about anything. Not even death. At least not mine. All that matters is Grace and our baby. My sperm. It's breaching Grace's egg.

Wait!!!!! He didn't reset me! There's starlight everywhere, bright as a meteor shower, pulsing the space around us. Is this *null* or kablooey? Wait! This must be *null*, because there's our baby, and I'm more breathless than a scuba diver with an empty air tank. It's a girl! Her adorableness is immeasurable. She looks like Pebbles Flintstone, only cuter. She's surrounded by stardust. I've never been this chill.

"Grace! Do you see her? Do you see our exquisite baby?" Why can't she hear me? I can't wait to tell Grace about this, and more importantly, how sorry I am for being such an ass. They say when you're gone, people will remember how you made them feel. I don't want to be remembered as a self-consumed, childish robot with delusions of grandeur. I want people to smile when they think of me. Fuck! My flickers make people feel good, so smile, Freddy, smile—and stop being a selfish a-hole. You're a father, Freddy, and Grace is a mother! If I can ever speak again, the first words out of my mouth will be, "I'm sorry Gra...." Wait! Is that calliope music?

"Now!" #3 shouts, as Fiona Fluid flies into Tick's shop, takes a huge shot of tequila, flashes her light beams igniting the booze, and spits the fiery mixture all over the crabs, instantly killing the invaders, who upon further inspection look like ticks, who upon further, further inspection, are in fact, Time Moochers!

"How did we wind up in a horologist's shop? Did someone light a Molotov cocktail? Is that a singing beluga whale? Who cares! You were right about *null*, Mother. None of this matters anymore. Fuck, that's not what I wanted to say at all. Grace! Grace, are you here?"

"I'm here, babe."

"Did you see our baby, Grace? Isn't she magnificent?" I ask.

"She's the most beautiful thing I ever saw," Grace says.

"Oh, Grace, I'm terribly sorry. Please forgive me. I've been such a selfish idiot," I say.

"I know, babe, but you're my selfish idiot. And not that I don't like how it sounds, but what's a horologist, I mean, besides a great spelling bee word, right?" Grace whispers.

"It's not what you think."

"Fiona! #3! Not to be an ingrate, but what in bloody Hades happened to—kablooey?" #1 demands.

62

Fiona

There never was a more insightful, more lovely human than Fiona Fluid, a face like a poem, body like a spin instructor, brain like a super-computer, and a wit like Lenny Bruce.

Fiona was an only child. She grew up carefree on Miami Beach and indulged in all it had to offer. Fishing, surfing, boating, snorkeling, swimming, skateboarding, clubbing, and her favorite activity; scuba diving. Suffice it to say, Fiona spent an inordinate amount of time in the water. She was so fascinated by ocean life, it led to her career as a prominent marine biologist.

During the day, Fiona was a professor at the University of Miami. At night, and on weekends, you could find Fiona diving the coral reefs between Miami Beach and Key Largo. It was on one of these scuba trips, the alien appeared. The alien claimed to be a time traveler and provided such a detailed account of key events in Fiona's life, including her first boy kiss, first girl kiss (with Trippin), first period, first shroom trip (with Trippin), and the day she first swam with wild dolphins, that the perfectly logical Fiona had no choice but to believe the alien.

Plus, Fiona loved music, as did the alien, who had a great set of pipes. The alien provided an explanation of a number of events which would unfold over the next few decades, all of which intimately involved Fiona. The alien's explanation went like this…

"You see, hon. You don't mind if I call you hon, seeing as were the only two girls here?"

"Fine, hon," Fiona says with an attitude.

"Ohhhhh. Gotcha. I see how calling you hon can sound condescending. Sorry, Fiona," the alien says.

"Just messing with you—hon!" Fiona giggles.

The alien snorts. "Oh, I like you. Where was I again?"

"You see, hon," Fiona says.

"Oh yeah, thanks, Fiona. You see, h…whoops, caught myself. You see, Fiona. So, what was I saying? Oh yeah, anyways, about your future. See in a few years, when you're 32, snorkeling in 32 feet of water, off 32nd Street on Miami Beach, you'll meet #1."

"That's a lot of 32s. Who's #1? What is this, math class?"

"Math class. You're a hoot, Fiona. Anybody ever tell you, you're a hoot? Anyways, #1 is the Creator and Creation of all things. He created me—and he likes the number 32."

"He's a God?"

"Well, he thinks so anyway, Fiona. Don't get me wrong, though, he's quite the looker, at least from my perspective."

"Interesting. Do you think I'll find him attractive?"

"Depends? How do you feel about orcas?"

"Orcas. The largest and notoriously most aggressive member of the dolphin family. I've always thought they were the most misunderstood cetaceans."

"Yeah, so anyways, he's an orca."

"An orca?"

"Yeah. He can turn into anything, a bird, plane, even a beauuuutiful human, but being from the water planet, Rolexa, he's an orca. Anyways, he's dreamy. Real important thing here, Fiona. When you meet #1, promise you won't tell him about me, about our conversations, about our plan?"

"Promise! What plan?"

"The plan to save your child, and the Universe?"

"Child?" Fiona questions, patting her belly and grinning. "Interesting. Who's the baby daddy?"

"Well, it ain't polite for a lady to tell, but I can give you a clue?"

"Give, sister!" Fiona says, laughing.

"Sister! Ha! You're so funny. Okay, sister. What's black and white and about to be all over you?"

From there, the alien told Fiona a laborious, alluring tale. The alien spoke very quickly, as if it were running along a train platform, and Fiona was on the train, and the train was heading in the wrong direction, and Nazis were shooting at them; and the tale was about *now, next, null,* and especially *how.*

How #1 was the first being in the Universe. How #1 was lonely. How #1 created a perpetual hourglass clock to satisfy his perverse need to track the eons of loneliness which passed. How the hourglass is powered by Rolexa's stars and is responsible for how time passes across the Universe. How #1 had so many bad memories of loneliness associated with the hourglass, he hid it away on Earth in the care of master horologist, Clock Tockington. How once the fitness watches came out, how #1 converted his time-keeping to digital and forgot about the hourglass. How *now, next,* and *null* work. How the alien befriended the Time Moochers of Timexa and discovered their devious scheme. How the Time Moochers learned of the hourglass. How the Time Moochers discovered they could travel through the hourglass to other planets, but only if the hourglass was in *null* space near a gargantuan source of power that was about to, but had not yet made the Universe go—kablooey. How said source of power would build up right before the *next* sperm of Fiona and #1's son Freddy, set on Rolexa time, breached the wall of Grace's *now* egg set on Earth time. How the Time Moochers didn't know exactly when this *null* space would open up. How thanks to her friendship with time itself, the alien knew it would be at 4:20 Earth time, somewhere between Rolexa's second indigo moon's eclipse and Rolexa's third silver sun's eclipse. How that was a long-ass time. How the Time Moochers, having no need for time, concocted an elaborate plan of invading Earth through *null* space while #1 was otherwise occupado, resetting Freddy and saving the Universe. How Freddy's *null* provided the miserable Moochers a time-free opportunity to travel to Earth and destroy the perpetual hourglass responsible for how time itself passes, thus having a timeless Universe all to themselves. How the alien discovered she could time travel because of her calliope songs. How the alien traveled back to the time of Rolexa's second moon's lunar eclipse and trained 5-year-old Tick Tockington to perform the task of holding the hourglass still. How that was as far as the alien got with the plan to this point. How the alien time traveled to meet Fiona to complete the plan to save Freddy, Grace, and the Universe. How Fiona would survive cancer. How much Fiona was going to love being a grandma. How the alien's name was #3, but Fiona could call her hon, if the mood struck. And finally, most importantly, how they really, really, really had to prevent—kablooey!

Fiona and #3 met every week for months, refining their plan. #3 regaled Fiona with mesmerizing stories from around the Universe. Fiona told the alien about life and love on Earth. They shared their hopes, their dreams, their love of music, how they would celebrate after they saved the Universe; tequila is involved. #3 sung beautifully haunting songs, which made Fiona feel like she too could transverse the Universe and time itself. Fiona and #3 became best friends and are to this day.

On the prophesied day, when Fiona was 32, while diving a coral reef in 32 feet of water, off 32nd street, an orca appeared in the warm waters of the Atlantic, nibbled Fiona Fluid's swim fin, transformed into the most handsome man she'd ever seen—and it was love at first bite.

63

To kablooey, or not kablooey, that is the question

"I was thinking the same thing, Father. What happened to kablooey?" I ask, and I can't get this stupid grin off my face, because I'm going to be a father—and no kablooey!

"Hey! Alien! Oh great, there's more of you," Tick says, releasing the remainder of the contents of his bladder. Can I let go of the hourglass now?" Tick asks.

"Oh yes. Great job, Tick. Sorry about the last 62 years. Didn't mean to ruin your life. Until this morning, I wasn't exactly sure what day the Time Moochers were coming. I'll make up for it, Tick. Promise," #3 says, blowing Tick a kiss.

"Freddy dear, and lovely Grace, what a gorgeous baby girl you're having. Permit me to explain what happened to kablooey, and unlike your father, I shall be concise," Fiona says.

"Ouch!" #1 says.

And then Mother speaks, very quickly, like she's running along a dock, and the rest of us are on a ship, and the ship is leaving port, and the KKK is shooting at us, and even though maybe some of us heard parts of this story before, it's science-fictiony, so perhaps people will understand it better when it's repeated, in a different way, by a different person. Well, you get it.

"Your father created a perpetual hourglass clock responsible for time across the Universe. #1 also used it to track his loneliness—poor thing. #1 ditched the hourglass on Earth in the care of Clock Tockington. This guy's," Fiona adds, pointing to Tick, "great-great-great-grandfather."

"#1 created fitness watches and forgot about the hourglass. The Timexian Time Moochers learned they could travel through the hourglass to Earth when Freddy was in *null* space, but only just prior to when Freddy's *next* sperm breached Grace's *now* egg. This would allow the Time Moochers the ability to travel through *null* space and destroy the hourglass, thus having a timeless Universe. #3 befriended the Time Moochers and learned of their devious plan. Then she traveled back in time, trained Tick to hold the hourglass steady, twice a day at 4:20. #3 time travels, tells me the whole story. #3 and I develop a plan of our own, yada yada yada, we kill the Time Moochers, save Freddy, Grace, the Universe, my grandbaby, and—I'm going to be a grandma!"

"Good of you ladies to fill me in. I still don't understand. I didn't reset Freddy, and not to be an ingrate, but what in bloody hell happened to—kablooey?" #1 asks.

"Men, always bringing a bomb to a knife fight. Freddy didn't need to be reset, #1. It was only his *next* that was out of whack. I found the perfect balance of *nexts,* which I extracted from your descendants. Some of them were quite the kissers. Whew! Where was I again?" #3 asks.

64

Kiss my alien a…

"Kissers," Grace says.

"Oh yeah, thanks, hon. Anyways, your offspring can kiss all right, #1, but let me tell you, that Bustella—those boys got nothing on her. The way she darts her little tong—"

"Get on with it!" #1 says.

"Sure thing, Daddy!" #3 says, adjusting her flippers and snorting.

"She gets to call you Daddy?" I whine.

"She most certainly does not!" #1 says.

"Anyways, Daddy," #3 snorts. "After I extracted #1's descendants' *nexts* into my frontal lobe, the perpetual stars passed through my noggin, scooped up a healthy dose of *nexts,* and some personality upgrades, deposited them into Freddy's head just as he and Grace touched hands, thus boosting the *next* level of Freddy and his sperm in order to balance the off the chart *now* of Grace's egg. Easy peasy! Pleasure to meet you, Grace, Freddy, and that adorbs little one of yours. She looks just like Pebbles Flintstone."

"A *next* transplant. Cool!" Grace says.

"No wonder my head hurt," I say, *because, ouch, that fucking hurt.*

"Sorry, Freddy. You were my first *next* transplant. Hell, you were my first anything transplant, and boy, do you have a hard noggin," #3 says.

"He takes after his father," Fiona says, giggling.

"Does not! And why didn't you tell me about all of this!!?? I am a God, after all," #1 asks.

"Don't take this the wrong way, #1, but you're not exactly a team player, and this was an all-girls on deck situation. The Time Moochers would only attempt travel when they knew you were otherwise occupado with Freddy and kablooey, and boy, were you. Everyone knows Time Moochers can't be killed on their own planet because it's timeless there. I mean you, #1, could have killed them, but you have the whole 'I'm a God. I have an aversion to killing thing' going on, which is a little odd for a killer whale, don't you think? Anyways, we had to wait until they traveled to Earth, where they were vulnerable. Then, when the Time Moochers made their move, Fiona swooped in and gave them what us girls call a tequila sunset," #3 says.

"Tequila sunset?" I ask.

"Cause it's the last drink they'll ever have," Mother says, high-fiving #3's flipper.

"Anyways, about kablooey, #1. See, Freddy didn't have to be reset at all. He's half Earthling and half Rolexian. Now that his *next* is balanced, he can live in both times zones and modulate between them," #3 says.

"Thank you for saving us, #3," I say. *In the old days, as in 3 minutes ago, I would have said thank you for saving me. See how I've grown?* "What exactly do you mean, modulate between them? I thought I would be free of *next* when this was through?" I ask, like a guy with gum on his shoe.

"Well, #3?" #1 demands.

"Modulating is easy," #3 looks at me lovingly, and says, "Okay, Freddy, close your eyes and repeat after me."

"Sure," I say, closing my eyes as a sign of trust, *because I've changed.*

"There's no place like home," #3 says, snorting.

The old Freddy would've gotten angry. The old Freddy would have screamed. The new Freddy, it turns out, has a much better sense of humor. I smile the biggest smile ever, and roar with a belly laugh rivaling Grandpa Santa's. Everyone joins in the ruckus. The laughter breaks apart all of the *next* stress I ever had, and my flickers surround us in clouds of stardust. I see purple pathways leading from *now to next*, from Earth to Rolexa, and all I have to do to move between them is smile! I smile at #3, and #2, who just appeared, kiss Grace, hug Mother, and shake Father's flipper.

"Seems as though I've been outdone, Fiona, #3. Congratulations and excellent work. You too, #2, although you certainly fooled me with all that rubbish about missing your target," #1 says as #2 comes slinking out of the shadows.

"Yes, #2 was helping us keep you distracted. Right, #2?" #3 says, winking at #2, who sheds a tear.

"No! I can't lie anymore. I didn't know anything about their plan. #3 is protecting me from my own incompetence, and any potential #2 references," #2 says.

"It's my fault, #2. I tricked you when I switched out the bogus coordinates #1 gave us for locating Freddy. It was his grocery list. Shame on you, #1! Anyways, I plugged in the right coordinates for finding the *next* descendants I needed to balance Freddy, but I couldn't tell anyone, except Fiona. Sorry, #2," #3 says.

"Grocery list! That explains the orange juice. I don't care. I don't know what's gotten into me. Probably all this kablooey talk. I'm a new whale. I've wanted to do this since the moment I saw you," #2 says, and kisses #3 passionately.

"Holy Abalone, #2! Wherever'd you learn to kiss like that?"

"I practiced on a plum," #2 says.

"A plum?" #3 asks.

"Told you," Grace whispers to me.

"This still doesn't explain how you time traveled, #3?" #1 asks.

"I tried to tell you, #1, but you never listen. That's why I told Fiona," #3 says.

"I do too listen!" #1 says.

"Be honest, Eddie, listening is not your strong suit, which probably explains all those unanswered prayers—from everyone in the Universe," Fiona says.

"Point taken, luv. You can time travel, #3?" #1 asks.

"See, #1, all the time I spent on the surface, communicating with other life forms, paid off. After a few centuries of sending my thoughts around and requests for stories, I found I could communicate with time itself. It's my singing, you know. It's quite lovely, I've been told. I even won a song competition on Saturn's Got Talent. The judges said I ran rings around the competition—Ha! You'd know, if you ever listened, #1. Anyways, talking to time is easy. First, I won over the seconds, then the minutes, the hours, after that, the days, years, centuries, even light years. And the stories they had to tell—past, present, future, fantasy, science fiction, espionage, mystery, and my favorite, romance. One day, time offered me the ability to traverse its continuum, and boy, did I," #3 says.

"Even I can't time travel, and I am a God. Besides, I created you in my image, so you don't have any greater powers than me," #1 says indignantly.

"Shame on you, Eddie. The Time Moochers wanted to take over the Universe, we tricked them, used your hourglass to do it, prevented kablooey, and instead of being proud of #3, all you can do is think about is your own creation outdoing you," Fiona says.

"A few moments ago, I would have said the same thing, Father."

"But—" #1 says.

#3 interrupts, "It's my calliope music, #1. When I sing at the right pitch and bounce my sound beams off the correctly organized configuration of stars, I can go anywhere, any time in the Universe. I can even control *next*. The minutes and hours explained the whole thing to me. Only those of pure heart, with an overwhelming sense of empathy, the ability to arrange the star charts to reach the past, present and future, and with a great set of pipes who can sing calliope music, have the gift of time travel. As far as I know, I'm the only one. Oh, and I can only time travel when the Universe itself, or some other cataclysmic shit, depends on it. You know, like to prevent kablooey, but not to meet a guy, or attend a Beatles concert; that doesn't work at all. Trust me. Anyways, I tried telling you, #1, but you never listen. Listening, #1! Listening! It all comes down to communication. Sorry, I didn't mean to be rude, Daddy. Don't worry, I saved a bit of somethin' somethin' to help you with that." #3 sings, and a single Rolexa star flies from her head into #1's.

"Calliope music? What is the meaning of this? Wait a bloody minute! Ah! You gave me a listening *next*! Brilliant, #3. Where'd you get it?" #1 asks.

"You wouldn't believe me if I told ya. Oh, I'll tell you anyways. From all places—a politician," #3 says.

"A politician! That's the most unbelievable thing I've heard all day," Grace says, as everyone breaks into laughter.

"Well, handsome, you don't mind if I call you handsome, 'cause look at you?" #3 says.

"Not at all," *the new me says.*

"So, handsome, what's next?" #3 asks.

The old Freddy would have employed two-dimensional thinking. The old Freddy would demand to go to Earth and use my stardust gene therapy to help cure all diseases known to man, thus boosting my ego. The new Freddy has other ideas. "Well, and only if it's okay with you, Grace, here's what I'm thinking." And by thinking, I mean using my upgraded brain with boosted *nexts*. "I'd like to stay on the spaceship and honeymoon on Rolexa, Grace."

"Honeymoon? You said he wouldn't lose his memory, #1. We're not married, Freddy," Grace says.

"My memory is fine, Grace," I say, and kiss her tenderly, *like Bustella.*

"Whew! Where'd you learn to kiss like that, Freddy?"

"Practiced on a plum," I say, softly nibbling Grace's ear. "#1. I mean, Father, as ship's captain, God thingy, whatever, will you do the honors?" I ask like a guy who's so in love, they'll get married by an Elvis impersonator, but would rather their alien father perform the ceremony.

"I'd be honored, Son. Check your pocket, lad," #1 says with a tear.

In my pocket, I find a splendid hourglass cut ring, glowing amber light beams. "Thank you, Father. It's perfect!" I say, smiling, and my flickers surround the ring with amber stardust. Do this right, Freddy. Down on one knee, Freddy. "Grace Whisperer. Would you do me the honor of—"

"HECK YEAH!!!" Grace shouts, and kisses me all over my face, like it's covered with cookie dough—and plums.

"Mother, would you be my best ma… *er* person?"

"Of course, Freddy dear. I'm going to be a grandma!" Mother says, unable to contain her excitement.

"And, #2, will you please give the bride away?"

"Uh, me? Sure," #2 says, sniffling.

"You okay there, #2?" #3 asks.

"Sure. Sure. I got allergies. Geez! Anyone got a tissue?" #2 asks, still sniffling.

"#3, would you please honor us with a song to walk Grace down the aisle?" I ask.

"You got it, handsome. I got just the perfect tune," #3 says, as calliope music flows from her mouth, and everyone freezes. "Too soon?" #3 giggles, as everyone breaks into laughter.

"Have you kids thought of a name for the baby yet?" Mother asks.

"Funny you should ask, Fiona. We haven't had a chance to discuss it at length with kablooey and what not, but I'm leaning toward Trippin," Grace says.

"Trippin! You can't be serious?" #1 says.

"Just yanking your tail, #1. Her name is Infinity," Grace says with a smile.

"Always the jokester. Infinity. Ah, perfect, like the tough little bird in the Matrix," #1 says.

"That's Trinity, Eddie dear," Fiona says.

"Ah, quite right again, luv. Infinity is a strong, lovely name, and with all the stardust in the little lass, she'll last forever. Hold on kids, we're off to Rolexa," #1 says.

"It's so magical, Grace, with all of the glorious colors, and, Freddy dear, you'll never run out of places to swim. The entire planet is water," Mother says.

"Sounds wonderful, Mother. I need to make a quick pitstop at the hospital, if nobody minds?" I ask.

"Hospital? I hope we didn't damage you, my boy?" #1 asks.

"Not at all, Father. I'm going to drop off my macular degeneration cure, along with a few notes on how to modify the compound to cure other diseases, and then head to Rolexa."

"But, babe, don't you want to stick around Earth? All of mankind will want to thank you," Grace asks.

"Nah. The note I'm leaving will say it's from an anonymous, but trustworthy source," I say, like a guy who's as humble as a nun.

"Oh, Freddy, I've never been so proud of you." Grace winks, flashes her elf ears, and whispers in my ear, "Or so horny."

The spaceship heads upward. Stars flow through the ship. What a rush! "This is amazing, Grace. Look!" I say in astonishment, as we breach the surface of a huge lake. "Lake Okeechobee!!!"

"Brilliant, #1. Everyone knows Miami is full of aliens, but who would think to look for them in Lake Okeechobee?" Grace says.

"We've been underwater the entire time, Father?" I ask, like a kid whose father is a cool orca alien God thingy.

"You can't very well expect to hide a spaceship in your atmosphere, lad, not with Captain Kirk and those new-age rocket blokes flying around space delivering same day packages and what not," #1 says, and everyone laughs.

65

For better or worse

A magnificent Miami moon hangs so low in the sky, you can nearly touch it.

The moonlight illuminates the orange, red, and yellow fruit on the neighboring mango trees, and filters through the seagrape trees lining the beach dunes. Drawn like sea turtles returning to nest on the same beach where they hatched, they arrive precisely at 4:20 a.m. and look at each other with a deep feeling of a shared experience. A fitting stage to celebrate their rebirth on the first anniversary since they were returned to Earth, on this very beach, as their best versions of themselves. They scamper excitedly from one to the other, like puppies at supper time. Rather than bragging on themselves like at a high school reunion, they ask questions about the other's lives, their hopes, their dreams, their happiness, their favorite music, because a little of #3 rubbed off *(not like that— Geez!)* on all of them as well. As it turned out, #3's upgrades were—perfect!

Leif quit his job servicing pools for his father and got a job in a cannabis dispensary on South Beach, where he shared his deep understanding of *now, next,* and Maui Waui. Leif did so well selling pot, he purchased his own dispensary, bought a house with a pool, and hired his father to clean it. Jerry continued to clean his own pool. June supervised, wearing a green bikini—that matched her eyes—and the pool.

Burt was reunited with Ernie. He returned to Earth with hilarious material about aliens and got his own Netflix special. Burt thanked Patricia for tending to Ernie in his absence, and boned her good for a few months, until he fell in love with his Netflix producer. Patricia was inconsolable, until she found comfort crying on her best friend Mariel's shoulder, during which time she discovered she was a lesbian. Patricia and Mariel were married on the sands of South Beach a short time later. Millie carried their rings on her collar down a seashell aisle.

Max gave up Sheila, became more charismatic, (if that were even possible), stepped-up his political career, and was elected— Governor of the State of Florida.

Bob ran into the governor on a tour of the Miami food stamp office. Bob pitched him on the idea of doubling food stamp benefits by adopting a state income tax on millionaires. The governor supported the tax, and appointed Bob to a newly created office of Governmental Compassion. Bob married Karla, who never lost those 15 pounds, and was never happier. They are expecting their own bundle of joy. The baby's due date—4-20.

Al lost his appetite for everything bad. For violence, for lumpy fettucine Alfredo, for the gangster business, in general. Al found his new passion—pornography. Contrary to what you must be thinking, Al enjoyed the artistic side of the industry, and went from bankrolling the films, to directing, and thanks to #3's fixing his *little stamina problem*, starring in them under the stage name—Al Daylong. Candy married Ensign Riptide and got a job on the cruise ship as an entertainer. Her show, Candy Cotton's Burlesque Review, is the highest rated in the fleet.

Harvey made amends with his children, renewed his vows with Helen at the Greynolds Park boathouse, wrote a best-selling book about self-forgiveness—and became a life coach.

Sam's letter to the editor about polluting the ocean with sewage outfall was published in the paper. The story was picked up by all of the cable news networks. The governor appointed Sam to head the newly created office of Environmental Conservation—where he immediately banned the discharge of wastewater into the ocean. Tim found six bales of weed, sold his boat, and retired to Everglades City.

Andy Tyler returned to Mt. Airy, and produced the blockbuster film, What Would Andy Do? Andy married Thelma Lou, who won an Oscar for her role as Helen Crump. Leon DeCapricorn was her co-star and was so taken by the experience, he moved to Mt. Airy, and ran for sheriff. He lost by two votes—to Andy Tyler.

Geronimo created a new outer space storyline for Bustella and Chunka. Their latest anime, Bustella Blasts Off, premiered in Tokyo and is #1 at the box office worldwide. Bustella taught Geronimo how to kiss—like a girl. Chunka fell hard for a Shiba Inu. They had their first litter of puppies—on 4-20.

Cliff quit his job and opened a therapeutic counseling center for children and adults who were abused and neglected. Jane was his first patient. Jane surrendered custody of Twan to Cliff. Jane made a full recovery and put her $20 million settlement to good use—funding Cliff's counseling center.

Ernest stopped writing and took up flying full-time. Thanks to #3—he no longer needed an airplane.

After their exchange of information, their eyes are drawn to the moon. It's pink tonight, and the craters are moving, forming the shape of an orca.

66

The honeymoon's over

"Father. May we borrow the ship?" I ask.

"Of course, but you only arrived on Rolexa last year. Where are you off to?" #1 asks.

"Rolexa is splendid, Father. We love it here. The crystal sea is magnificent. Thanks to you, Grace and Mother can breathe underwater, so I finally have dive buddies. I especially like it when you join us on our adventures, Father. We've ridden seahorses the size of elephants, played tag with golden sea monkeys bigger than King Kong, visited the indigo moons, floated in the mystical southern lights that set the planet aglow in pink, green, and lavender. And the best part is wherever we go, we're surrounded by perpetual stars. I mean, how couldn't I love living on a water planet, because I have—"

"Don't you dare say gills, lad," #1 interrupts.

"I was going to say, a special affinity for water, and along those lines, there're plenty of other water planets out there with life on them, Father. In medical school, they teach you all the parts of the

"

body. What makes them tick. They don't teach you to listen to your body, your inner voice, and ours are saying, there're a lot of galaxies out there in need of an eye surgeon and a psychiatrist," I say like a guy who finally grew the fuck up.

"Ah, good thinking. Use your gifts. You're welcome to leave Infinity with us. Between Fiona, #3, and #2, you'll have all the babysitters you could ever use. And I wouldn't mind watching the little bugger myself," #1 says.

"Thanks anyway, Father. In fact, #3 is babysitting today. As much as Infinity loves #3 and her singing, our baby is coming with us," I say.

"Quite right, lad. Just where she belongs, with Mum and Dad," #1 says, tossing me a vial of stardust. "Here you go, my boy. This will put the ship in hyperdrive anytime you need to return to Rolexa post-haste. Have fun out there until Infinity's first birthday and then straight back to Rolexa. I wouldn't miss our little one's birthday for all the stars in the Universe."

"Thanks, Pops," I say, like someone who sincerely likes their father.

"Freddy lad, might we have a word?"

"Of course, Father. Please excuse us, Grace?"

"A father-son moment. How adorbs!" Grace says.

"It's been wonderful having you here, Freddy. I know this won't make up for the years I wasn't there for you, but as the son of the most omnipotent being in the Universe, it's time for you to know the meaning of it all," Father says, transforming from orca to human form.

"Cool," I say, trying to sound nonchalant. Inside, I'm aflutter. I'm floating here waiting for the self-proclaimed creator of all things to enlighten me, but he's just floating across from me with a dopey grin on his face.

Say something, anything, Pops. Awkward! Come on already. Meaning of life? Spit it out, Pops. Nada! The old me would be thinking he's going to tell me time is precious, eat dessert first or some other Zen bullshit, so why is he wasting my time? Thank God that was the old me.

I've changed. I learned what Mother tried to teach me. Never underestimate anyone. People, even your parents, can surprise you. He's just smiling at me. Well, I don't want to be rude. I smile back like *the fucking ray of sunshine I've become*. He keeps smiling. Now he's flickering.

Wait! He flickers?!!! Fuck! He flickers like me! He never flickered before. Well, how do you like that? I am a chip off the old block, after all. I grin like the Mona Lisa. I flicker. He smiles and flickers like the light beams of 3 Rolexa suns. Our flickers meet in the middle of the one-foot space separating us. The flickers greet each other like long-lost friends, and freeze. I can't fucking breathe — and I love it. We're in the *null*. Trust me, being breathless in the *null* is the best. Being breathless with my Father is enlightening. I see #1 for who he is, a well-meaning, loving, slightly flawed, mildly witty, pacifist killer whale, alien, God thingy, or, as I prefer to call him Pops.

"Wait! That's it Pops? Smiling is the fucking secret to life?"

"'Tis, my boy. I hope you weren't expecting some Zen stuff about time being precious? Every single-celled Rolexian ninny knows that."

"Nah," I say like a guy who finally stopped underestimating people, and orcas.

"Truth is, all you have to do is smile, lad, and the Universe becomes a better place," #1 says, his smile never faltering.

I smile back, not saying a word. We swim back to Grace, smiling, filling the room with flickers. I take Grace's hand. She smiles at me and Father.

"I'll have whatever you're having," Grace says, and Father and I smile at her. "Geez, Louise! What are you two on? Did you beam down to visit Trippin without me?" Grace jokes.

Fiona enters the chamber. "What's with the goofy looks, boys? What did I miss? Did you guys do Ecstasy without me? Hang on, what's with the vial of spaceship stardust? Freddy Fluid, Grace Whisperer, are you kids going somewhere?"

"Yes, Mother," I say, smiling.

"I understand, Freddy dear. Have a great trip, and don't forget those stardust vitamins, Grace. They really help breastmilk production," Fiona says. *(In the old days I would have said, Ewwww! See, I've grown.)*

"Thanks, hon! You don't mind if I call you hon?" Grace says, kissing Fiona on the cheek, and winking.

"Take good care of them, hon," Mother giggles to Grace. "Hang on, dears. I can't go months and months without seeing my grandbaby," Mother says. "Eddie, a little help here. Please, dear."

"Quite right, luv. Now, where is my bloody tech sorcerer when I need him? Chip, you daft wanker, get in here, please," #1 shouts as he transforms back to an orca to intimidate Chip.

"What now, you lazy sod of a whale?" Chip says, laughing as he beams into the room.

"Ah, good of you to come, Chip, you bloody nob of a human," #1 jokes.

"Like I had a choice, twit!" Chip retorts, and they both laugh.

"How are those new vision bubbles coming along, Chip?"

"I've got them perfected, #1. Tick helped me. Who knew a horologist would know so much about computer tech?"

"Ah, Tick Tockington. How's the old chap doing?" #1 asks.

"He's very happy to share Moses' harem; especially since you transported Midge here for him. He did mention something about Moses cheating in gin rummy?" Chip says.

"I knew it, Fiona! I told you bloody Moses cheated. Now, about those vision bubbles, you ninny."

"You're good to go, #1. You can use the vision bubbles to see back and forth from any galaxy in the Universe. I call it Startime, you know, like Facetime, only no roaming charges," Chip says.

"That's bloody brilliant, for a ninny, that is," #1 says.

"Even better, #1, you can travel anywhere in the Universe through the bubbles in the blink of an eye. I've rigged them so only you, the royal family, and myself, of course, can use them. We don't want any plonkers running off willy-nilly."

"Quite right! Good job—for a wanker. Freddy, Grace, take this along and keep in touch," #1 says.

"Oh, none of this keep in touch stuff, Eddie. I want to see my grandbaby every day," Fiona says.

"That's a bit unreasonable, Mother," I say, still smiling.

"Once a week, Fiona. Promise," Grace says.

"Can't blame a grandma for trying," Fiona says.

"Chip, you twit, what's this dolphin doing here? Did you screw up the new vision bubbles already?" #1 asks.

"Don't ask me, tosser. I like my fish with chips and malt vinegar," Chip jokes.

"I'm responsible, Eddie dear," Fiona says.

"You, Fiona?" #1 questions.

"Damn! Get a load of you, baby. Tall, dark, and darker; and look at that tail. Hey, sugar, I'm Dicksee."

"Wonderful, a dyslexic dolphin," #1 says.

"'Xactly, baby," Dicksee says.

"Exactly what, Madame?"

"'Xactly dyslexic, baby. There's nothing I like more than dicks. That's why Mama named me Dicksee."

"Really, Madame. Your mama certainly has a foul mouth," #1 says.

"Oh, that ain't the half of it, brother. See, when Squirt was ready to pop—"

"Dicksee, language, please," Fiona says.

"Sorry, sugar," Dicksee says.

"Madame, are you telling me you're Squirt's daughter?" #1 asks.

"Hell yeah, baby! You knew Mama? That's cool, sugar. Any friend of Mama's is welcome at my place, and by my place, I mean," Dicksee says, rolling over and pointing at her underbelly.

"Madame, that doesn't explain your presence here," #1 says.

"Eddie," Fiona interjects, "I beamed her up for that birthday surprise you always wanted."

"Birthday surprise!? Birthday surprise? I recall no such—"

Grace interrupts, "Hey, #1, for the most brilliant creature in this Universe, you're a bit slow on the intake. Freddy, did the same thing when I gave him his 18th birthday surprise."

"Huh?" Father and son question.

Fiona whispers in #1's ear. "Oh… Birthday surprise! Bloody brilliant, luv," #1 says, eyeing Dicksee like a New York tourist ordering the last slice of Key Lime pie—in a greasy, overpriced Miami Beach diner.

"I still don't understand," I say. Grace winks and puts on her elf ears. "Ewwww!"

"Get with the times, dear!" Mother says.

"Fine, but Ewwww. (*Sorry, but this is Ewwww worthy.*) Well, Mother, Father, we're off," I say, like a guy who just got the keys to a fucking spaceship!

67

Neat little bundle

On the spaceship.

I wish I could tie this into a neat little bundle. I wish I could say I have one speed now, that I've found middle ground. Truth is, since #3 gave me new personality traits, boosted my *next*, and after spending a year on Rolexa, I have too many speeds to count. *Now, next, null*, Rolexa time, Earth time. I can modulate between all of them. It doesn't make me special. Why, you may ask? Because anyone can experience *now*, and even *null*, with the proper techniques, although they can't move between Earth and Rolexa time, nor have the advantage of knowing what the future holds. Thankfully, between my *next* and #3's time travel, we keep pretty current on the future.

I wish I could say since my *next* got under control, Bad OCD vanished—it hasn't. Bad OCD sticks around like a bad penny, but it has improved. I still get anxious on occasion, like last night, when I thought the tiny mole on my back was a melanoma. Turned out to be a bit of kelp that washed off after a swim in

Rolexa's crystal sea. The good news is Grace continues my training and mastery of meditation, breathing techniques, voo, and progressive relaxation; no needles, though—no, thank you!

Being able to be 100% truthful with Grace about everything I hid from her reduces my stress, too. While I didn't lie by withholding my secrets, I gotta tell you, I felt like a con man before, and although Grace shouldn't be treating her husband, she is the only psychiatrist on Rolexa, and boy, do I need one. Honestly, everyone should have their own shrink.

Knowing my origin story, getting to know my father, and understanding my gifts; all of these things keep me balanced. When Bad OCD dares to show up, like your nosy neighbor right after you built a room addition on your house without a permit, I have a secret weapon. Her name is Infinity. She's the most beautiful creature in the Universe. I'm not being egotistical about our daughter. Ask anyone—she's heavenly. Infinity came into the Universe on 4-20, swathed in stardust, which envelops her to this day like a cozy blanket. I spend so much time with Infinity and Grace, and am so blissed out of my fucking brain, Bad OCD is well—fucked.

"Look, Grace, first stop, Earth! That was quick," I say.

"This ship's got more moves than Michael Jackson, babe."

"Take her in for a landing, please, Grace, and try not to wake Infinity. I just got her to sleep."

"Aye, aye, Captain. I love it when you order me around, Captain Babe."

"And I love you wearing those ears when we're in the spaceship," I say, *because, well, you know.*

"It's the least a little Vulcan Princess can do," Grace says with a wink.

I momentarily turn to mush, and pull it together. "You are the better pilot, Grace." *I never would have admitted this before my next and personality were balanced.* Besides, as much as I love flying this ship, I've got my hands full. Full of love, that is. "I can't stop looking at her, Grace; even when she's sleeping. If there ever was something to use your eyes for, it's looking at babies."

"Speaking of eyes, babe, I heard on satellite news, thanks to a certain anonymous scientist, macular degeneration has been eradicated."

"Wonderful news, Grace. It wouldn't have happened without you, and you, Infinity, you precious angel." I smile, and my flickers join Infinity's stardust blanket for a little jig around the ship, lighting it up like the Rockefeller Center Christmas tree.

"The news also reported they're fast-tracking FDA clearance of the technology for a multitude of illnesses, even cancer. I'm so proud of you, babe."

"Nonsense. It was very much a group effort, Grace. I'm thrilled people will keep their vision, because I can't get my eyes off of you, Infinity, you little—"

"Sorry to interrupt the love fest. We're here, babe."

The beach gatherers turn their attention from the orca shaped moon crater to a round clear grapefruit sized spacecraft whizzing past, leaving a trail of stardust. The spaceship does a double loop de loop in and out of the surf and sticks a perfect landing in the middle of the gathering. Then grows to the size of one of those giant beach balls they throw around at concerts—*you know the ones.* The spaceship gets even bigger, the size of a fairytale stagecoach, which used to be a pumpkin, but instead of Cinderella, out pops an extremely graceful woman who looks like an elven princess, and an exceptionally handsome man.

The man smiles broadly, like a politician, only he isn't kissing babies, he's holding one—in a stardust blanket. His smile grows, and stardust flickers fill the ocean air like sparks from a beach bonfire—*after you throw in a carton of sparklers*. The gathering stare in silent amazement until one brave soul approaches.

"Hey, chica. Is he God?" Bustella asks Grace.

"Nah," Grace whispers in Bustella's ear, then pauses for dramatic effect, and adds, "Just his son, and granddaughter."

"Jesus Christo! Bustella says and crosses herself.

"I'm not Jesus, Bustella,"

"Whew! 'Cause you look just like him, or his muy caliente brother," Bustella says, crossing herself again and taking a knee.

"So, I've been told. Please stand, Bustella. We're all brothers and sisters here, except for my enchanting wife, Grace."

"Hello, all," Grace says, waving her arm in that little parade float beauty queen manner that makes me want to—*never mind*.

"And this little bundle of starlight is Infinity. Isn't she the coolest?" I say, blubbering. I wipe away my happy tears with one hand and Infinity floats out of my arms. "Whoops!" Laughing, I retrieve our daughter. "Her gravity is still set on Rolexa. At any rate, my name is Freddy, Freddy Fluid. I want to thank you all for loaning me your *nexts* and your special personality traits. Turns out to be just what the doctor ordered. Right, Grace?"

"Absolutely, and I want to thank you too," Grace says, winking at every single one of them—*those lucky folks*.

"If not for loaning me your nexts…" Freddy says.

"Kablooey!" Leif says.

"Exactly, Leif. Without all of you, we wouldn't be standing here today with Infinity. Speaking of standing here, it's marvelous! I've never been able to stand in one place long enough to feel the Earth through the soles of my feet. Seems I had to go to outer space to get grounded on my own planet. What a glorious sensation. Arghhhhh! 10 seconds on Earth and I'm back to talking to myself."

"You're not talking to yourself, Freddy. We can all hear you. Glad you finally got some soul, babe!" Grace says.

"Very funny, Grace. Isn't she the funniest?"

"Don't give up your day job, Grace," Burt quips.

"You must be Burt. I never met a comedian before. I thought you'd be funnier. Well, what I'm trying to say everyone is we want to express our eternal gratitude from the bottom of our soles, and souls," I say.

"It's cool, Freddy. Happy to help. Based on our little reunion here, we're all better off for it," Cliff says.

"I'd appreciate the opportunity to pay you back for your kindness. If any of you have a request, please tell me," I say with a beaming smile.

I realize I haven't stopped smiling since Infinity was born. Unless—you count last night with the melanoma scare, last week when I discovered Rolexa has sea worms (yuck), and last month when I was convinced, I had early onset Alzheimer's because I forgot where I put Infinity's orca doll. *Well, you get it.*

Yep, Bad OCD keeps its distance, but every once in a while, it creeps in like a cat burglar. Father asked me if I wanted him to cure my OCD. As much as I enjoy things that are cured, like bacon, pastrami, and macular degeneration (*in the old days, I would have said—you're welcome*), I told Father my OCD made me a better husband, father, and surgeon. I have everything a human or Rolexian could hope for. I discovered who my father is. Mother is alive. Grace is by my side. *Now, next, null,* and even Bad OCD are under control. We have a spaceship and can explore every galaxy in the Universe. Infinity is exceptional. There is nothing more I could want or wish for—except, I hope Infinity takes after Grace.

The last thing this neat little bundle needs is to take after me. #1 forbid! Don't even think it, Freddy.

Just look at her. Other than her stardust flickers, and being able to breathe underwater, she's perfectly normal. Everything about her oozes Grace. Don't give it a nanosecond thought, Freddy. I smile upon the hushed gathering with love in my heart, and stars fill the air. A child's voice breaks the silence.

"I wanna play with Baby Yoda," Twan says.

"Hello, Twan. Easy peasy," I say, smiling, summoning my vision bubble from the ship with my flickers. The glistening bubble floats before me, and I speak. "Father, someone here wants to play with Baby Yoda."

Before Father can transport through the vision bubble and shape shift, Infinity smiles, floats out of my arms again, disappears into a cloud of stardust, and transforms into Baby Yoda. Mother, Father, #2, and #3 through the vision bubble, the gathering on the beach, along with Grace and I, watch in amazement.

We're all dumbfounded, as Infinity, in the guise of Baby Yoda, soars to the heavens and organizes the innumerable stars in the sky, based on their shape, size, and color. A giant hourglass full of blinking Rolexa stars appears in the firmament. Then Infinity transforms back to her baby form, smiles, winks, opens her perfect tiny mouth, and out comes the most miraculous music, and it sounds like—a day at the circus. *"Zalk me!"*

About the Author

David Raymond is a Miami native, and best-selling author. David spent his public service career directing large governmental social service systems, including the Florida Department of Children & Families, and the Miami-Dade County Homeless Trust.

David holds a Master of Science degree in Mental Health Counseling and completed the Harvard University, John F. Kennedy School of Government Executive Education Program. Prior to working in the social service field, David taught middle school marine biology, and was an environmental laboratory technician testing Miami's ocean waters.

Following a distinguished career, David successfully wrote over $1 Billion in grant applications, and three novels to date. David's hobbies include playing guitar, learning the banjo, kayaking, fishing, reading, hiking, and experiencing the wonders of nature.

David lives in Biscayne Park, Florida with his mystical wife Amy, and their forever goofy Aussiedoodle, Starry. David and Amy are blessed by their extraordinary children, Mia, a gifted psychotherapist, Abraham, a legendary native fishing guide, their wondrous daughter-in-law, Yudith, a teacher and mother, and their magical grandson, Ryder.

David's books are set in South Florida, with locations in Miami and the Everglades popping to life.

Acknowledgements

My heartfelt thanks my supportive, charming, lovely, and wise, Aunt Lynn (Geth) who I have known and loved longer than any other person on Earth. If not for her, my books would still be locked away in my computer.

I must acknowledge my amazing cover designer, Ana Chabrand, and illustrator, Leila Charur, for their gifts of transforming my stories into works of art. For the second book in a row, Ana's art concepts have influenced my storyline in a delightful manner.

Thanks as well to my editor, Mckenzie Lyn Graveline for the enumerable hours spent on how to best represent numbers in a book about time and OCD—even if we angered the APA style gods in the process.

Grateful acknowledgement is made to my friend and colleague, Eileen Bryson who actually reads absurdist fiction and likes it! Eileen's supernatural beta reading and proofreading skills make me a better writer— and make it look like I really paid attention in freshman English. (*I did not.*)

My infinite gratitude to my wife and partner in life, Amy, who is the air in my lungs, the beat in my heart, and tolerates a guy who could easily be mistaken for the illegitimate lovechild of Sheldon Copper and Guy Noir.

Finally, this book serves as a tribute to my multi-generational obsessive-compulsive disorder, which has been both my superpower and kryptonite. Love you, Buddy. (*Yes, I call my OCD, Buddy—deal with it!*)

Books by David Raymond

It's Like Having Sex With God

The Mermaid of Arch Creek

Time Noir

www.davidraymondbooks.com